Surfacing

A Magical Journey Out Of The Darkness And Into The Light, In Surfing And In Life.

Tiffany Manchester

Copyright

Surfacing

by Tiffany Manchester

Cover Art by Roy Ruiz

Printed in the United States of America

Second Edition, 2022 (First Edition, 2017 *Surfer Girls Kick Ass* under ISBN 9781543911947)

ISBN: 9798802101766

For more info check out: www.tiffanymanchester.com

Surfacing

Zoe Smith is flailing in her career as a professional surfer on the WSL (World Surf League)...as well as in her relationship with Derek. She needs to make a change. But what?

Stuck in a funk, she heads home to Australia at the end of the competitive season, uncertain of her future. Will the end of her relationship also signify the end of her career, or will her life take a turn for the better?

Luckily, with the help of a best friend, a boy crush, a strange encounter with an angel, and some much-needed soul-searching, she finds herself on a magical journey out of the darkness and into the light...in surfing and in life.

*** * ***

"OMG I just finished your book and I absolutely loved it. Like really really really loved it. It's as good as The Way Of The Peaceful Warrior!" - Michelle Melendez

"A crazily relatable and inspiring story that caused me to reflect on the concept of courage and how I can relate it to my own life." - Ruby Meade

"Finally a book that I don't want to close! Surfacing is one of those books you are afraid

to finish reading because it's too good to be over." - Janine Reith

"It's the EAT, PRAY, LOVE for surfers!" - Liz Davison

"A very relatable feel good story for surfers and non-surfers alike. You won't want to put the book down!" - Brisa Hennessey, Professional Surfer

Also By Tiffany Manchester

Pack Light, Travel Light, Be The Light

Tish, 23, freshly home from Africa is already seeking her next adventure. She is sick of the city, the tight grip of mainstream society, and her disapproving parents. There has to be more people like her out there. But who are they? And where?

Desperate to find her tribe, she heads out into the Canadian wilderness where she discovers the thrill of being on the river and the challenge of navigating whitewater armed only with a paddle and her fellow rafters. Little does she know it will be the spark lighting the way to new, often harrowing adventures.

Along with her constant companion Red Fran, she finds herself avoiding death on her moped in Taipei, getting lost hiking the Annapurna Circuit in Nepal, being stuck in the jungle in Ecuador for three days with nothing but two mangos and a bottle of rum, and tackling the craziest rapid yet in Uganda... as well as finding the love of her life.

But the biggest adventure of all? Having to face her true Self, and her fears, every step of the way.

Dedication

To all my salty sisters striving for success in surfing and in life -
you've got this! And to all of the pros, who have inspired me to
surf harder, train harder, and smile along the way.

Preface

When I began the writing of this book, all I knew was that it was about a pro-surfer. I honestly had no idea how it was going to unfold. But as the words landed on my screen, and as Zoe (the main character) embarked on her incredible journey, I realized that the story wasn't being solely created by me. While my personal experience of heartbreak, of my adventures as a professional athlete, and of my awakening and healing in Hawaii are all weaved into the details - the angels, the fairies, mother ayahuasca, the ocean, and other beautiful energies were all there to infuse their love, support, and guidance into the process.

Use this book to empower your mind, body, and soul... and become a better surfer!

To get the vibes going, here is an excerpt from a poem I wrote with the angels:

Believe in your truth
And watch your life thrive
Forget about the how
Keep your eye on the why

Preface

You were born to feel good
Know every day drama free
Live your life so on point
Others can't help but see

All you've got is the present
So let the past go
Take care in each moment
True love is the goal!

xoTiff

Part One
FACE THE FUNK

Chapter One

'Epic fail' was all I could say to Derek as I emerged from the steep ocean trail onto the main road of Honolua Bay. He was standing at the top waiting for me.

I stared at the ground, my head hung low, trying to avoid being spotted by the small crowd of onlookers who were mingling next to their parked cars on the edge of the hillside. I couldn't *see* the disappointment in Derek's eyes, but I could *feel* his sense of despair as he searched for something to say. He had no wisdom for me and, unfortunately, settled on, 'Yeah, what happened to you out there?'

The best I could manage was to ignore what felt like an idiotic comment. In fact, in that moment, I decided I should ignore him altogether. So that's what I did.

This competition was over for me. I'd been eliminated in Round Four to someone I'd thought would be a very beatable opponent. Sure, she had plenty of talent and lots of potential, but I didn't think she'd be able to pull off an 8.53 in the last minute of our heat. *I had this... I had this!* I grumbled to myself.

But I didn't. Bailey, the fresh and enthusiastic rookie had just beaten my ass. So now I had yet another piss-poor result to add to my string of piss-poor results from this year's World Tour – a blow to the ego for a top-ranked athlete like me. And to top it all off, it was the last event of the season. Ending on a low majorly sucked.

In past years when I'd been eliminated early on, I was much better at dealing with it. Quick mental recovery from a loss is part of the game you have to learn to play as a professional athlete and as an ambassador of the sport. At least, it is if you want to survive. And you have to know how to survive before you can thrive. Sure, I'd still get pissed off, but I was better at masking my frustration with a smile while I brought the loss back into perspective. In the end, I knew I had to manage myself and keep it together.

Yet this was my fourth 'bad' finish and I was on the verge of imploding. I'd lost confidence in so many ways this season. And right now, I just couldn't fake it anymore. I felt like a failure and wanted to bury my head in the sand.

But no, this was the professional surfing tour, where hiding was not an option. Being in the limelight comes with the territory, which means signing autographs, cameras following me everywhere and doing post-heat interviews. I pulled down my hat and hid my eyes with a gargantuan pair of sunnies, not willing to risk anyone seeing the truth about how I felt.

'Zoe, what happened out there today? The conditions seemed a little bit challenging for you.'

Damo was an ex-pro surfer turned commentator. He held the mic to my mouth and awaited my response. I had to dig deep to find words that I wouldn't later regret.

'Um, yeah, well... I don't think it was so much the conditions as a series of my own mistakes. There were actually some nice waves that came through, but I couldn't seem to find my rhythm out there today. It just wasn't my day.'

'It's the last event of the tour. Do you have any plans for the off-season?'

'Um, I don't yet, actually. I mean, I'll head home to Aussie and then see what happens.'

I was trying to be chipper – but I wasn't fooling anyone. I made barely any effort in engaging in the interview and just wanted it done.

'Well, you've already qualified for the Tour next year, so big congrats, Zoe. Enjoy the break!'

I was grateful that Damo let me off easy, though I probably didn't give him much choice. I smiled, gave a thumbs-up to the camera and quietly mumbled 'thanks' as I walked off the inter-view area and made my way to where I'd left my gear, hoping desperately not to run into anyone who'd want to talk. That was a pretty unreasonable expectation when you're in the middle of a world-class competition at one of the best beaches and most popular surfing destinations in the world... Maui, Hawaii.

Luckily, the other competitors were busy doing their own thing. Aside from a few nods and quick hellos, people appeared to feel my vibe and get the message to leave me alone as I crossed through the VIP area and entered the locker room. I put on my headphones and cranked up the tunes as I gathered my stuff, making an effort to shake off my bad attitude.

It worked. Well, it worked for a few minutes anyway – which was just enough time to put on a happy face, hug a few of the ladies who were moving into the Quarterfinals, and wish them good luck. The competition was to continue through to Finals and crown a champion today. Normally I'd stick around to watch, but on this occasion I just couldn't bear it.

I found Derek and together we headed to the car. He strapped my board bag onto the roof while I threw my other bags into the back seat. I plopped into the front and rolled down the windows to let out all the hot air. Or was it all just *my* hot air? Derek started the car, then glanced over at me as he pulled onto the street. Maybe *glared* at me would be more accurate. It was hard to know for sure.

'But for real, Zoe, what happened out there?'

In my foul mood, I'd decided that it *had* to be a glare. I mean, it was obvious that what he was really asking was: how idiotic can you be? I snapped at him in response – no, in *defense* – to his imaginary attack.

'Dude, can you just drive?'

I stared out the window and fixated on the sparkles of the ocean as the bright sun reflected off of the water. I watched it pulse unapologetically inward, towards land. We drove along the coast, passing palm tree after palm tree, the waves rumbling in from the distance and exploding onto the rocks.

That's pretty much how my head feels right now, I thought to myself. *Like it's about to explode...*

'Zoe, don't ignore me. Please!' Derek begged. 'I know there's nothing I can say, but still, what are you thinking?'

I looked over at him and noticed his shoulders hunched. I could tell that he was desperate to get something out of me, so I gave in:

'I'm thinking I've digressed as a surfer, which doesn't make sense because I'm doing everything you've been telling me to do, so I'm freakin' *pissed*, Derek!'

I baited him. He took the bait. And here we go again...

'Oh, I get it. You want to blame everyone else? You want to blame me, right?'

Derek's voice was calm as he spoke. He may even have been right. But can you blame me for not wanting to hear it?

'Do you really want to piss me off right now?' I threw back at him.

'Well, c'mon Zoe, of course not, but you were the one out

there, not me. You've already proven that you can win, so what happened?'

'Ugh!' was all I could say before crossing my arms and staring back out the window in frustration. We spent the rest of the drive in silence.

We were staying in a guest house on some oceanfront property owned by a friend of Derek. It was a small, quaint, cabin-like structure about 100 yards from the main house. The land was beautifully manicured with flowerbeds, plants, and fruit trees galore. That's one of the many amazing things about Hawaii – if you have some land, you can grow a lot of your own food without much effort. Seriously, throw some papaya seeds into the yard and *voilà!*

When we arrived back at the guest house, I placed my board bag along the side of the house, kicked off my *slippas* (Hawaiian for flip-flops) and left them at the door. Derek followed suit, then carried the cooler of food and drinks to the kitchen counter. Without saying a word, I dropped my other bag and headed straight to the bathroom to take a shower. I was anxious to rinse off the day, but to be honest also keen to avoid more unwelcome conversation.

As you can tell, things hadn't been going that well for me, and placing 13th today was one of my worst competition results to date. I'd been a professional surfer since I was 15, ranked in the top 6 for the majority of those years, and a proud winner of one incredible Championship title two years ago at just 21. At 23, and with the position I took from this season's final competition, my overall ranking would now be 9th in the world – an absolute piss-poor result for a recent champion. And certainly for me. With only the top 10 out of 17 qualifying for the next Tour, I was *freaking lucky* to have made the cut.

I probably sound like a total brat, but these past two seasons since winning that world title, well, I just haven't been able to get my shit together and I don't know why. I've been on an emotional rollercoaster, and now that rollercoaster is flying off the tracks. I dunno, maybe all the pressure to do well, as in *winning every single heat,* has gotten to me.

Argh! This is no bueno! I thought to myself, shaking my head in disappointment and stepping into the shower. I plunged under the showerhead and let the water gush over my back for a couple of minutes before turning up the heat. I don't know why, but I like the water to be so hot that it's almost at the point where it stings, like when you first step into a steaming hot tub. It's a mixture of pain and relief at the same time. Know what I mean?

I stood there with the water soothing and scorching my back simultaneously, wondering what I was going to do. Oddly enough, I wasn't wondering what to do about surfing. I was wondering what to do about Derek...

Yes, my surfing career was an issue that needed to be dealt with, but the season was over so for now thinking about that could wait. In the meantime, my relationship was weighing on me heavily, and I had to admit I'd reached my tipping point.

I sighed, feeling bummed that it had become such a drama.

Chapter Two

By 18, I'd already completed two years surfing at the professional level and was moving up the ranks fast when I started dating Derek seriously. To be honest, I think my success came as a bit of a surprise to the industry. It's pretty safe to say that all of the other girls on tour had been taught to surf as early as age four. For many of them raised in a surfing family, like Clara or Marissa, the ocean was their backyard, which meant they had already logged thousands of hours on a surfboard, with mum or dad or uncle teaching them the ways of the water and encouraging them to engage in contests.

But that's not how I began. I didn't even learn to surf until I was 11. This, not surprisingly, had made me the underdog. And considering where I came from, underdog was an *understatement*.

Born in the mountains of Colorado, snowboarding was my thing in the winter; skateboarding the rest of the year. I loved the mountains – especially when it came to making fresh tracks with my dad, early in the morning after a big dump of snow. Equally I loved going to the skatepark with my mom, who would hang out watching me for hours while I goofed around and worked on my moves. I loved my life in Colorado. I had friends, freedom, and fresh air...

But right after my 10th birthday, my parents suddenly split. And just like that, my world was turned upside down. As it happened, my mom had been having an affair with some dirtbag from her office, and when the dirtbag moved to Florida, she decided she couldn't live without him. So she left us. She *abandoned* us. Abandoned her family.

My dad was devastated, obviously. Yet, despite his pain dealing with the situation, he always made sure he was there for me... a confused little girl who missed her mom terribly. I had nightmares for months afterwards. I was scared to be left alone, and found it hard to believe that it was all really true. I kept willing her to return, and prayed every night that she'd be home when I woke up in the morning. There was a hole in my heart that left me feeling empty, depressed, and alone in this big scary world.

I tried to sleep in my dad's room as much as possible, but he was worried that I'd never be able to manage on my own if it became habit, so he held strong in tucking me into my own bed. Inevitably, I'd wake up in the middle of the night freaked out, and when he heard me yelling, my dad would rush into my room to soothe my wounded soul. I don't think either of us got much sleep during that time, which, as you can imagine, made me a total pain in the butt 10-year-old and him a fairly cranky father.

I don't mean to depress you! There was a bright side to all of this. The excruciating experience we went through brought us much closer together. He got a job offer back in Australia, where he came from. He hadn't been able to get excited about anything in the year since my mom had left, but with this offer, there was a change in his demeanor. I sensed a lift in his spirits, which, in turn, lifted mine.

And since I'd never been anywhere outside the United States, suddenly I became an enthused kid hopeful of a new (and happy) adventure with my dad. Plus, I was excited to see where he grew up.

While I was scared to leave behind everything familiar, including my friends, I guess somewhere in my heart I was wise enough to know that this move to Australia was what we both needed.

And it was.

Arriving in Sydney, I was in awe of everything. We stayed in a hotel downtown near Darling Harbour while my dad got his job sorted at his corporate headquarters. He took me to the aquarium, Sydney Harbour Bridge, Taronga Zoo and loads of other places, too many for me to remember now. I felt like I was at an amusement park every day, taking in the new rides, smells, foods, and people! After a couple of weeks at the hotel, we loaded up his new company car, and drove over the renowned bridge towards northern Sydney and into the beachside suburb of Manly.

It was the end of January, and even though I knew I was missing prime snow season, I was too shocked by the fact it was summer in Australia to give the snow much attention. *Who knew?* The air was warm, the sun was bright, and the beaches... OMG, I loved the sand! It wasn't my first time seeing the ocean – I'd been to Miami a few times to visit relatives – but I *had* forgotten how much I loved the beach, swimming and playing around in the shore break.

Our new home in Manly was a small, two-bedroom bungalow in a neighborhood a few blocks back from the beach. The foliage around the house was overgrown and weeds were taking over the flowerbed by the front door. Inside, it was already furnished, which was helpful because we'd sold or junked pretty much everything back in Colorado. I loved my room instantly and it overlooked the cutest backyard area, which was always full of chirping birds.

We unpacked our small stash of stuff over the weekend and did our best to settle in and get our bearings so that my dad and I would be ready for work and school on Monday. That week was overwhelming; even though the kids and teachers at school were friendly, I felt shy and awkward because I had a hard time understanding their strong accents! I did enjoy being able to walk to and from school instead of having to take the bus all the time. I'd put on some Britney Spears and zone out.

On Friday of that first week, I met Sophie, who scared the crap out of me on our first encounter. Apparently, she'd been calling my name repeatedly from behind as I was walking home, but with the music blasting through my earbuds I was completely deaf to my surroundings. But that hadn't deterred her; she insisted on getting my attention by running up to me and tapping me on the shoulder. Caught off guard and shocked into awareness, I tripped over my own feet before turning around to see who it was.

'Oh geez, sorry Zoe. Didn't mean to scare ya.'

I pulled out an earbud. 'Ugh, oh, hi.' I blurted out embarrassed.

'I'm Sophie? We're in the same class?'

She had long, braided blond hair and glasses. And freckles... *lots* of freckles. She was friendly and outspoken, which I'd noticed in class, so even though she didn't know *me*, I felt like I already knew *her*.

'Oh hi. I'm Zoe.' I smiled at her and then looked back at the ground, not knowing what else to say. Everything was just so new in my life that I didn't really know how to respond to any of it... even something as simple as making a friend.

'Yeah mate, I know. Cool. Well, I think we live pretty near

each other. I'm just down that street.' She pointed towards the next corner.

'Cool. I'm just down that way...' I said, pointing ahead.

'Well, I'm going for a surf tomorrow morning, if you wanna come? It's just a short walk down to the beach.'

I perked up immediately.

'Yeah! That would be awesome! Um, I have to ask my dad. Do you mind if maybe he comes with us?'

'Yeah, no worries. My mum comes with me too sometimes.'

From that day on, Sophie and I did pretty much everything together. And if it wasn't for her, I'm seriously not sure I'd be the surfer I am today.

Chapter Three

The essence of surfing has the potential to be an incredibly uplifting experience. Even more so when you approach the sport with the understanding that it isn't all about catching waves. As a young and super active grom, I had no qualms about paddling out even when the ocean was flat or the waves were sparse. Something in me just had a need to be out there.

Sometimes I'd sit on my board and stare out at the horizon, lost in thought, dreaming up dreams and breathing in the salty air. I guess I'd needed something in my new life to replace snowboarding. And surfing was that something. I could pour all of my energy into it. I adapted quickly to the sport. Maybe it was because of my skills and experience on a snowboard, maybe it was from the similarity of skateboarding, maybe it's because I was young, agile and fearless. I dunno, maybe it was a little bit of all of those.

Finding my rhythm with the board was the easy part, but when it came to dealing with *people* in the water... my learning curve with surf etiquette was far more profound. When you add a crowd into the mix (which is inevitable at popular surf spots), you add an entirely different element to the experience. And that element is human aggression. You never know what mood someone is going to be in, nor how they're going to react when someone drops in on them (highly likely at *some* point during a session). It's the same as when someone pulls out in front of you on the road and cuts you off – it's stupid and dangerous and it royally pisses you off!

Anyhow, I happened to be one of those super annoying people one afternoon while we were out for our post-school surf session. This was about three years after I'd met Sophie and had been surfing heaps that entire time. By accident, I cut someone off. It happens! What can I say?

Now truth be told, as a 14-year-old girl in the water, I probably got away with *a lot*. It's a male-dominated sport, and a lot of the older men were protective of us girls, so they went easy on us, while also making sure that other people didn't give us a hard time. Even so, Sophie taught me early on the appropriate way to act, so I paddled up to the guy straight after and apologized repeatedly for cutting him off.

'My bad, my bad!'

(I've found it best to apologize with exaggerated sincerity *and* a big smile... It usually softens the other person up a bit.)

To my relief, he didn't seem fussed at all.

'No worries, eh, it happens.'

'Yeah cool, thanks!' I was feeling awkward now, because I noticed how cute he was.

'Right, I'm Derek by the way.'

And I mean *really* cute. His short brown hair was a welcome change to the often longer blonder locks of the Aussie surfer, and his brown eyes were expressive when he spoke.

'Oh. Um, I'm Zoe.' Awkwardly, I raised my hand to gesture 'hi', and then turned around and paddled away out of embarrassment. (*What the hell was wrong with me?*)

A few waves later, Sophie and I headed in. It was time for food.

'Who was that guy, Z? He's totally cute.'

'Derek? I think? I know, S, he *was* really cute. But I freaked out and paddled off! Oh my God, I'm so pathetic. Ugh!'

Walking away from the beach, both of us laughing, we were stopped in our tracks when we heard someone calling my name. We turned in unison to see who it was, accidentally smacking our boards together as we did so.

'Hey Zozo, watch out!' S belted out unapologetically.

'Ugh, sorry!' My head was down as I examined her board, worried that I had dinged it.

'Holy crap, Z, it's the guy from the water!' S exclaimed, no longer seeming to care about her board.

'Huh?' I looked up and saw him running towards us.

He was wearing a pair of blue shorts and a gray long-sleeved t-shirt, and I could tell from his darker hair that it was him.

'Hey Zoe!' he said, slightly out of breath.

Sophie nudged me with her arm, trying to get me to speak.

'Oh hey, um, this is my friend Sophie.'

'Hey, nice to meet you!' S said in her always-friendly tone, to which he responded with a nod and a smile.

He looked back at me and continued, 'So I was wondering if anyone is teaching you to surf?'

'Uh, I guess I'm just learning as I go, but S here is the one who got me on a board in the first place, so she's pretty much taught me what I know. Oh and I watch a lot of surf videos.'

'Cool, well, my uncle runs a surf camp over the summer and I was thinking you should join... Both of you, if you like. It's really fun!'

'Um, maybe? I dunno, I'll have to check.'

'Sure, of course,' he said as he held out a piece of paper with his number already written on it. 'Maybe we can meet up and I can give you more info?'

But I just stood there, staring at his number. S had to nudge me again to get me to move. I came to and took the paper from his outstretched hand.

'Sweet, well, call me later, okay? I'm free tomorrow. Bye!'

He turned and sprinted back towards the beach.

'OMG, Z!' Sophie squealed with excitement. 'You totally have to call him!'

'I know, I know, S! I will... maybe!'

I walked home with the paper held tightly between my fingers, careful not to let it get it wet, secretly ecstatic that a guy had chased me down to give me his number.

So that's how Derek and I met.

And yes, I ended up joining the surf camp... Duh! Sophie couldn't join because she was going on a family trip, but the camp was a ton of fun and I improved a lot over that summer. Derek's uncle Greg was our awesome coach. He was athletic, average-sized, but robust. He had silver hair and his skin was weathered from years of sun exposure. He was kind, a great teacher, with helpful insight on my surf skills. I was flattered to have his attention. And he got on brilliantly with my dad.

During the days, Greg would film us groms surfing. Then after the session, we'd go back to his place for a video review while he assessed our rides. That's when we learned a lot of the technical info. Things like swell direction, how winds affect the tides in one section of the wave versus another, body positioning, stuff like that.

Derek was a gem. He was so easy to be around. Plus, he was from California so it was nice to talk to someone about America again, especially the cultural differences with Australia. I guess he liked me too, because miraculously, by the middle of the summer, I'd become his girlfriend. I'm pretty sure Greg and my dad thought it was cute, but for me, it was terrifying. I'd never had a boyfriend before. Sure, I had lots of guy friends because I was a tomboy, but I was never the one *with* the guy. Nonetheless, I felt super comfortable with him and I liked that he wasn't distracted by anything else when he spoke to me.

So just like that I had a coach, a boyfriend, and a summer of catching waves every day. It was a dreamy couple of months to say the least.

But as the summer came to a close, Derek had to go back to California. He had only been visiting his uncle for a few months. The trip was a gift from his parents. But now he had to go back and finish the school year at home.

I was bummed, obviously, but S returned to Manly after her summer holiday at about the same time, which made the initial pain of 'missing my boyfriend' a little easier. I was distracted for a while by all the catching up we had to do.

As it turned out, Derek and I didn't do too well with the long distance thing. I mean c'mon, we were so young! We kept in touch from time to time, but our connection just sort of fizzled out after about a month.

On the plus side, my dad and Greg had made an agreement that Greg would continue to coach me throughout the school year, and I tell ya, he took coaching very seriously! He entered me into as many contests as possible and 'worked the system' on my behalf, introducing me to some of his connections, which landed me sponsorship with one of the local surf shops in Manly.

Fast-forward a few years of consistent training, lots of competitions, a bunch of wins on the junior surf tour, the Qualifying Series, and one insane fourth place finish as a wildcard on the World Championship Tour, I had become a notable competitor. When I reached my goal to qualify for the Women's

World Championship Tour, this rambunctious 18-year-old was more than ecstatic.

Starting in mid-March and ending early December, the Tour consists of 10 competitions that take place around the world: three in Australia, one each in Brazil and Fiji, two in California, and one each in Portugal, France, and Hawaii. A world tour in the truest sense. Hello dream life!

Chapter Four

Halfway through that first season on tour, I was in California for one of the contests at a place called Huntington Beach. To my surprise, Derek showed up, having recently moved there from Santa Barbara. Huntington Beach was his new local surf spot.

I can't tell you how amazing it was to reconnect with him! We'd grown and changed, had new experiences, yet he still felt comfortable, familiar. It was fucking awesome! By the end of the second competition in California at Trestles, we'd decided to give our relationship another go.

But with my hectic schedule and his full-time job, we didn't get to see each other much. So it was incredible when he joined me at the last event in Hawaii that season. I *loved* his optimism and enthusiasm for what I was doing! Plus, he was an amazing surfer, so I always valued his feedback.

Needless to say, life on tour was insanely different from the life of a regular 18-year-old who would be heading away to college for the first time. Man, by this point I had already explored new continents, partnered with some cool sponsors, gained media attention, and had a solid following on my Instagram account.

S and I were still super tight and I valued every video chat we had, but I'm sure you can agree it's not the same as hanging out in person! She'd joined me at lots of events in the first few seasons, but once she moved to Byron Bay just south of the Gold Coast and became a full-time lifeguard, her schedule kept her busy at home.

By the start of the next Tour year, Derek made a leap of faith and quit his job to travel with me full time. You might say it was a risky move considering our lack of experience as a conventional couple, but hey, he'd been wanting to make the transition to being a freelance writer so it seemed like the perfect time to go for it. I'd been able to stash away some of my earnings as an athlete from sponsorship deals and prize money over the first few years, which enabled me to foot his travel expenses. It was an easy 'yes'.

Traveling on the World Surf Tour is a mind-blowing experience. Imagine insanely long plane flights, constant movement, shuffling gear, competitive stress, and a myriad of other considerations that come with the role of professional surfer. As glorious as it all looks from the outside, it can definitely take its toll if you don't learn to adapt to the chaotic lifestyle.

Personally, I love being on tour. The continual change of location appeals to my adventurous side, and even though I don't always have a chance to be a tourist in the culturally diverse places we visit, I do always relish the excitement of new smells, new swells, new people, and new food.

Now, bring someone else along for the ride and you never know how things will play out. Will they be able to handle the craziness of it all? Can they cope with spending all day at events, watching, waiting, socializing? Can they adapt to last-minute changes, lugging loads of luggage, limited personal space, and an alarming amount of crowds and fans?

This is not something you can predict, because as my dad once told me *clarity comes from action, not thought.* In other words, sometimes the idea of something ends up being a lot more appealing than the reality of it, and on the flip side, sometimes it's even *better* than you imagined it would be! Either way, you'll never know unless you actually try it out for yourself.

As for Derek and me, well, let's just say that our partnership was full of bubbles and feathers. It was light-hearted and easy... at least at first. He seemed to enjoy the people he was meeting. He got to surf a ton of new waves. (Important!) He'd go off and do his own thing when he wanted to, venturing out to explore the local scene or surf a less crowded spot elsewhere, or stay back at our accommodation and focus on writing. We had a lot of fun.

I think a lot of it had to do with the fact we were still individuals within the relationship. We could live our own lives independently, yet still feel supported at the same time. I guess I'd say it was a healthy relationship based on mutual respect.

The excitement of having a partner by my side was *ah*-mazing. I loved knowing he was right there to wish me luck as I headed into the water, there to watch my every move while I was mid-competition, and there to greet me when I was done. He was my date at events, my buddy during travel, and my boyfriend morning and night. I was stoked!

And somewhere in the first year of our relationship Derek had also become my coach. It wasn't like we sat down and discussed the parameters of this new role though. It just happened naturally. I mean, he's an amazing surfer, and was already watching my every move, so it was easy for him to pinpoint my weaknesses and strengths. Plus, he'd spent so much time being coached by Greg that it was natural to jump into the role.

This added element to our relationship wasn't a problem at the beginning, when we were all good. But it sucked when I didn't feel like my coach was in my corner anymore. And that's what it had been feeling like for a while now. For instance, he used to encourage me to work on an air reverse because it had been one of my big goals for ages. He was all for it! He'd spend tons of time coaching me through the many elements that make up this particular move, and he knew exactly what went into it, because it's a maneuver that's super common for all of the pro men. But he hadn't seemed motivated to do this lately. In fact, he even went so far as to say that it's too hard for the women to get any air and maybe it's better to focus on more attainable goals... *WTF?!* Thinking back to it, that moment crushed my soul.

So that's what was on my mind, as I stood under the steaming hot shower, contemplating my major fail in the Championship. Thinking back over our relationship, wondering where we'd gone wrong and how we'd ended up here. I felt all of these realizations flooding into my brain like a tsunami. The loud sirens that I'd been denying about our relationship were now blasting so loud that I couldn't ignore them any longer.

I let out a sigh, wondering why I wasn't willing to see these not-so-trivial matters until now. You know, like the fact that it *really does matter* that we were clearly not on the same page in terms of what we wanted our future together to look like. Or the fact that he loved socializing and spent most evenings out, doing *who knows what*, while I preferred to stay in.

And to be honest, I didn't even know how or when this deterioration of our relationship had begun, but what I *did* know was that it had gotten worse – and that it couldn't go on like this. A part of me was desperate to shove this truth back down to the pit of my stomach where it had come from, but there was another force that was stronger, and it refused to give up.

So I turned myself over to it.

I let go.

I let go of my need to hold on. I let go of my need to control the outcome. I let go of my fear of being alone. I let go of the guilt, the drama, the worry, the doubt...

And I surrendered to the tears that started pouring down my face. I sobbed and sobbed and sobbed in the safe space of my scorching shower, where the streams of falling water were a message of encouragement to cry, to join the outpouring in an emotional as well as physical sense, giving me comfort in the process. It was the release I had unknowingly, yet desperately needed.

A few minutes or hours later (I had zero clue as I'd lost all concept of time), the tears dissipated. Along with the stress, the mental clutter, and the emotional drama. A weight had been lifted off of my shoulders, and I felt relief for the first time in ages.

It gave me clarity. And with this newfound clarity, I knew exactly what I needed to do.

Chapter Five

I stood under the water for a couple more minutes to enjoy the peace that had been evading me these last few... well, more like many, *many* months.

'Alright then,' I said to myself as I turned off the shower, feeling rejuvenated.

I dried off, put on my fave pair of super comfy jeans and pulled out a red tank top that had 'Aloha' written across the front in yellow writing. *Aloha* is the Hawaiian word for hello and goodbye. In Hawaiian language, it means love, compassion, and breath, among other similar sentiments, and it seemed like a good shirt to wear for what I was about to do.

I ran a brush through my long, blonde waves, taking my time, staring at myself in the bathroom mirror until I realized I was in procrastination mode. Okay, so I was scared about what I had to do next, but it was time to stop prolonging the inevitable. I put down my brush and walked out to the living room to talk to Derek, who was on the couch with a beer, fiddling around on his phone.

I sat down beside him, crossing one leg on the couch so that it was easier to face him.

'Hey, can we talk?' I felt nervous.

'Sure,' Derek replied solemnly while continuing to stare at his phone.

I waited patiently, and silently, trying not to fidget while he finished whatever he was doing. He must've finally realized that this was going to be one of *those* conversations... You know, the serious kind that don't involve other distractions. He put his phone on the coffee table in front of us, then leaned back on the couch and turned his head to face me, giving me an awkward smile before saying, 'What's up?'

Here goes, I thought, taking a big inhale before starting...

'Derek, I don't know how to sugar coat what I want to say, so I'm just going to say it. And please, if you can, wait until I'm done before you respond because I want to be able to get it all out without being interrupted.'

I paused for a moment, psyching myself up before continuing. Derek nodded in silence, giving me the go ahead.

'This thing we're doing, whatever it's turned into, isn't working. I'm completely lost and confused, and I don't know who I am anymore. I'm not just lost in terms of our relationship, but also as an athlete. The thing is I don't know what the deal is with *us,* but what I *do* know is that I'm not the happy person I used to be.'

He was watching me intently, looking more and more uncomfortable by the second. But he kept silent, so I continued...

'As for surfing, I've been feeling disconnected with my rhythm. I don't read the water or trust my instincts anymore. I second-guess myself and hesitate. And it's because I'm relying on you to tell me what to do. And while your intentions are good, of course, the reality is that it's not translating into success for me. I feel like a loser out there in competition and it sucks.

And I'm embarrassed about my performance this season. And, well, I can't keep doing this!'

Derek was so good at listening. I really appreciated that about him. I let out a big exhale and said, 'Okay, I'm done.'

He nodded his head a bunch of times, which is something he does when he's letting new information sink in. The truth was I had more to say, but it felt like that was a good place to stop. *This was just getting started, after all*, I thought, *I need to pace myself.*

After a couple of long moments that were drawn out by an uncomfortable silence, he finally spoke:

'Yeah, Zoe, I agree with what you're saying. I think I understand where you're coming from.'

'You do?' I said, surprised that we had finally come to an agreement on something this year, and that it was *this* of all things.

'And, well, I've been wondering if the Pro Tour is really what you want to still be doing.'

WTF?! I thought. I replied abruptly along the same lines, 'Huh?!'

I sat upright on the couch, realizing that we weren't coming to an agreement *at all*. He sat up too, reacting to my movement. He continued to speak, but now his voice had raised a few notches:

'I mean, c'mon Z, isn't it time to move on from the Tour and focus on real life?'

My mind was doing flips. Oh man, this conversation was heating up fast. Instead of snuffing out the flame, though, I stoked the fire by jumping on his ridiculous statement and matching his aggravated tone.

'What on earth are you talking about? You *know* how invested I am in my surfing career!' I shouted.

'Okay, okay!' he said, gesturing that we should lower our voices.

'Look Z, I love you, and you know I'm your biggest fan! I *chose* to be a part of your world and I've enjoyed it too. C'mon, you have to know that, right?'

He spoke more gently now, in a helpful attempt to douse the drama. But as he brushed his hair out of his face with his fingers, I could see that his brow was moist. He was not generally a nervous sort of guy, but whatever, I was too distracted by my thoughts to give it more than a fleeting observation. I had to focus...

'And now?' I was being harsh and short-tempered, even with those two small words, but I was feeling defensive and couldn't help myself.

'Well, I... I just think there's more to life than traveling around from competition to competition. It just seems like the sole purpose of your life has become all about winning events and adhering to the demands of your sponsors, and it's killed the simple joy of surfing.'

His words trailed off, but he continued to look me straight in the eye, and I could tell he was relieved to say how he really felt. Even though it was a kick in the face to me.

'What the *fuck,* Derek?! Why have you been spending so much time and energy on me when you don't even want it?'

'Because *you* wanted it, Zoe. This has been all about you, remember?'

Okay, I got that. But I'd been thinking all along that he wanted this too, otherwise why would he have quit his job to join me?

'Well then, what is it that *you* want, Derek?'

He sat silently for a minute, and even though I was anxious, I knew it wasn't a good idea to rush him. So I leaned backwards, resting my back against the couch, nervously shaking my leg and staring at the wall, waiting for his response. I'd like to think I was being patient, but, hey, I probably wasn't.

After an extremely long minute, he finally spoke.

'Well, I think I *do* want to be with you, Zoe, but not so much like this. I want to get married and have kids and travel around the world doing whatever we want, whenever we want...'

'Argh!' I couldn't help myself, so I threw my hands to my head and looked at him with disbelief.

'Oh my God, I can't believe this is happening! D, we've had this conversation before and you know I have no interest in getting married or having kids right now. I'm only 23 and I'm a professional surfer!'

'I know, I know, but 23 isn't *that* young. And besides, I'm ready to do more than what we're doing now. We're so chained to your schedule and, to be honest, that sucks sometimes. I know it was awesome at the beginning, but it's kind of gotten old for me. Plus, I'm having a hard time focusing on my writing. I think I need some new inspiration to get my creative flow going again. And since you're obviously stuck in a rut, I figured... I *hoped* you'd be ready for change too.'

We both fell silent, Derek waiting for me to say something. I was too angry to reply.

He reached over and placed his hand on my knee, hoping, I think, to reconnect with me so that we could work through this drama amicably. But no, not me. Instead I brushed his hand away and quickly stood up from the couch. I don't know why I did that. Maybe I just needed to get up and move around to shake things off.

'Ugh!' I said finally with an air of frustration. 'I don't know what to say, Derek, except that surfing is still my priority.'

'Oh. I see. Well, I guess I thought that maybe you'd have a change of heart around the Tour now that the season is done and you have the time to redirect your focus.'

'No man, I have to get my shit together and prepare for *next* season. I'm still in the game, Derek. I *did* qualify for the Tour again, remember, even if it *was* just barely?'

Our tones seemed to have come back down to an almost-normal level of conversation, which was good, but I honestly wasn't expecting it to have gone in this direction. I mean, I knew on some level that Derek wanted to move forward, since we'd had a few discussions around marriage etc., but I didn't realize there was *this* much urgency to it.

'Don't you see a life beyond your surfing career?' he asked, looking up at me as I paced back and forth in our small living area. His forehead was all scrunched and his eyes were wide – a tell-tale sign that he was frustrated. In an attempt to ease his discomfort, I stopped pacing and sat my butt back down next to him.

I was nervous, because I knew I *had* to be honest with him even though he wasn't going to like what I had to say. *Geez... Why does this have to be so hard?* I thought to myself, as I looked up at the ceiling, not quite ready to face the music. Every bone in my body was trying to get me to run away from this conversation. Why is it so hard to say how I really feel?

Somehow, I found some words.

'Well, right now I see a life *with* my surfing career. I see love, I see money, and I see fun surfing adventures with a partner by my side. But Derek, I don't know that I even *believe* in marriage, first of all. And second, I'm not sure I want kids, so it's kinda hard to go down that road with you right now... if ever. D, I'm sorry.'

Derek slouched forward to bury his head in his hands, moaning inexplicably. I had no idea what to do except rest my head back on the couch and stare up at the ceiling.

The truth was out, and to be honest, I hadn't expected to end up on the topic of marriage and babies; I hadn't been thinking that far into the future. It made me wonder; had I been too self-absorbed to realize how he felt?

The silence was deafening but I had nothing more to say. With his head still resting in his hands, Derek finally mumbled:

'Well, I guess I have something else to tell you then.'

'Oh okay. What is it?' For some reason, my heart began to race. What *else* could he possibly have to say?

He lifted his head up and glanced over at me, quickly blurting out, 'I've been having a... a connection... with someone else.'

'Excuse me? A *what*?!' My voice rose with each word, afraid that I already knew what he meant. Still, could he be any vaguer?

'A *connection*? What does that even *mean*, Derek?' I tried not to yell.

He seemed tongue-tied as he grasped for some words.

'Derek, you better spit it out before I lose my mind.' I was trying to calm down and stay seated on the couch so that things didn't heat up again.

'Yeah, well, I met this girl last year, when we were in California for the Trestles competition and...'

'And *what*? What do you mean in California *last year*?!' I really needed him to pick up the pace and I couldn't care less that he was struggling. Lucky for him he managed to pull it together, looking down as he spoke.

'Well, I was visiting a friend, and he had invited a few people over. She was there, and we ended up spending most of the night talking. It's not like anything happened, but then I saw her again this year and, well, we got to talking again, met up one night, where she kissed me... and I kissed her back... and I liked it.'

He spoke quietly, sheepishly.

'Well, this isn't fucked up *at all*. One minute you're telling me you want to marry me and have kids, and the next minute you're telling me you cheated on me. Are you sure that's all that happened?'

I was acting angrily and I didn't care.

'No, nothing else. I promise.'

'But you weren't planning on telling me what happened?'

'It's just... I've been trying to move past it and I wasn't sure it was necessary to share. But I guess deep down it's been bothering me. So since we're being honest...'

'Wow, how generous of you, Derek,' I said flatly. 'So what's the deal with her now? Are you keeping in touch?'

'We've exchanged a few emails, yes.'

'Jesus, this is so messed up.'

The anger had turned to upset, and the tears began to well up.

'How [*sob*] could you [*sob*] do this?'

'Zoe, I'm so sorry. I didn't mean for this to happen. I love you and I've been trying to make things work. But I guess... hell, I don't know!'

'Never [*sob*] mind, Derek. I don't need [*sob*] to hear anymore. I think our time together is [*sob*] done.'

Without waiting for a response, I got up, walked out the back door and plopped myself in the big hammock that overlooked the ocean. I needed space to calm down.

By the time the sun was settling down behind the horizon, so were my nerves. I was still super pissed that Derek had cheated on me, even if it *was* just a kiss. But it sounded like there was more to it, at least emotionally. That was what had made me feel worse. Still, I *had* planned to break up with him, so what difference did it make?

My mind was having its own internal battle; one part trying to accept what was happening and move on, the other clinging to the anger and the hurt, even a sense of abandonment.

Because that's what it felt like to be cheated on; like my trusted mate left me to go and secretly connect with someone else in the way he's only supposed to connect with *me*. Horrible.

When the sky was dark and night was finally upon this dreadfully long and painful day, I went back inside to face the music. Derek had made us dinner, and even though I should have completely lost my appetite, somehow I hadn't. A small consolation.

Between moments of silence, more sobbing, feelings of disappointment, betrayal, sadness, guilt, and a myriad of other sentiments experienced on both ends, we managed to hash things out and finalize our break-up. It wasn't easy, considering how raw I felt, but as luck and timing would have it, we were meant to leave Hawaii the following day, so we were forced to alter our plans immediately.

Change happens with the speed of thought. I saw this on a bumper sticker many years ago and it always stuck with me. It seemed applicable to this moment. The original plan had been for us both to stay with Sophie and her family, like we usually did. Instead, Derek re-routed his flight back to his home in California, where my dark and twisted mind suspected he'd be hooking up with this other woman in no time.

Needless to say, my night was sleepless.

Chapter Six

I got up around 6am the next morning. I hadn't gotten much rest, as you can probably imagine. I was too upset or confused or angry or whatever to be able to relax enough to fall asleep. Derek had spent the night on the couch, so I walked quietly past his snoring body and snuck out the door.

The *ohana* (a term Hawaiians use for 'guest house') where we were staying came equipped with two bicycles, so I hopped on one of the cruisers and pedaled my way down the street, towards one of the coffee shops in Lahaina.

Emotionally, I was in a difficult space. I felt the rug of my life being pulled out from underneath me. My relationship had failed *and* my surfing career was flailing, but the wonderful scent of the plumeria flowers and the sound of carefree birds welcoming the new day calmed my mind as I meandered down the empty, early morning streets.

I was only in Hawaii for a few more hours, and I wanted desperately to enjoy the magic of the land. Its *mana*. Its energy. An energy that I knew would give me strength if only I allowed it. And God knows I was going to need as much strength as possible to get through what I anticipated would be an emotional day.

Derek and I drove to the airport together, which was a pretty dumb idea considering how weird and painful it was between us. But hey, it seemed like the most logical thing to do since we both had to be at the airport around the same time.

We sat in silence as he drove, me resuming my position staring out the window. About half an hour into the 45-minute drive, I glanced over at Derek, who kept his eyes fixated on the road. I realized we were both feeling distant and sad, so I focused on the excitement of going home. Even though I had only lived there for a few short years before traveling all over the world and joining the Tour life full time, Australia definitely was home to me. My dad, unfortunately, would be away on a six-month trip in Kenya for work, so it was a major bummer that I wasn't going to be able to see him. But I *was* going to reunite with S and her parents and brother, and I knew that being in the familiarity of the Smart family was just what I needed right now. In fact, I felt a hint of relief at being able to see a little sliver of magic during this painful moment of the heart.

We arrived at airport departures, and as I was unloading my stuff, another well of tears began to stream down my face uncontrollably. I looked over at D who was pulling my board bag off the roof of the car for the last time, and I felt a pang of regret for not wanting what he wanted. *Why?* I thought to myself. *Why is this happening?*

Derek put my bag on the sidewalk and looked up to see the wet mess of my face. He reached out and pulled me into his chest. I wanted to pull away and maintain my distance and anger, but I couldn't. Despite our parting ways, I just wanted to feel his love.

'I'm sorry for hurting you, Zoe, I didn't mean to,' he said softly as he squeezed me harder.

With my face still buried in his chest and sobbing on his t-shirt, I told him, 'I know. I'm sorry too.'

Derek let go and walked back around to the driver's side. As he got in, he looked up to give me one more smile and a 'take care, Zoe' before getting in and driving away to return the rental car. The tears continued to roll down my face as I threw my backpack over my shoulder, grabbed my surfboard and bag, and made my way inside the airport to check in for my flight.

A hui hou, Hawaii. Until we meet again.

Chapter Seven

I had a window seat in the third row of the economy section of the plane. *One day it's gonna be first class all the way,* I said to myself as I put my backpack under the seat in front and settled into my chair. It's a 10-hour flight to the Gold Coast, but I'm only 5'4" and used to flying long hours in tight spaces. I had done this particular flight many times before so I knew I could handle the journey without much fuss. Still, I secretly hoped nobody would sit beside me. I put on my headphones, turned on one of my playlists and closed my eyes, ready to zone out.

Flying, I've discovered, is great for personal reflection, and so I've come to cherish these moments of personal quiet time in between the craziness of contests. Even now, knowing that I was carrying a lot of darkness in my heavy heart, I was surprisingly okay with feeling my emotions. Besides, so much had already come out in the last 24 hours that I figured the worst of it was over.

I must have drifted off to sleep at some point, because the next thing I remember is being rattled awake by an annoying little boy behind me kicking the back of my seat with his teeny tiny shoes. *Stupid brat,* I thought as I turned around and peered through the gap between my seat and the one next to me. I saw some messy blonde hair on the head of a... 4-year-old? It's hard to say when you don't pay attention to that sort of thing. I kept staring straight into his squinty dark eyes until he stopped fidgeting long enough to notice me. Our eyes finally locked and I proceeded to give him my 'look'. He stopped kicking immediately. I turned back around, feeling quite satisfied with my non-verbal communication, and noticed the guy next to me was getting his drink from the steward.

'Ooh, I'll have a rum and coke, please,' I said when she looked my way.

Nothing like a little alcohol to help lighten the mood, right? I pulled down the tray table in front of me before reaching over to take the miniature bottle of rum and sad cup of ice that my mysteriously beautiful neighbor was passing over to me. I glanced over half-heartedly to meet his gaze as he introduced himself.

'Hey, I'm Teo.'

'Oh hi, I'm Zoe.'

Holy crap! This was my reaction as I looked into his crystal blue eyes. They were absolutely mesmerizing. I swear to God I felt as though he was staring straight into my soul, which made me feel extremely vulnerable. So vulnerable that, of course, I turned away quickly and concentrated on pouring the rum into the plastic cup. After taking a few sips, I carefully placed the cup back down on my tray, studiously committed to *not* looking back towards Teo.

I gazed out the window, in awe of the vast darkness of the sky. It made me think about the movie *Interstellar,* and I recalled how blown away I was at the infinite possibilities of the Universe, then at how narrow-minded we are about the concepts of time and space. *We can't even begin to understand what's really happening 'out there'*, I thought.

Wait! I was having a dream before that kid woke me up! A memory was triggered by the thought of the movie. I remembered that the dream I'd been having was about feeling confined, trapped in a glass box on a busy street. I was banging on its walls, trying to get the attention of the people happily milling about around me. They were laughing and talking to one another, and everyone was floating or flying around me. But they couldn't see or hear me. It was horrible!

'The feeling of entrapment isn't pleasant, is it?' Teo said nonchalantly, clearly oblivious to the fact that he was trying to strike up a conversation with someone who didn't want to chat. Or maybe he *did* realize but didn't care. Regardless, I continued to gaze out the window even though he had caught my attention. I didn't want to be enticed, but something about him was drawing me in, so I tried discreetly to get a better look at him out of the corner of my eye. I noticed his long, lean legs, which took up most of the space in front of him, and I assumed this was the 'entrapment' he meant. His black hair was short but shaggy, and I wondered if...

Damn, so much for discreet! Our eyes met. (I tried not to look, I swear!) He seemed thoroughly amused by my avoidance technique as he waited patiently for a response.

'I don't know,' I replied, giving in. 'I guess so.'

I still *wanted* to be irritated, but he chuckled at me in such a sweet way that it would've taken too much effort to maintain the façade.

'Well, your thoughts are painting a much clearer picture than *I guess so.*'

I frowned in confusion. *What? He was reading my thoughts?*

'Yes, I am, and you were dreaming about being stuck in a

box. But don't worry about that for now. Let's just stay focused on the task at hand.'

Huh? Something strange was happening here. Something *real* strange. And my instincts, my *tough* girl instincts, wanted to put up a wall and block him out immediately. But once again, things went in the opposite direction and I felt compelled to participate. I didn't know how or why or what – it's just what happened.

'What's the task at hand then?' I asked curiously, giving him my full attention now.

'The task is to look at how you feel, based on the decisions you've made, and to realize that you don't like what you've become.'

And *bam!* Just like that, he punched me in the gut... metaphorically speaking. But he didn't stop there:

'Let's take it a step further and think of that box as a symbol of your self-imposed limitations.'

'My what?' He had me royally confused yet completely enthralled.

'Your thoughts are the cause of your disappointment and upset. Nobody else is to blame for the reality of your situation.'

'I'm not sure I'm blaming...'

But before I could finish my sentence he silenced me with a stare that was far more effective than the one I'd given to the kid behind me. I didn't feel any contempt in it, and maybe that was the difference.

'There's a part of your mind that wants to play the victim in the experiences you're having. But this is not the *real* you. This is the part of your mind we can call your *ego*. You are aware of this term, yes?'

'Er, yeah, of course.'

He continued, 'Anytime you have a negative or fearful thought, it's coming from your ego. And because you don't want to take responsibility for how this thought makes you feel, you blame others for it instead. For example, you blame Derek for making you feel hurt and betrayed and angry because of what he did to you.'

'How did you know?'

'Focus, Zoe, focus.'

Okay, so what is he saying? I wondered. *Am I living in a self-inflicted box? And if so, how do I escape?*

Turbulence hit and I woke with a jolt. My eyes shot open and I looked immediately to my right. The middle seat was empty, just as it had been when the flight had taken off. Right at that moment, the steward leaned over her cart and asked if I would like something to drink.

'Um, yeah, I'd love a rum and coke, thanks.'

Chapter Eight

I spent the remaining hours of the flight in deep contemplation. Or was it confusion? Was there even a difference? I still wasn't sure if I'd been dreaming or something else. What the heck had happened? I mean, obviously it *must've* been a dream, but how did it feel so freakin' real?

I decided that whatever it was or wasn't didn't matter. What did matter was that I needed to deal with this damn *box* full of self-imposed limitations that I was apparently stuck in. That much rang true at least. I mean, I knew I was in a funk, but I was the one responsible for getting there. I made a decision right then and there to free myself from my ego – from the fear and doubt that had me placing blame and playing victim to my circumstance. Yep, any and all self-imposed limitations had to go. It felt good to make this decision in my mind. *But now what?*

I realized it was going to require a little bit more effort beyond the decision itself. *But what kind of effort?* I pondered away at this for a little while and acknowledged my enjoyment of alone time. And since being alone would require me to steer clear of distractions, I thought it would be a good way to start this new process of 'figuring things out'. Yep, solitude was my friend.

Plus, without Derek in the picture, even though I already missed him, it eliminated much of the distraction. Whether I *had* been selfish in our relationship or not (the jury was still out on that one, if you ask me), there was no doubt in my mind that I'd poured tons of energy into it, which now made me see how out of touch with myself I had become. *Wow! I have so much me-time to catch up on! Where have I been?*

It was so weird. Just taking this brief moment to turn the attention back on me, gave me instant clarity. *No wonder I haven't been performing well! Geez! Why did I concede so many of my non-negotiables in my relationship with D?* I vacillated between sadness and excitement as I came to grips with this new perspective. Yes, Derek's role had come to include being my coach, and yes coaches are hired because the athlete believes the coach knows better, but in the process of listening to him, I had stopped trusting my own instincts. And this new pattern had decidedly rolled into our romantic relationship as well.

Why the heck did I become insecure in so many aspects of my life? It was a profound question, if I do say so myself, and the anticipation I felt in finding the answer helped me feel better, like I was on a journey rather than a detour. I took note that relationships could be either super helpful or super distracting. I decided that mine had started out helpful, only to become a distraction, and immediately began to feel a cloud of negativity hover over me. *Ugh! I can't believe I let him do this to me! How could I be so stupid?*

But before I could venture any further down the well of self-pity, the stupid brat behind me began kicking the back of my seat again. I swiftly turned around to yell at him (c'mon, I was in no mood for this), but instead my elbow knocked over my drink, spilling the melted ice and remnants of the drink onto my tray.

'Argh!' I wanted to scream out loud but was able to keep my frustration to myself as I used the little napkins to wipe up the mess. The lady sitting in the aisle seat kindly handed me a cleansing wipe that she pulled out of her purse for me.

'Oh, uh, thank you so much,' I said politely.

'No problem, sweetie. I have two little grandkids and these wipes are a lifesaver!'

I could tell she was proud. *Okay Zoe, c'mon, bring it back. Focus. What did that guy... Ted? No. Teo? Yes, that was it. Is that what he meant about the ego and playing the role of victim?* I felt a flash of inspiration despite the lingering negativity, and decided that the only way to crawl out of this state of confusion was via a personal declaration – a declaration that would help me to regain confidence. But how?

Well, what if I only said 'yes' to the things I wanted to say yes to? I also wanted to give myself permission to change my mind whenever I desired. I figured this would be a good way to get back in touch with who I was and what I wanted. But then I wondered if this would even be possible given the obligations I had with my sponsors and fans, especially when I already knew that some of those obligations weren't appealing to me, like, *at all.* Safe to say I didn't know how this was all going to work out. A miracle, perhaps? All I *did* know was that, for now, I had to pay attention to how I felt about any work I was being asked to do, either by others or of my own accord. *From this point on, I officially resign from saying 'yes' when I really mean 'no', and that's all there is to it.*

I reached down and fumbled around in my backpack looking for my pen and 'everything book', where I would journal, doodle, write my to-do lists, all sorts. I opened the notebook to a new page and stared at it blankly, waiting to be magically inspired. Feeling ridiculous and even embarrassed by my own lack of creativity, I thought back to life B.D. (before Derek) and reflected on my optimistic I-can-do-anything attitude and my excitement for all of the awesome that I *knew* was ahead. My, how things had changed...

I closed my eyes and took a long, deep breath in. I held my breath for as long as I could, trying to maximize the amount of air I could hold in my lungs. And then, as I slowly exhaled, I wrote down the words that came to me:

I WILLINGLY RECEIVE ABUNDANCE IN ALL ASPECTS OF MY LIFE, THROUGH THE UNIVERSAL GATEWAY OF MIRACLES AND MAGIC.

I read it a few times, clueless as to where it had come from and not even understanding exactly what it meant. But hey, maybe I didn't need to? It came to me *and* I liked it, so wasn't that a good enough start? Besides, the idea of experiencing more magic was like music to my ears, especially because everything had just gotten too darn regimented, even in my supposedly free-spirited line of work.

So there it was, a declaration that had come out of nowhere. Or had it?

I closed the book, leaned back, and shut my eyes.

Part Two
Find A New Flow

Chapter Nine

The long flight helped me to shed a layer of my old 'self', the way a snake sheds its skin. And even if it was just a teeny tiny thin little layer, it was enough for me to own the fact that a new chapter of my life had just begun.

You may be thinking, 'Duh, you broke up with your boyfriend and then got on a plane headed to Australia! Of course, it's a new chapter, Zoe.' But I'm talking about change on an internal level. It's like when my mom left and I couldn't move on until I fully admitted to myself that she wasn't coming home.

Well, the page had definitely turned. Derek and I had broken up *for real*, and there was no turning back.

After waiting 15 minutes for my oversized luggage and spending another 15 getting through customs, I finally entered the arrivals area of the already bustling Brisbane International airport and headed straight outside with all of my stuff. Ah! The subtropical onshore breeze was heaps better than that freezing cold air-conditioned airport...

I'd already texted Sophie when the plane landed, so I proceeded to the pick-up zone, sure she was already driving around here somewhere. She was also up to speed that Derek wouldn't be with me, because of the brief email I'd sent her before the flight to let her know that we'd broken up. I stood by the curb to make sure she could spot me, and also because I didn't want to sit down again. My back was sore and I needed to stretch it out while I had the chance before sitting in her car for the next two hours.

She pulled up in a fancy, shiny, dark blue Land Rover Discovery, yelling 'Zozo!!!' out the window. This was her fave nickname for me, among many.

'Fancy car, chica!' I said with a grin as she got out and walked around back to give me a hug.

Sophie was around 5'9", so she had a good 4 inches on me, along with a strong, well-built frame. She stooped, wrapped her long arms around me, and gave me a real good squeeze.

'Awww babe, it's so good to see you!' she said, hugging me even tighter.

'You too, S, thanks for picking me up.'

We chucked all of my bags into the spacious SUV, hopped in and began the drive down the coast.

I spent most of the ride 'home' listening to Sophie. I think she could tell I wasn't in the mood for an extensive conversation just yet. I was tired, and still emotional from the last 48 hours. I mean c'mon, a break-up, a long flight, and a strange encounter with a beautiful soul was all too much to verbalize at that point, at least in a way that wouldn't come across as crazy. Plus, the motion of the car was rocking me into a doze. Luckily, S's acute observation skills and emotional intelligence spared me the frustration of having to chat, as she filled me in on life since we last spoke properly about a month ago. She caught me up on her family, like how her little brother was an avid skateboarder and surfer now, which meant he was always getting texts from random girls crushing on him, and like how her mum was killing it in her online jewelry biz, and her dad was still happy doing his real estate thing and playing golf.

'S, your family is always amazing!' I meant it too.

'I know, I'm pretty lucky, hey?' she said with a big grin.

That's one thing I loved about S. She didn't hide the fact that she came from an extremely generous and supportive family. It's rare to see this kind of dynamic nowadays, I think, not to mention the fact that her folks are still happily married. I liked that she was proud to own it.

After being on the road for a couple of hours, we made the turn into her driveway. Sophie's family lived in a town called Lennox Head, just south of the ever-popular Byron Bay. Her parents' house is ridiculous in its modern beauty. The spacious, two-storey home was a mere 30 yards away from the beach, accessible straight off the back deck. S had her own self-contained apartment on the beach level of the house, with a separate front and back entrance. The family had moved to Lennox from Manly around three years earlier, and I don't know if her parents gave her this space as a way to keep her close or to keep a close eye on her. Either way, she was one lucky bitch!

I followed S through the front door and then veered into her spare room on autopilot. It was the room I would call 'mine' for the next three and a half months. S wheeled my hefty surfboard bag to the other end of the apartment and dropped it by the sliding door that faced the beach. It was so good to be in a place that felt like home after having traveled for the last eight months. S walked in and stood beside me as I stared down at the bed in front of me.

'Well, babe, welcome home!'

'Thanks, S. Hey, I think I need to pass out for a while...' I managed, my eyes already half-closed.

'Go for it, hun!'

She turned around, closing the door behind her while I splayed face first on the queen-size mattress and passed out almost immediately.

Chapter Ten

I woke up with a dry mouth, a headache, and the excruciating sound of a car alarm. Ugh! I lazily dragged my arm towards my face and squinted my eyes in order to get a clear visual of my watch.

'Crap... It's still on Hawaii time!'

My tired brain didn't have the capacity to even *try* to remember the time difference, so I just rolled myself off of the bed and started to rummage through my bag, searching for my toothbrush and other bathroom essentials. Once located, I dragged my ass to the adjoining bathroom, peeled off my sweaty, stinky airplane clothes and kicked them into the corner by the sink, before stepping into the shower and closing the glass door behind me.

Ah, yessss! I took my sweet time, enjoying the warm water as it cleansed and awakened both my body and my mind. After toweling off, I pretty much dumped my bag out onto the floor, searching for some clean clothes. I never got around to doing any laundry during my stint in Hawaii, so a fair amount of my stuff still needed a washing. I settled on a light purple long-sleeve shirt and pair of running shorts, then wandered into the kitchen to get some water and see if anything was going on. Sophie was on her laptop at the kitchen table.

'Well, hello there, Zozo. Feeling better?' she said looking up and giving me a big, enthusiastic smile.

'I'm not sure yet,' I said as I grabbed myself a glass of water and plopped down on a chair on the other side of the table from her. 'What time is it?'

She glanced down at her screen and came back with, 'Quarter past four, babe.'

I looked at my watch and did the math. 'Holy crap, we're like 20 hours ahead of Hawaii.' I don't know why I was so surprised, because I'd already done this Hawaii-to-Australia thing multiple times before.

'Wowzers, that was quite the nap, and I'd still totally be passed out if I hadn't been woken up by that car alarm.'

'Yeah, well, better you're up now anyway, so you can start getting over the jetlag. Besides, my parents are expecting us upstairs for a barbie in a couple of hours, if you're keen. And I need you to catch me up on this whole Derek thing before then. Gimme the deets. What happened?'

After first helping myself to some cereal, we went for a walk and I filled her in as best I could. My brain was still super foggy, so even though I left out a lot of the emotional nitty gritty, she got the gist of the situation... which was enough for now. With that out of the way, we returned to the house to kill time before dinner. S did some work on her laptop, but all I could handle was some Netflix on the couch.

'Let's do this, Zozo!' S was giving me the five-minute warning.

'Right on! But first I need to brush my hair and change my clothes. I don't want to look like a surf bum right off the bat you know. Gotta make a good first impression!'

'Ha, it's years too late for that, mate!' she said as she put her hand in the bowl of grapes on the table in front of us and proceeded to toss one at me. I was too tired to flinch and it landed right in my half-full glass of water with a big *plop!*

'Nice!' I said sarcastically as I got up and turned around to head back to my room. Not three seconds later I felt another grape hit my back. I looked back to give her my half-assed stink eye, but she was too busy laughing at her own hilariousness to notice.

Such a nutter, I thought to myself, happy to know some things will never change.

I wore my 'good' jeans for the occasion (meaning they fit snug and were fairly new rather than old, baggy and full of holes), along with a black, form-fitting top that was plain but nice enough. I had even put on some gold hoop earrings and some pink lip-gloss. I don't know why, but I was a little bit nervous to see Abby and Peter – that's Sophie's mum and dad – even though they're like my second family and I *know* they love me to bits.

S opened the downstairs sliding doors onto the deck and proceeded up the white staircase to the main house. The first person I saw as I reached the upstairs balcony was Abby. Her hair was blonde, but this time around she had a few extra silver streaks. Judging by the wrinkles on her face, you'd think she was in her 50s, but I'd always found it hard to tell. She loved the sun and had been an avid sailor for over 20 years so her skin was a tad weathered. She wore some cool patterned yoga pants and a plain white t-shirt. But what I noticed most was the gold chain with a turquoise pendant she wore around her neck – something she had made herself, I was sure.

'Zoe!' she squealed with excitement when she saw me, putting her drink down on the barbecue. She bypassed her daughter, who was standing between us, reached her hands out and gave me a warm hug, which came with a huge whiff of... what was that scent? Lavender, I think.

'Hey Abby!' I replied with excitement. 'It's sooo nice to see you... and to be here!'

She pulled back to get a good look at me, leaving her hands on either side of my shoulders. She looked me up and down, then stared straight into my eyes, holding my gaze. After a few seconds, I felt shy and looked away. Luckily, right at that same moment S's dad stepped onto the deck from their living room, holding a wine glass in each hand and loudly stated, 'Hey, Abby, stop eye-gazing at Z. You're making her feel uncomfortable!'

At 6'3", Peter was the tallest in the family, and impressively fit. Aside from golfing, he was a runner. He had been bald since I'd known him, which must've been about 12 years by now. He had dark brown eyes and a big grin. He loved his family more than anything, so it always meant a lot when they were all together, usually for Sunday dinner.

'Hey Peter! Thanks so much for having me...' but before I could say anything more he interrupted with, 'Oh please, we love when you're here. Anytime, love. Anytime, aye...' And with that he handed me one of the glasses of wine and S the other. 'Now, if you'll excuse me, I have some cooking to tend to.' He turned and went back inside the house.

'Geez, S, your parents look amazing.'

'Yeah well, they've definitely gotten more sarcastic with age... so watch out Zozo!'

'Oh please, I'm way too boring for them!'

'No kidding, babe. Taking the piss out of you is like shooting fish in a barrel. Ha!'

We both laughed and some of my wine spilled on my top. *Classic*, I thought to myself as I wiped the liquid off of my shirt with my other hand. S just rolled her eyes and continued to giggle.

When dinner was ready, we sat at the table inside the house instead of the deck, as the wind had gotten pretty strong. It was quite a spread. Chicken and veggie shish kebabs, spinach salad with strawberries, walnuts, and a raspberry vinaigrette, some homemade spicy bread (Sophie's specialty, made with jalapeño), and of course, more wine. We were just starting to dig in when Sophie's brother Seth walked in the door.

'Sorry I'm late, I was at the skate park and lost track of time.'

'Just clean up, get your butt over here and say hi to Zoe,' Peter hollered at him.

How cool is that? Instead of bitching at him for being late, Peter's main concern was to make sure Seth gave me some love.

'Oh heya, Z!' he said with enthusiasm as he put his stuff down and washed his hands in the kitchen sink. He came over to the table and bent over the back of my chair to give me a kiss on the cheek.

'Wow dude, you've grown... And you've got major facial hair!' I was bugging him already, as was the norm, but it was true. His scruff scratched my skin when he planted one on my cheek. 'Wait, how old are you?'

He kept his head down and ignored me as he walked to the other side of the table to sit down. He's probably the only person in Oz who I can successfully torment, so I don't hold back.

'Nineteen.'

'I hear the ladies are all over you these days. Got a girlfriend?'

He blushed and just shrugged his shoulders.

'Don't worry. I'll get it out of you later... one way or another!' I said with a smirk.

As we ate, I realized S must have already shared some info in regards to my break-up, as they didn't bombard me with any questions about Derek. Instead, they kept the conversation light and positive, with much of the focus on Seth. Dinner with my second family was a comforting entry into this new journey I was going on and I was super grateful for it. By the time we were done with ice cream, I could barely keep my eyes open, so I excused myself from the table and took myself to bed.

It was a surprisingly happy albeit brief first day back in Oz. It was good to be home.

Chapter Eleven

I must've zonked out the second my head hit the pillow, because when I woke up in the middle of the night I actually had to pause and get my bearings. I'd say that's pretty normal for anyone who travels as much as I did.

'Dammit!' I muttered as I looked at my watch. 2am.

Recovering from jetlag can be tricky. People have all sorts of theories on how to adjust to a new time change. But for me, the most effective technique is also the most obvious one: stay awake until it's time for bed, and stay in bed until it's time to get up. Of course, that's easier said than done.

I'd had a long flight with little deep sleep, so it hadn't been hard to pass out initially. But my body was still on Hawaiian time, which meant that after a few hours of rest it wanted to be awake because it was morning in Hawaii, even though it was the early hours in Oz. Staying true to form, I was determined to stay in bed until I fell back to sleep. My body was stiff and tired from sitting upright on the flight for so long – but I knew I could do it. And I did. Though instead of entering into a deep slumber, I drifted in and out, falling into some crazy dreams, waking up for just long enough to figure out where I was before rolling over and entering into another strange and vivid scenario.

In one of these scenarios I was alone, staring into a vast blue sky full of white, fluffy clouds. I was in the middle of a spiral staircase, and when I turned around, I saw that the staircase was part of a castle made of dark stone. I turned back and there he was... Derek. He was floating in the air in front of me, with another woman whose face was blurry so I couldn't tell who she was. They were laughing, oblivious to my presence. I reached out with my hand, calling out to him, but they both drifted away together, and I was left there, alone and crying... feeling abandoned by love.

In another one, I was watching surfers at what looked like Pipeline, that infamous wave on the North Shore of Oahu in Hawaii, but it wasn't shaped in quite the same, perfect way. I was in the water too, but not on a board. Instead, I was treading water with my head barely above the surface. Suddenly a surfer on a huge tsunami-sized wave came towards me. She was on my surfboard, driving down the line right past me. She was fierce and unstoppable, and I had to duck under the wave to avoid being run over. I felt jealous of her unwavering confidence.

I woke up, disturbed by my dreams, and rubbed my eyes; I could see it was still dark outside. I let my eyelids close but this time I couldn't fall back to sleep. Something felt weird to me, like someone was here. Was it just my mind playing tricks on me after my freaky dreams? I opened my eyes again, making sure not to move my body while I scanned the room. As I glanced towards the window about three feet from the foot of the bed, I saw a figure. I couldn't see much in the darkness... but I was sure it was the silhouette of a man. Lying there motionless, I was frozen in place while my eyes were glued wide open and my mind raced.

Surely, I'm dreaming, I decided, *or I'm going crazy... or I'm seriously in trouble...*

And then he spoke.

'Be still the mind.'

The words were softly spoken as they came out of his mouth, and even though he was on the other side of the room, it felt like he had just whispered directly into my ear. As though he was telling me a secret that only *I* was allowed to hear. Freaked out, I wanted to scream and yell for help, but something stopped me. Instead, quite the opposite happened, and I felt a lovely sense of calm wash over me. I realized I'd heard this voice before. It was familiar. Distinct. Compelling.

Was it? Could it be...?

'Yes, Zoe. It's me, Teo.'

I took a moment to let it sink in before sitting up, unafraid now, even though there was a strange man in my room who had appeared out of thin air. I was confused, but calm, a strange emotional combination. It was one of the weirdest experiences I'd ever had.

'You have forgotten about me for some time now, Zoe, but I have been with you always and everywhere, since the day you were born.'

'Confusing' seemed to be the word of the day, alongside 'strange'. All I could manage was, 'Um, huh?'

'I am your guardian angel, Zoe.' Teo was not fazed by my uncertainty.

I was squinting, desperate to get a clearer view, but his silhouette was so faint he looked more like a ghost. My efforts were useless. He continued before I could say anything else.

'When you were a little girl, we had countless conversations. You accepted my presence without question, for you did not distinguish between the physical and non-physical realms.'

Physical and non-physical realms? What's he talking about? I couldn't get my head around any of what he was saying.

'Soon enough, however, you began to learn the ways of your environment. You listened to your elders; people like your parents and teachers, who encouraged and even demanded that you pay attention to their rules, perspectives, and beliefs. This is normal. This is how the mind becomes deeply influenced by the physical realm, or *life on Earth*, as you know it to be called. Your ability to see *beyond* began to narrow, eventually blocking out the non-physical spiritual realm, of which I am a part.

The influences of your immediate surroundings began to consume you, and by the time your 5th birthday was upon you, you were no longer able to *see* me. But now, dear Zoe, your recent circumstances have caused you to begin questioning many perceived realities. Your mind is more open, as is your heart, which means you are now willing to remember.'

Remember what? I wondered.

'Remember what you already know...' he replied with a soft whisper.

I still had no clue how to respond, but in that moment I was *wide* awake, and felt so very *alive* in the quiet of the night.

'I must go now, Zoe. That is enough for now. But I will see you again. In the meantime, you needn't worry about deciphering this conversation, or my presence. It will all become clear to you with time. For now, simply *believe* there's more to life than meets the eye.'

And then he was gone.

Chapter Twelve

I woke up bewildered, as the memories of my middle-of-the-night visit from Teo came flooding back to me. I sat up suddenly, wondering if it actually had happened. Was it real or was it a dream?

Then I remembered Teo's request: *believe there's more to life than meets the eye.*

Well, I wasn't ready to discount that it was a dream, so I decided, at least for the time being, it could be both.

I wasn't sure what 'believe' really meant, but I did come to the conclusion that in order for me to believe there was more to life than meets the eye, I'd have to ditch the doubt. Okay then. So what doubts did I have? The first one that came to mind was fear. I was afraid of what would happen if I believed in an experience that was so inexplicable. It was beyond the realm of my understanding and I wasn't sure how I felt about something I couldn't control.

Whew! It was all too mind-boggling to deal with right now, especially this early. First things first – I needed to get salty. I put on my bikini, board shorts and hoodie, grabbed a chocolatey energy bar from the kitchen and threw it in my backpack with a water bottle. I found my wetsuit, some wax, grabbed my fins and a fin key, and stuffed them all into my bag as well. Finally, I pulled out my 5'10" round pin and opened the sliding door that overlooked the beach.

'Ah!' I inhaled the fresh early morning air as I closed the door behind me and made my way around to the main road. I jogged up to the parking area, which was the easiest way to access The Point.

As a self-proclaimed introvert, I prefer to get my day started while everyone is still sleeping. I'm not one to thrive in the hustle and bustle of crowds and voices and chaos, so it's always better for me to hit the surf for dawn patrol, when it's still relatively quiet. One of the many reasons I love surfing is because the ocean feels cleansing to the soul, and I've learned that when I feel anxious or frustrated or angry about some silly drama, or when I can't make a decision about something, jumping in the ocean for a surf or just a quick dip *always* lightens my mood and clears my head. So if I was going to sort this 'belief' stuff out, I most definitely had to get out of my head... and into the ocean.

I walked down the path and dropped my stuff on the rocks, close to where I could check out the waves. I sat down and began to gnaw on the energy bar from my bag. It was chewy, and a bit chalky, but these things were a staple for me so I was used to it by now.

Seven Mile Beach in Lennox Head is particularly famous for this righthand break at Lennox Point. This morning, the waves looked 'fun size', which for me meant shoulder-to-head high. They were fairly clean, and I was surprised to see there were already about 25 people out, which I thought was a bit much considering it wasn't even 7am. I'd honestly thought I'd be one of the first five in the water.

Even though it was early summer, the water temperature in December still hadn't warmed up enough for me, so I put on my long-sleeve spring suit. Fins in and board waxed, I strapped my leash around my ankle and carefully made my way down the rocks towards the water – board under arm and hair blowing in the wind.

So as I mentioned, the Lennox Point wave is a right point break. That means it breaks onto the rocky point and starts to crumble from the right, moving left. When most people start surfing, they try to catch the wave and ride it straight into shore. But a good, rideable wave actually moves in a specific direction – either to the left or to the right.

Now, what separates a *good* surfer from an *excellent* surfer is they understand that surfing requires not just skill and technique, but also a creative ability to read and feel the dynamic movements of each wave. No two waves are alike, so you have to adapt to each one individually, then make little corrections from moment to moment like adjusting your stance, speed, and rhythm. In other words, in order to maximize the 'surfing potential' from each wave, you have to develop both your left (analytical) and right (creative) brain hemispheres, which means it takes a strong head *and* a soft heart to get really good out there. Pretty cool, right?

I paddled my way to the point and took a couple of smaller waves on the inside, before heading to the main break. I lingered on the outskirts of the line-up to watch how the waves were breaking and how people were positioning themselves. There were a handful of locals dominating, and as it became more crowded with each passing minute, I knew I had to join the mix. It was now or never.

And then I noticed a set in the distance. It was coming in from a different angle and I happened to be lined up perfectly for it. I turned around and paddled hard to get into position. I snagged the first wave, etched in two smooth warm-up carves right off the bat. Then I had to stall and wait for the wave to reform so that I could pick up speed and get in one really sweet cutback before surfing off the back of the wave just as it broke in front of me. *Yeeewww!*

In the line-up waiting for another, I contemplated my experience. Every wave is different, so you have to feel for a new connection with each and every one, and then within every *moment* of each wave. To do this, you *gotta* let go of your thoughts, because thoughts are distractions that pull you away from the moment. Yep, thoughts get in the way, alright. They take you out of the present, which makes it near impossible to adapt and react to the wave's continual ebb and flow. If you're not focused, you're pretty much f*cked. It's that simple.

Wow! I thought. The best way to surf with both style and grace is by being fully present with the wave, from moment to moment. That's when the magic happens. That's when you're 'in the zone' and everything else around you melts away. It becomes effortless, where there's this feeling of connection that's...

Ooooh, is that what Teo meant by 'believe'? I wondered. *Are we talking about a higher power, when he says there's more to life than meets the eye?*

I sat on my board, pondering away when I heard a voice in my ear. It was Teo.

'Yes Zoe, wonderful! When you spend your time focusing on what you *should* have done or said, or *should* be doing or saying, you are simply stuck in the past or future, instead of focusing on the now. These thoughts occupy your mind and pull you out of the present moment. Therefore, you become *un*aware, making it quite impossible to connect with the perfect rhythm of the perfect moment available to you. Remember, *every* moment is perfect when you connect with it fully.'

I looked around but he was nowhere to be seen. What the heck was going on here? It was hard not to be in disbelief. I mean, how was he just showing up out of nowhere? Where was his voice coming from? And also, I couldn't hear anything else around me. It was like someone had hit the mute button on the world, no joke! The sounds of the ocean – completely gone. It felt like time was standing still.

And then Teo's voice continued.

'Zoe, the Universe has everything sorted out for you, and in truth, you need do nothing. Indeed, this is what it means to be *in the zone*. When this is forgotten, you begin to live from a state of fear. You think you're all on your own, that you need to control everything. Every decision, every thought... the outcome of your life now depends solely on your own ability to take charge of it, which would seem very scary indeed. But this, sweet Zoe, is backward thinking. You are not alone at all. The Universe has your back 100% and is always conspiring in your favor. It gives you signs and opportunities and ways to change your mind about how you see your life and your 'self'. With trust, you can turn any seeming tragedy into a gift.'

Like with Derek? I wasn't speaking out loud, but my thoughts were loud and clear.

'Exactly. You can respond to your experience with Derek in many ways. It just depends on how you choose to perceive it.'

'So how do I trust in the, um, Universe, when it feels like things are falling apart? I can't just sit back and do nothing... can I?'

'We'll get to the doing part later, Zoe, but for now, trusting requires a little bit of faith, and faith requires a lot of patience.'

I struggled to grasp all of this information.

'Um, Teo, how is it I can hear you but I can't see you? This is mighty odd, and I can't believe I'm not freaking out. I mean, seriously, this is really *really* weird, and I'm still not sure I understand who you are and where you came from.'

'Zoe, you are believing there's more to life than meets the

eye, and this is why you're not freaking out. You are also trusting this experience because, deep down, you have faith. You feel familiarity with this experience, even though you may not consciously remember it. With belief there is trust, and with trust there is faith. Don't worry; you don't have to have it all figured out at once. We'll take our time. We'll ease into it. Have patience, Zoe. I love you.'

And in an instant the sweet sounds of the ocean were once again loud. And I knew Teo was gone.

Chapter Thirteen

I stayed in the water for over an hour after Teo's visit, mulling over his words in between waves. I knew for sure that patience wasn't a strong quality of mine. I'm more the type of person who, when she wants something, wants it now. And besides, I thought that my impatience was actually a good quality, because it meant I didn't waste time when it came to going after my goals. I would get this laser focus and drive to achieve whatever it is I wanted. On the other hand, I got frustrated if I wasn't seeing results or achieving those goals fast enough. I don't know if this has more to do with my expectations or something, but I tended to feel like a failure much of the time.

And then I remembered the saying 'patience is a virtue' and wondered, *might it actually be true?*

A small wave lined up in front of me so I took advantage of it and rode it into shore. I slid off my board as I got to the best exit area, and carefully maneuvered around the slippery rocks and up to where my stuff was. I was a bit chilly, but it was nice to feel so refreshed, which always helps to rinse off the 'jetlag fuzzies'. I picked up my stuff and chugged some water while cruising back to the house.

After rinsing off in the outdoor shower (conveniently located on the back deck), I dashed to my room and threw on a t-shirt and my comfy jogging pants, then went straight to the kitchen and helped myself to S's food.

'Let's see... eggs, tomato, avocado, toast. Coffee. Perfect.'

I put the coffee on to brew while I made scrambled eggs. As soon as I sat down at the table to eat, S came out of her room and plopped down on the sofa.

'Hey you. Do you want a cup of coffee or something?' I said.

'That'd be tops, hun, thanks.'

I got back up and poured her a cuppa, adding a little bit of milk.

'Thanks, just how I like it,' she said as she reached up and took the mug. A few minutes of silence passed while I stuffed my face and S sipped her coffee, before she finally broke the silence.

'What's up, Zozo? Something on your mind? I mean, apart from the obvious.'

It's no surprise she could tell. She knew me well.

'Well kinda, yeah,' I replied. 'I've been thinking about the concept of patience. Like, as in, practicing patience as a way to increase my faith.'

I wasn't ready to mention Teo yet. That part I was going to keep to myself.

'That's pretty deep, hun. Faith in what?'

'Um, faith in a higher power, I guess. You know, in that there's more to life than meets the eye.'

It felt a bit weird to say it out loud. Plus, even though Sophie and I were super close, this wasn't the kind of stuff we normally talked about. Heck it wasn't the kind of stuff *I* normally talked about.

'Okay, I'm intrigued. Tell me more,' she said.

Alright, I thought to myself, *she seemed interested enough.* It felt safe to continue.

'Well, it's like, I was doing so well before I met Derek, and of course it was great to be with him and have a partner with me, but it also seems like it all totally backfired. You'd think I'd have been doing so well on tour with him around, but instead I've been seriously sucking over the last year or so. And then we broke up anyway! So it made me wonder, what was the point of it all? What was the point of all the work I put into the relationship?

But now, ever since I got on that plane and have had some time to think things over, I'm wondering if everything that happened with D was meant to happen. Know what I mean? I guess that's how I *want* to feel, but I'm having a hard time wrapping my head around it. I'm still upset, and well, pissed off when I think about him, to be honest.'

S nodded her head, acknowledging that she understood what I was saying. And then she spoke.

'So you want to see the experience as positive instead of negative?'

'Yep, I do. But I don't know how faith or patience fits into that. Does that make sense?'

I looked at S quizzically then, hoping that I didn't sound like a freak. S grinned at me.

'Hey, remember last year when I called you because I was bummed about that friend who was desperate to borrow $1,500, and promised to pay me back within three months, but then completely avoided my calls and ended up leaving town?'

'Yeah I remember.'

'Mate, I felt totally ripped off by someone who I thought was my friend.'

'That was bullshit for sure!'

I was enthused when she said this, glad to know she didn't think I was a nutter. I remembered that story clearly too, because it's crazy hard to upset Sophie. She's just so damn nonchalant about life, and sees the best in everyone. But this... this had really gotten to her bad.

'I was pissed at her for ages,' S went on, 'not to mention pissed at myself for feeling she'd taken advantage. I blamed her for everything. I carried this feeling around with me every time I thought of her. And you know I'm not one for hating, right? Babe, I *hated* hating! It made me miserable. But over time I realized that I didn't want to hold grudges and continue to be angry. So I sucked it up and eventually was able to take some responsibility for my part in the experience.'

'How exactly?' I asked.

'Well, I realized that it taught me an important lesson about taking the time to listen to my instincts before I say yes to anything. My gut was telling me no, but because I felt bad for her I did it anyway. In retrospect, that was a terrible reason for doing it.'

'Okay,' I nodded, starting to see where this was going.

'To take it a step further, it taught me what kind of people I want to surround myself with, whether it's as friends or colleagues or both, yeah? Look, I do get it, babe. It took some time for me to get to this place too, but when I finally realized that blaming her wasn't going to get me anywhere, it forced me to look at my own my shit, instead of focusing on someone else's. Namely, that I don't need to participate in other peoples' problems!'

I thought about it for a minute. Even though I thought her friend *was* to blame, what S was saying made sense too, I guess.

'Did it give you more faith?'

'Aww, yeah, I think so, because a few months later, when we were hiring for lifeguards, I suggested that we have a three meetings rule before we make any decisions. We took our time and it helped us sort out the right people for the team. It brought some real good quality to the process, which was perfect for me in terms of gaining respect from my boss, who gave me a promotion shortly afterwards. But you know, I don't think I would've had the knowledge to do that, or even the confidence to suggest it, if I hadn't gone through that other experience first. It gave me faith that everything works itself out in the end, even if it doesn't feel like it at the time.'

I couldn't believe how much S had to say on this topic. And still she wasn't done...

'Z, if you want to feel more optimistic, tell me what's pissing you off first. That way I'll know what we're working with, which will help us to see where you need to change your mind about the situation.'

'Hmm, good question,' I said as I thought about it. 'Well, when I was on the plane I had a moment of optimism actually, at least for a couple of hours... until the reality set in. Ha!' I laughed awkwardly.

'Good on ya, mate, a sense of humor!' Sophie was smiling as she sipped her coffee.

'Yeah right, well, I think what pisses me off is that he had a certain way he wanted me to train, and so I did what *he* wanted me to do, because he was coaching me. But I didn't like what I was doing a lot of the time. I figured I *had* to do it because I had decided that Derek knew better, because he was a better surfer than me.'

'And now?' she asked.

'Well, looking back, I'm not so sure that was a good idea. And then, in our personal life, I dunno, he kept talking about life in California and getting married and having kids, and something about it always felt like he was trying to pull me away from the scene!'

I was heating up as I let all of this out, feeling irritated now.

'Right, that's a pretty big contradiction, hey? You know, him being your coach yet wanting you to quit at the same time?'

'So how do I trust the process? How do I have faith when it all feels like crap?'

The more I let my feelings out, the more I realized how upset I still was.

'Hun, if you don't mind me being straight up about what I'm hearing,' and she continued without pausing, 'it sounds to me like you gave all your power to Derek.'

I looked away briefly, contemplating what she had said, and realized it was true. I mean, I was already somewhat aware of this, but the way S said it... well, it spoke to me on a deeper level.

'Sounds about right' was all that came out, because honestly, this conversation was starting to bring me down.

'Yeah, so how can you take your power back now?'

Sophie must've known by the tone of my voice that I was about at my threshold, but she wasn't one to back down when it came to getting to the bottom of an issue. And while I admired that she wasn't afraid to deal with uncomfortable situations or conversations, sometimes it was just hard to swallow her direct, no-nonsense approach. It made me miss my dad's gentle chats, and the way he would nudge me towards seeing something more clearly. Right now, I wished he was here with me instead of away in Africa. In any case, I tried to keep going.

'Uh, well, Derek's not here anymore so I suppose breaking up was the first step!'

'Righto Z, great start! What else?'

'Hmmm, I shouldn't assume that somebody else has all the answers, even if I consider them to be more skilled than me. I can take their thoughts and suggestions into consideration, but I don't have to take their word for it, especially if my instincts are telling me otherwise. And as for my personal life, well, I better be really clear about the fact that surfing is my priority. No matter who comes into my life.'

Sophie was nodding her head, smiling, and I was so relieved to feel understood. It instantly lifted the dark cloud that had been looming over my head.

'Thanks S, I'm one lucky chica to have you as my friend!'

'Right back at ya!' she grinned.

And I began to see it would all get better.

Chapter Fourteen

I did my best to stay awake the rest of the day by distracting myself with unpacking. Bit by bit, I found a place for items that had lived on the road with me for months. My clothes met with a drawer for the first time in ages, my soggy bikinis made their way from a plastic bag in my backpack to a hook in the bathroom, and my shoes and now-empty luggage found some floor space in the closet. By the time I was done, I felt completely settled in. And it felt great.

One of the cool things about being *on* tour is when you're *off* tour in-between seasons. It's like being on summer holiday! I guess this may seem weird, especially if you adore the idea of living the kind of nomadic lifestyle that I live, but for me it's the exact opposite! It's a novelty for me to live a 'normal' life. You know, one that means being in the same place for an extended period of time, and where I get to appreciate the little things, like having a routine, a favorite cafe, a jogging route. And of course, when I entertain the idea of getting to see friends and family on a regular basis, it's awesome. The comforts of home are highly under-rated, if you ask me.

Then again, I *have* created a kind of 'home away from home' at the regular events on the WSL circuit now that I've been to each place multiple times. Let's see... There's the Bonjour Café in France, which makes the best *café au lait*, the lovely Hotel Cascais in Portugal, and I always look forward to the friendly local community at the Namotu Island Resort in Fiji. I know, I know, I'm pretty damn lucky.

Anyway, who do I want to catch up with while I'm here? I pondered. I hadn't made much of an effort in the previous couple years because Derek was always with me, so we'd mostly stay in and read or watch Netflix. My introverted side loved it!

Ha, I'm so slack! But not this time, I decided. *Nope, this time I'm going to make an effort to be... what do they call it? Oh yeah... 'social'.*

I grabbed my phone from the floor, sprawled onto the bed and began scrolling through my list of contacts, looking for names of friends in the area. Unfortunately, it quickly became apparent that, aside from Sophie, I didn't have many mates around. Duh, I was only here because S had moved here from Manly! But then again, I didn't have many friends in Manly these days either. I mean, I hadn't even been in Australia for heaps of time before I'd started touring. In case anyone needed proof, my American accent still lingered.

I switched to Instagram for a more entertaining distraction. Looking through my feed, I thought about the fact that I desperately needed to post some photos. I had completely ignored Insta this past month, and knew it was poor form to abandon my amazing followers who were waiting to hear from me, not to mention my sponsorship considerations. But my heart just hadn't been in it.

How was I supposed to post beautiful, happy photos when I wasn't feeling remotely beautifully happy? And I certainly couldn't post pics of the way I *really* felt, because that's not what people wanted to see from me, right? I know I could've faked it just as easily, but I didn't want to. It didn't seem like the right thing to do.

Oh well, I'll get to that soon enough, I thought to myself optimistically. I let my phone drop onto the bed and stared at the ceiling. Nothing doing. Just staring, letting my mind wander. It was relaxing. Eventually, my eyelids grew heavy and sleep took over.

I have no idea how long I passed out for, but I know I still would've been, if not for the flash of light that startled me awake. I opened my eyes, expecting it to be the afternoon sun. And while there *was* a blindingly bright light that shone from the window and onto my bed, everything else around me was dark. What the...? I reached over and turned on the lamp next to my bed, which only blinded me even more.

'Ah, dammit!' I said out loud, covering my eyes with my hands as I sat up and leaned back against the wall. I waited until the odd, burning sensation in my eyeballs subsided before opening them again. But this time, standing in front of the magical shining light was – yep, you guessed it – Teo.

Okay, now things were making sense!

'Aces to you for a grand entrance, Teo,' I whispered loudly.

I squinted, struggling to get a clear view of him while I spoke, but the light made it difficult to make out many details. What I *could* see was that he was wearing a collared, button-down shirt, white I think, and dark pants. I recognized the face I saw on the plane, mainly from the chiseled structure of his jawline and from the way strands of hair brushed along his chin, but that was about it.

'Can you come closer?' I whispered. 'I can barely see you.'

'You will begin to see me more clearly throughout the days. Have patience, sweet child. As your trust and faith increases, your fear will slowly melt away, and I will come closer.'

I listened to what he said, interpreted it, and responded, 'So what you're saying is that this is all I can handle?'

He laughed gently while nodding his head in agreement as I felt the word 'self-talk' enter my mind. I couldn't see his eyes clearly, but I knew that he was looking straight at me, and that this word had to have come from him.

Now, I don't know if you've ever had any encounters with angels, but I tell ya, it was impossible to argue with this one. I was consumed by the love emanating from his presence.

'You know, this is all very surreal, Teo, and normally I'd be totally freaked out about a stranger showing up in my room unannounced, but I feel so warm and safe with you here. You are... so... beautiful.'

'That's because I'm a reflection of your potential, Zoe. You are also a beautiful being full of light. You are also able to emanate a sense of warmth and love that extends far beyond your sight.'

'Wow, that seems impossible,' I replied.

'It *is* possible. This feeling you have when you're in my presence is your natural state. You must be patient with yourself as you uncover the blocks that prevent you from embodying the truth within you.'

I always needed a moment to let his words sink in. They were so profound and often difficult to accept. I mean, who talked like this?

'Teo, anyone who knows me well knows that patience is a concept I don't care to practice. I mean, when I know what I want, I want it *now*. And anyway, I thought we already covered this.'

'Yes, exactly,' he said.

A long silence was shared between us and I felt comfort in that moment, even though I knew I was being a major brat.

What can I say? I was rebelling against the very thing I wanted to experience for myself.

He broke the silence a few minutes later saying, 'Today is about positive self-talk.'

I wisely decided I would be better off to just listen, so I kept my mouth shut, nodding my head in agreement instead. Teo smiled and continued.

'Self-talk, in a general sense, is what you say to yourself from moment to moment as you go about your day. For example, you are eliminated early on in a competition. What do you normally say to yourself?'

I suspected he wanted me to respond.

'Oh, um, well, I've been pretty hard on myself. I get angry and tell myself I suck, and then, uh, I probably take my frustration out on Derek.'

'Yes, and then what happens?'

'And then I avoid talking to everyone else and feel bad about myself. And jealous, and moody, and competitive in a bad way.'

I honestly couldn't believe the words that were coming out of my mouth. I wasn't one to admit these things out loud. Not even to myself. Maybe Teo was like my own personal truth serum.

'Yes, Zoe. This is a decision you make based on how you *choose* to see your 'self'. On the other hand, you could choose to see yourself in a different, more positive light. What else could you choose?'

It felt hard to think of something positive. I was so used to reacting negatively that it had become my go-to response. Nothing was coming to me, so I looked up and let out a big sigh, as I realized how far into the darkness I had gone...

'Good, Zoe, you are beginning to see the thoughts you have been choosing to think, and how they have been affecting you. Now, let your mind come back to the light, and choose again.'

'But how do I find something positive out of a negative experience?' I was stumped.

'Zoe, try to embrace the experience as a gift, by always seeing that there is something to gain from it. For example, think about what happens when someone gets lost on a road trip. They could become upset, focusing on the wrong turn and lost time, and its inconvenience. But they could choose another perspective. They could see it as a fabulous detour to a new place, a new adventure. And maybe this person ends up running into an old friend, someone with whom they've been wanting to reconnect. There are *countless* possibilities. In other words, *you* get to choose how you want to feel, based on how you interpret any given situation.'

'So you're saying I need to change my mind about how I see things?'

'Yes. The difficulty for humans with this particular lesson is that most people are controlled by their emotions. For example, you are happy when things go your way in competition; you are unhappy when they don't. Unfortunately, this kind of mindset makes the experience of joy possible only within the framework of a seemingly positive experience. As a result, one goes through life feeling insecure, craving success yet averting failure all at the same time. It's a fear-based way to live. But Zoe, viewing an experience as negative or positive is all in the eye of the beholder. It's a choice you make, nothing more and nothing less.'

I was starting to understand what he was saying, albeit still a little fuzzy. That's probably why he added:

'Zoe, the easiest way to practice positive self-talk is to have faith and patience that everything is working out in your favor.'

'Hmmm, the patience thing strikes again!' I said sarcastically.

'Think of it this way, when you feel anxious that something

is not happening as quickly as you desire, you begin to think that nothing is happening at all, and so you become frustrated.'

'And that's when I lose faith?' I said, starting to understand on a deeper level what he was getting at.

'Yes. When you begin to lose faith, you have a tendency to become even more frustrated, doubtful, and hard on yourself. You might say something like, *what's wrong with me?* Or, *what did I do wrong?*'

'Let me get this straight. What you're saying is impatience *leads* to negative self-talk and loss of faith?'

'Yes. Ultimately, it means you're turning your back on the Universe because you're turning your back on your Self.'

'So if I focused more on having patience and maintaining my faith no matter what's going on around me, then it would be easier to practice positive self-talk?'

Phew, that was *a lot* to take in, but I think I got there.

'Well done, Zoe, yes. Remember, faith is about maintaining a sense of peace *regardless* of your external experiences. It comes from trusting that there is a higher power working diligently on your behalf, to give you *exactly* what you need. We'll get to more of that later, but for now, focus on saying nice things to yourself even when your first reaction is to do the opposite. Watch yourself closely, Zoe. Be diligent with your thoughts.'

Chapter Fifteen

Mentally speaking, a lot had happened since returning home, and I was feeling overwhelmed by the gazillion thoughts cluttering up my mind.

Teo's visits had helped me realize that I was being way too hard on myself. And because of it, I'd become a rather negative person. I don't know if it was obvious to others, but I suspected it was, at least to those who were paying attention. Plus, my break-up was still an open wound. I missed Derek terribly, and being in this house kept reminding me of him, which made it hard to shake the gloom.

But now that I was taking to heart what Teo had said, I realized he was right. I *was* my own worst enemy. It was the wake-up call I needed to kick-start a shift in both my behavior and my outlook on life. I didn't want to be a drag; I wanted to be a positive influence in the industry. This new intention lifted my spirits, and there was no-one better to share it with than the ever-optimistic Sophie. So when I told her of it, she, of course, was all for joining in on the ride. Together, we decided that in order to get down to the business of positivity, it would require a full week of fun. And since she was the one who managed the lifeguard schedule, it was no problem for her to adjust her shifts accordingly.

During our dedicated fun week, S caught me up on her boyfriend/girlfriend escapades. She had no sexual preference, and her stories about guys and girls were super hilarious. Her happy outlook on life was inspiring. She was *always* stoked, and I swear this has been the case since the day we first met. We took lots of walks on the beach. Sometimes her bro joined us, sometimes her mum, sometimes her dad, and sometimes all of them together. We cruised the shops and cafes in Byron just up the road. I started to read *An Autobiography Of A Yogi*, handed to me by S's mum after a sporadic heart-to-heart one morning. And I chatted with Dad on the phone, watched the *Twilight Saga* (which I secretly fell in love with), and ate more than my fair share of gelato. I ate more than my fair share of everything, in fact, including a memorable Christmas Day barbecue over-looking the beach on the back deck at the Smarts.

And of course, we surfed heaps, having a blast and goofing off just like we used to back in the day. No pressure, no drama, just plain ol' fun. Okay, okay, I'll admit I still had to continually re-remind myself to relax! The old me was annoyingly incessant in its attempt to creep in and stress me out. This, I learned, was the fast track to negativity.

Luckily, Teo's encouragement to practice patience had helped me slow down and smell the flowers, so to speak. Which, for me, meant trying to relax without putting any pressure on myself. Besides, I'd been back in touch with Greg, my old coach, and I knew he was bound to kick my ass into high gear once we started working together again. *Why rush it?* I figured.

'For now,' I declared, 'I give myself permission to fully enjoy the simple things in life.'

It gave me some relief. But to be completely transparent here, I still felt a shit ton of resentment when I thought about

Derek. Meh. I was *trying* not to let it get to me, which had to count for something, right? I was doing my 'Teo homework' by focusing on positive self-talk, which I'll have you know was *a lot* harder than it sounded. Especially since I came to realize my addiction to negativity. The difficulty I was experiencing in breaking this pattern had forced me to see, yet again, just how far into the darkness I had gone. I'm tellin' ya, it took *a lot* of effort to be nice to myself.

But it was working. I think. I felt... lighter? Yeah, I think that was it. Lighter.

Chapter Sixteen

This break had started out as a simple sabbatical – time away from life as 'Zoe the professional surfer' – but when I woke up on the day that marked two weeks after my arrival, I felt a sense of urgency that couldn't be ignored. Just like that, I had the unstoppable drive to start pre-season training. My determination to kick ass was as fierce as ever, but so was the pressure to perform. And once again, I felt the weight of the world drop heavily onto my shoulders.

Dammit, I thought, annoyed as I walked up the beach with my backpack full of surf gear to meet up with Greg.

Greg lived in Lennox these days, his house half a mile south of where I was. Greg and Peter, S's dad, were business partners and mates from way back when, so it was no coincidence that he'd moved from Sydney's Northern Beaches around the same time as Sophie's parents. We decided to meet at The Point.

Truth be told, I felt hesitant to hire Greg as my coach again, considering the fact he was now my *ex*-boyfriend's uncle, but when I saw his smiling face from a few feet away, I was instantly reassured of his solid, non-judgmental character.

'Hey hey, Zoe. Welcome home, love. How's it feel to be back?'

'Hey Greg, it's good to see you!' I said, gently putting my board down and giving him a hug.

I noticed that he was quite a bit bigger than the last time I'd seen him, and as we hugged, his newfound 'softness' was slightly disconcerting, as was the shallowness of his breath, which I could hear when I had my ear against his chest as he squeezed me. In all the years I'd known him, he'd been a fit man. Yes, he was a bigger, stockier guy – but always fit. I wondered if something was up, but really, how would *I* know? And what could I say?

I decided to avoid the possibility of an awkward conversation, and over-compensated with enthusiasm instead.

'It's so great to be back, Greg! I do miss Dad, but staying with Soph has been a lifesaver! God, I just love the Smarts! Such a great family.'

'Good to hear, darl.'

He gave me one more big squeeze before letting me go, and I almost lost my balance as he did. *He's still strong, which is good*, I thought to myself. But I couldn't shake the funny feeling that all was not okay with him.

'Shall we discuss our game plan?' He got right down to business, as he usually did. Not much of a small talker, this guy, which as you may have realized by now was fine by me.

'We've got just under three months until Snapper, so what do you reckon?'

Snapper Rocks was where the first competition of the season was held every year. It was just over 100km north of Lennox, in a popular surf region of the Gold Coast.

'I reckon I want to win...' And then paused ever so briefly before adding; '...everything.'

'Of course you do, Zoe. And if you don't mind me saying,

from your final ranking and what I know about you and Derek, it looks like you had a tough season.'

I heard myself sigh as my head dropped and my shoulders slouched, indicating a most obvious sense of defeat. But he was spot on, and I had to give him an honest response.

'Yeah, it's been a tough *year*. I guess you know about Derek and I parting ways.'

I was staring at the ground for the most part, only lifting my head slightly to see if I could catch a glimpse of his reaction, in case there was one. He said nothing. Maybe he wanted more of an explanation? Probably. But that was as far as I got, and with each passing moment of quiet, I grew more and more uncomfortable. I *had* to break the silence.

'What about you, Greg? What's been going on with you lately?'

The focus was on him now and I was hoping he'd fill me in with the truth.

'Honestly Zoe, things are *interesting* right now. But I'm hanging in there.'

I suspected this was all the information he was willing to share right now, just like I'd shared very little of my full picture.

'Okay, okay, good.' (What the heck else was I supposed to say?)

And then he brilliantly changed the subject. It was definitely *way* too early for awkward.

'Well then, Zoe, are you ready to do whatever it takes?' His voice was more upbeat now.

'Hell yeah!' I replied enthusiastically as we gave each other a high-five. We sat down on the rocks overlooking the surf to go over the details. As it turns out, Greg had conjured up an entirely new training regime.

Over the next couple of weeks, life became super intense – both on and off the water. Greg had me doing a combination of strength and metabolic training, which included kickboxing workouts with a local trainer. And while training had been par for the course in years past, Greg seemed to bring a whole new intensity to his job. I sensed he wanted this for himself as much as he wanted it for me. He was serious and wasn't holding out any room for error on my part. I worked hard, allowing him to push me beyond pain and comfort... And to the point where I scared the crap out of myself a bunch of times in some pretty big wipeouts.

'C'mon Zoe, get it together!' was something I began to hear on the regular, along with 'focus!' and 'take charge of yourself!' These were just a few of the comments he hurled at me during the first 12 days or so. I took his words in my stride because I trusted him. I mean, his coaching had done wonders for me in the past, like when I qualified for the Junior Tour. I had to believe he knew what he was doing now too.

I slept hard and fast on these nights, too tired for anything else. Soph had been working a bunch too, taking up some extra shifts to make up for our days off together, so at least I didn't feel as though I was missing out on anything.

One glorious sunny day, a few weeks into the new program, Greg had me sit really deep at The Point. The waves were double overhead, which was deeper than I was comfortable with at this feature, not to mention deeper than a lot of the top local guys who generally take priority. That's a lot of testosterone to deal with. I swear to God I could feel their angst being thrown my way, which meant the pressure was *real* when it came to committing *and* charging hard when a set wave came in. And if I didn't? Well, I'd be committing social suicide in the surfing hierarchy.

Here's how it'd go down: I'd feel embarrassed, more than likely piss someone off who could've ripped the wave I chumped, and then I'd paddle away with my head hung low.

In case you hadn't figured it out by now, I was super nervous, and even slightly shaky. Had my skills recently improved? I suppose so. But the timing didn't feel right and I wasn't sure I was ready. It was the same feeling I get when I imagine myself surfing optimum Pipe; I knew I was good, but I wasn't sure I was *that* good.

A set was rolling in and I let the first wave pass without hesitation. Judging from the previous sets I'd observed, I knew the first wave wouldn't hold and that the third one would work best, so that was my plan. But as the second one appeared, all the boys next to me were yelling at me to go. My heart was pumping and I felt pressured to do it. The game was on. And there was no way I was going to crumble in the face of fear, so I turned around and paddled my ass off to catch the wave. Greg was on shore with the video camera, and I swear I could hear him yelling at me too, though I couldn't decipher *what* he was yelling.

I popped up as fast as I could, pulled in tight to the wall, and immediately started pumping down the line of what looked to me like a ten-foot face. Unfortunately, it quickly became apparent that I was too slow, and that it was already too late. The wall was closing out and I was under the seam of the wave with nowhere to go. Talk about worst-case scenario. This was the exact place I *didn't* want to be. Much like, say, if a piano fell from a window and you just happened to be standing on the spot right underneath where it was going to land.

The wave hit me on the head and its impact threw me off my board. I was pitched into the air before freefalling into what felt like concrete. *Whabam!* I was in a washing machine now, tumbling around... and around... and around. The power of the water held me down and I was at its mercy, feeling terribly pessimistic about the miserable plan it undoubtedly had in store for me. But all I could do at this point was hold my breath, wait, and do my best to relax so as to conserve as much air as possible.

Once the violent tossing subsided, I opened my eyes to see if I could get my bearings, even though I was still being held underwater. *The set must've passed*, I thought, still trying not to panic even though my lungs were screaming for oxygen. I climbed my way up to the surface, ready for air the second my head broke through the water. It was just enough time to get a breath in before the next wave came down on me.

Again I was underwater. This was the ultimate practice in patience. And trust. And faith. I'd probably only been under for 10 seconds this second round, but I swear those seconds felt like forever.

I came up and once again gasped for air. I yanked on my leash with my leg to bring the board back to me, grabbing it and immediately pushing it under my body so that I could paddle out of the 'break zone'. I was surprised it was still in one piece. I hustled my way to shore, even though my body was tight from lack of oxygen and I was painstakingly out of breath.

I pulled the leash off my ankle and ran sloppily up the rocks, slipping and stubbing my toes the entire way.

Greg was heading towards me, but he was slow-moving, and I took off in the other direction before he could catch up to me. With my board under my arm, I dashed down the street, towards home, as far away from him as possible.

By the time I arrived at the back porch, I was so out of breath that I was wheezing. My head was throbbing from the wave crashing on my head. I was sweating inside my wetsuit and completely parched.

I dropped my stuff on the back patio, not giving a fuck about damaging my board, and rinsed off in the outdoor shower. I stayed in long enough to catch my breath and cool off, but not too long, because I wasn't sure if anyone was around and I needed to avoid conversation at all costs. I needed to hide.

What just happened? That was just one of the many thoughts rattling through my brain. As soon as I felt clean of sand, I ran into my room, threw the towel on the floor, hung my bikini in the shower and chucked on the first item of clothing I saw – an oversized t-shirt.

I began pacing.

Oh my God, oh my God, oh my God... What is happening??!!!

I felt strangely nervous and excited at the same time, but I didn't know why. I'd surfed big waves plenty of times; I'd been *beaten down* by big waves plenty of times.

That's just how it goes, I thought. *That's how you learn. Pushing past your comfort zone is how you develop skill. That's a given... So what's different this time?* I wondered.

While the pacing was helping to clear my head, it was doing nothing to alleviate my headache. But I couldn't stop. I paced. And paced. And paced some more. And eventually, I realized the difference was in my state of mind.

Nothing is as it seems. Everything is the opposite of what I thought. This isn't how I want to live my life.

And once again, change was upon me.

Chapter Seventeen

I continued to hang out in my room while the adrenaline rush of the morning's event dissipated. By 10am, my headache was mostly gone, but it was now my grumbling stomach that had my attention and was begging me to feed it. I went into the kitchen and yanked open the fridge, looking for something enticing to eat. But no, I shut the door, feeling disenchanted by its contents and figured I'd take myself out. Just then, S and her mum walked in with some delicious looking boxes. Perfect timing.

'Hey babe!' S called out as soon as she saw me. 'Mum and I just had brekkie and we brought back treats!'

'Yes!!!' I replied enthusiastically. 'Starving over here!!! Whatcha got?'

'How about some fluffy pastries?'

She placed the two boxes on the counter and then opened their lids to reveal a mouth-watering assortment of baked goods: one apple strudel thingo, a couple of muffins (carrot, maybe), a croissant each, some chocolate chip cookies, and a mini-loaf of banana bread.

'Oooh, yes please! You rescued me just in time – I'm so

hungry!' I said as I grabbed one of the muffins and took a bite of the warm, moist piece of heaven.

'Here's your latte, darl!' Abby said, handing me the take-away cup. 'S wasn't sure if you'd be back from your training session yet, but my spidey senses told me you were here – so I went ahead and got you one.'

'Well, your spidey senses were right on, Abby. Thank you so much!'

I took a sip and smiled, nodding my head in approval of the vanilla latte.

'Someone's spunky this morning, huh? Have a good sesh with Greg, babe?' S asked as she walked around the counter to get a knife from the kitchen, pulling my pants down as she made her way back to the table.

'Hey!!!' I screeched, yanking them back up with one hand, the other still very much committed to the muffin. But S began slicing the strudel into bite-sized pieces, ignoring me, and fully pretending nothing had happened. Her mum on the other hand giggled away, enjoying, I presume, our ever-present childish antics.

'So it was good?' Sophie asked again as she put the knife down.

'Um, yes and no...' I said, my words trailing off as I looked away, wondering what to say. 'I'm not really sure what happened, to be honest, but I think some would call it, like... maybe an epiphany?'

'Oooh, I love epiphanies!' Abby said enthusiastically. 'Do tell!'

We sat down together at the table and they started nibbling at the strudel while I finished scoffing the muffin, doing my best to collect my thoughts before putting them into words.

'Well, I guess I'll start with the big news first. Get ready, because it's a bit of a shocker. I've decided not to train with Greg anymore.'

I said this with my mouth still full, hoping they wouldn't catch everything I'd said. Maybe I was embarrassed or worried about how they'd react. Maybe it was because it would be real as soon as I said it. I swallowed the muffin and took a sip of the latte. More thought-gathering (AKA stalling time). Building up to the peak, I continued.

'In fact, I've decided not to work with a coach at all. Or, for that matter, *anyone* who's going to tell me what to do.'

My words came out with such conviction that I surprised even myself. Soph and Abby were cool as cucumbers, prompting me to elaborate with their continued silence and unwavering eye contact.

'I had a big wipeout today and I guess you could say it, er, rattled some sense into me. I know Greg and I are still just getting started, and at first I was really excited to work with him again, but something about it just doesn't *feel good*. I had so much fun the other week with you,' I said, looking up at S, 'and I really needed that. It was so sweet to be free of the constraints of a grueling training regime. And S, remember when you mentioned that I'd given away my power to Derek?' She nodded, confirming the moment. 'Well, this morning's event made me realize that I had once again given away my power, only this time it was to Greg. And surprise! I decided to trust him more than myself. I went against my instincts. I know this sounds a bit dramatic, but it felt like my beat down was punishment for it.'

Abby and Soph both gazed at me in the same way, with their heads tilted, eyes wide open and attentive, smiling as they heard me speak honestly. *Like mother, like daughter*, I thought to myself. *They are both so good at making me feel like my voice is important.*

'That's an incredible realization, Zoe,' Abby said.

'Yeah definitely, babe,' S said, nodding in agreement. 'So are you thinking of quitting the Tour too?'

'No way! Actually, I just realized all of this like an hour ago, so I haven't given much thought to how exactly I'm going to go about it. But I still want to go on tour next year. I love surfing and I love competing and everything that goes with it. I just need to do it *my* way. I mean, I just repeated the same pattern of putting myself in the hands of others. First Derek, then Greg. And both experiences have reiterated the same two things. One, I still want to be a pro surfer; and two, I need to do it *on my own terms*, even if I don't know what that looks like yet.'

I was fired up by my monologue, a sure sign of confidence.

'I want surfing to raise me up, not drag me down, otherwise, what's the point? I dunno, I think a part of me has known this for a while, but I felt like it would be selfish, so I didn't want to admit it to myself. I mean, my life is awesome and I've been so lucky to be a part of an elite sport, with my dad, Greg and Derek all supporting me the way they have over the years. And you guys taking me in... All my sponsors believing in me... Deep down, I guess I've felt as though I don't have the right to feel dissatisfied.'

So there it was. Another truth exposed. I looked at them and smiled a happy, unforced smile.

'Zoe, sweetie,' Abby finally spoke, 'I'm so proud of you. You deserve to be happy no matter what you're doing. The Universe supports you, and you can certainly find a way to do the Tour on your own terms. You are such a bright light! You know, I've learned a lot over the years, having a husband and kids, building my own business, so I know how easy it is to put the needs of others before your own, especially as a woman.'

She took a moment to look over at her daughter before

turning her gaze back towards me, wanting, I think, to be sure we were both listening before she continued.

'I've had to learn to take charge of my life in a way that ensures my needs are met, as well as the needs of my family, so I understand what you're saying. This is a very important lesson you're learning right now, Zoe, and I encourage you to follow your heart closely on this one.'

She finished by asking, 'What else have you learned since you got here?'

I inhaled and pondered her question for a moment.

'Well, aside from giving away my power, one thing I've noticed is that I'm always in my head, over-thinking and over-analyzing every move and every decision. It's exhausting! You guys know me, I usually prefer to keep things kinda quiet and chill, but with all the training, competitions, sponsorship obligations, Derek, etc., there's just so much to do all the time that I haven't had any quality time to myself. I never get any peace and it stresses me out! I think it's made me become resentful of the people I have to deal with all the time, even though I know they're only there to help me. I dunno, I feel like an asshole to think this way. I mean, isn't it selfish? My life is so awesome, isn't it a bit screwed up for me to complain about it? Or even worse, to feel like it's sucking the life out of me? Most girls would kill for my lifestyle.'

'Zozo,' S chimed in, 'you have the right to feel the way you feel, and you have the right to do what *you* need to do for *you*. It's just a matter of deciding what you want and going for it. And deciding what you want includes taking into consideration how you want to feel as you go about getting it. Mum's always telling me and Seth to feel good about what we're doing. It's what really matters.'

'That's right, sweetie,' Abby added, 'When I'm at a crossroads, I see two options: change how I feel about the situation or change the situation. And what I mean is... Oh crap!'

Abby was looking at her watch now.

'Ladies, I've got to go.' She stood up and looked over at S, 'Your father is taking me sailing and I'm not ready at all!' She then reached over to grab one of the boxes on the counter, looked back at me and said, 'Zoe, you've got this! And I'm just going to take some of these treats with me or Petey will be very jealous! We'll catch up soon, okay? Kisses!'

She blew us kisses as she walked out the back and hopped up the staircase barefoot.

'Oh my mum is hilarious!' S said, laughing at the fact Abby had left yet another pair of sandals at the front door.

I started giggling too, 'You guys are the best!'

'So what now, Zozo baby?'

'I guess I have to call Greg. I kinda took off on him and he's probably a little disconcerted. Oh God! What am I gonna say?'

'Are you sure it's what you want?' S said in a surprisingly more serious tone. 'I'm only asking to help you feel solid on your decision. It'll make the process a whole lot easier if you're not second-guessing yourself, hey?'

I sat back in the chair, crossed my arms and looked up at the ceiling – which, to me, represented a blank slate. It was weird, but I liked the way the ceiling felt – like a white, expansive canvas. There was a world of possibilities on that canvas and it was mine for the taking.

I exhaled with a big sigh, looked back at S, and said, 'Yes, Soph, I'm sure.'

Chapter Eighteen

I took me a solid hour to work up the courage to call Greg. What can I say? I was scared! To help ease the fear, I practiced a calming technique I'd learned from Derek ages ago, and had used regularly both before and during heats.

I inhaled deeply. As I exhaled, I imagined all of the built-up tension and nervousness leaving my body in the form of bubbles. And in those bubbles were words that described what was bothering me. 'Stress'. 'Fear'. 'Doubt'. I did this for a few breaths. The more bubbles I imagined leaving my body and floating out into the ether and dissolving into thin air, the better (and clearer) I felt.

'Righto, it's now or never...' I said to myself as I picked up my phone and dialed.

'Zoe?' Greg answered before the first ring had even completed its turn. 'Are you okay? Is everything alright?'

'Oh, hey Greg,' I said with slight hesitation, unable to spit anything else out. *C'mon*, I thought to myself, *it's safe to say how you feel, Zoe.*

I glanced down at the pointers I'd written down just in case I blanked on the phone.

'I'm fine, Greg, I'm fine, and I'm sorry to run off like that. I'm sorry if I scared you. I just, um, had to leave.'

'Zoe, this isn't like you. You know I'm here to help, right, mate?'

'I know, I know, Greg, you've been amazing, but that's sort of the problem. I need you to listen while I say what I need to say, okay?'

'Go ahead, Zoe,' he said in a deep, serious-sounding tone, 'I'm listening.'

'Okay, well, a lot has happened this last month, as you know, and I've finally figured out what I need to do.'

I took a breath and continued.

'I need some time away from everything, including coaching. It's not that I don't think I need training, because I know I do. It's just that I need to take control of my life again, and I don't know how to do that when I put myself in a position of doing what other people are telling me to do. I guess you could say I'm a bit lost, and I need to find myself again. Does that make sense?'

'Zoe, was it something that happened this morning that triggered this sudden change of heart? Was it because of your wipeout? I know it can be tough to get back into the rhythm, but it takes time. That's part of the process.'

I felt like Greg was fishing for answers, trying to justify my decision in his mind that it was about the wipeout, when that was really just the tipping point. I needed to get this across to him. I felt stronger and more confident now that the conversation was rolling.

'Today's session taught me exactly that, except I'm completely out of rhythm with myself. It's not about finding my flow again with *you*, or anyone *else*, it's about finding my *own* flow. Today's experience was just the tipping point really. I didn't want to catch that wave but I felt like I *had* to, because that's what *you* wanted. But it's not what *I* wanted.'

'But if you had been on point faster, Zoe, you would have made it through the close-out section and...'

'Yeah, Greg.' I raised my voice to cut him off. 'Sure, if I'd made the wave I may feel differently right now, but I didn't make the wave. And what's more, I didn't feel ready for that wave. Regardless of how it turned out, my point is that I didn't want to go in the first place! And I just don't want to keep training that way. I have to listen to me and only me from now on. Or at least for the next couple of months. I'm so sorry to do this to you and I feel terrible about it. I didn't plan for this to happen, and I'm not trying to upset you. I know you care about me, and I know your intentions are good. But again, this has nothing to do with you. Can you understand?'

'Well, I'd be lying if I said I thought it was a good decision. But ultimately, it's up to you, Zoe, and I'll support you either way. But are you sure you're not just jumping to conclusions right now? Do you want to take some time to think things through a bit longer? Maybe check in with me tomorrow?'

He was making me own my decision, but part of me couldn't help but wonder if his tight grasp had more to do with his needs. I knew there was something he wasn't telling me, but I didn't even want to go there at this point. All I wanted to do was be done with this conversation so that I could move on.

'Thanks Greg, but no. I need to roll with it right now, and trust myself. I'm not saying it's an easy call, but it feels right. And I need to start listening to my gut.'

Again, there was a pause, but I could hear Greg's heavy, congested breathing on the other end until he finally spoke.

'Well, okay then, Zoe. Best of luck to you. If you change your mind, or if you need anything, just let me know. I'm still here for you, Zoe, okay?'

'Thanks so much Greg. And thanks for everything. I really appreciate it.'

'Righto,' and he hung up the phone.

I chucked my phone on the table, plopped down on the couch and stared at the wall in front of me again, feeling excited, giddy even... Until reality set in. It felt like that first moment when the drugs start to wear off.

Holy crap, what have I just done?

It was the tiniest lapse in confidence, but it was enough to feel the doubt trying desperately to work its way in.

Did I just make a rash decision without giving it proper thought?

Fear is such a creep.

What if I just made a huge mistake to think that I could compete well in the upcoming season without a proper coach?

I hate this doubt.

No! No! No! No, negative thoughts. Ego... I'm onto you.

I had to shake it off and find a way back to positive self-talk – and fast. I decided to get off my ass and go burn off the latte and muffin with some exercise. I jumped up, filled my water bottle, and grabbed S's bike. Maybe some fresh air would reset my mind.

Chapter Nineteen

I rode quickly, gaining as much momentum and speed as I could, using it to bust through my emotions. It felt like I'd entered a time warp as I cruised through the entrance of the park, because all these memories came flooding back to me, about when my dad used to take me to a similar one in Manly when we'd just moved here from Colorado.

We usually went on a Saturday because that's when the local market took place, so we'd stock up on lots of fresh produce while also having a ride. I'd convince my dad to buy me some cookies, and inevitably beg him to let the crazy 'magic' lady give me a 'reading', but he'd never let me. She was always there, with her big frizzy gray hair and wrinkled skin, perched on her grass mat in the far corner of the market with what I later understood to be tarot cards. She sat tall, cross-legged, and always wore the most colorful knee high socks, watching the crowd and waiting patiently for someone brave enough to approach her. I loved to sneak over to the sidelines and eavesdrop when she was with someone, listening to her barely audible voice and hardly ever hearing what she was saying. From what I saw, every customer seemed to walk away smiling.

There was also a skate park at the back, where I loved to hang out, just as I had loved the one in Colorado, where my mom would take me.

I rode the path directly through the center of the park until I arrived at the back corner, where it turned into native forest and the trails began. The trails were a no-go for bikes, because they were too narrow to safely accommodate both hikers *and* bikers, so when I got there I dismounted and locked my bike to the empty rack next to the main path. I'd never been on any of these trails before, so when I approached a fork in the road, I wasn't sure which of the three paths to choose.

I pulled out my drink bottle and paused there for a minute, casually shaking a packet of flavored electrolyte powder into my water. The sun was high and the sky was clear blue, completely devoid of clouds. My eyes stung as I watched a flock of birds glide overhead. Then I noticed a bright purple butterfly flutter past me. I watched it closely as it zigzagged towards the left hand trail.

Ah, what the heck, I thought, giving myself permission to follow the direction of the butterfly.

I meandered along the trail for close to half an hour and had yet to see another human, which I found odd. The trees had become thick and had crowded out the sky from my view; my skin was thanking me for the relief from the hot sun. I stopped to hydrate again, and noticed ahead of me the most gorgeous ray of sunshine blasting through the trees. It was mesmerizing! I followed its ray of light downwards to see where it met the earth. There, I saw a massive Moreton Bay fig tree, its crazy meters-wide root system blocking my path, instructing me to go no further.

'Wait a minute, I recognize this light!' I exclaimed aloud as I bounded towards the tree and around to its other side. There, standing beneath the beautiful glimmering light, was Teo.

'Unbelievable!' I yelled out gleefully. I felt a sudden surge of love flood my body, making me want to jump up and down in joy. (But I didn't. Because that's weird.)

'Zoe,' he said. 'Look how far you've come! I'm so very, very proud of you!'

'Teo!' I ran towards him and threw my arms around him without hesitation. He wrapped his arms around me and I gladly allowed myself to be enveloped in his embrace. What followed was pretty much the most amazing feeling ever! I can't do it justice with words, but imagine feeling every cell in your body tingle simultaneously. It was a sensation of love that made me feel complete, like nothing was missing from my life.

While nestled into his warm embrace, I felt a myriad of emotions bubbling to the surface; they tumbled out in the form of tears. I didn't mean to cry, obviously, but I couldn't help it. The kindness and care I felt in his presence and in his arms stripped me of my tough, protective shell. But it was okay. I was a willing participant by now when it came to anything 'Teo'. And as long as he continued to hold me, I continued to sob away, melting into him.

After some time – whether it was a minute or an hour, I couldn't tell – my sobs turned into a quiet whimper and Teo pulled away gently. Still holding my hands, his eyes dropped to meet mine. As he was so much taller than me, I had to look up to meet his gaze.

'I... I'm so happy to see you, Teo! I've thought about you so much and now you're here! And I can see you! And I can touch you!'

He smiled the most heart-warming smile I'd ever experienced. So heart-warming, I felt my heart was about to explode. His voice was soft and soothing, as he said, 'I have been with you this whole time, Zoe; of that you can be sure.'

He released one of my hands, and guided me towards a wooden bench that I swear wasn't there a minute ago.

'Come, sit down, Zoe. Relax for a moment. You've just had a major emotional release and your body needs to rest.'

He was right. I *was* feeling a touch feeble. I sat by Teo in silence for a few minutes. It was pleasant. Peaceful. But it wasn't long before my mind started chattering again.

'So how come I couldn't see you all this time that you've been with me, but I can see you now?'

'Shhh, stay in the moment, sweet Zoe.'

I took a deep breath and let out a sigh, realizing how quickly I could let myself get distracted, and ruin the peace and quiet with my thoughts.

'Of course I will answer your question, Zoe, but for now, let's just be here and enjoy our surroundings, shall we?'

'Oh, okay.' I said compliantly.

I lifted my legs up and crossed them as I leaned back on the bench and settled into a comfortable position. Teo relaxed his posture too, leaning back on the bench with me. I wasn't really sure what we were *supposed* to be doing; all I was able to do was fixate on his glorious face. His hair was dark as the night, a silky texture that shone as if his head had a galaxy of its own. I noticed his chiseled jawline had no hint of stubble. The pinkish tone of his skin was perfectly smooth, porcelain-like, except for the two little dimples that became more prominent when he spoke. And his...

'Do you see that butterfly?' he asked sweetly, diverting my attention elsewhere. I took his cue and followed his gaze over my right shoulder. I searched around with my eyes for this supposed butterfly, but all I noticed was a mossy tree stump.

'Ummm, no?'

And then, all of a sudden, that same bright purple butterfly fluttered off the corner of the stump and flew towards us. Teo held out his hand and it gently landed in his palm.

'Wow!' I gasped. Its heart-shaped wings flapped gracefully, almost seductively, drawing me in with the shimmer of silver that seemed to throw sparks into the sky like a firefly. It had my utmost attention.

'OMG, I saw this butterfly earlier, before I took this particular trail! It's *why* I chose this trail! It's so beautiful! But this can't be the same one?'

'Hold out your hand, Zoe.'

I held out my left hand. With a few flaps of its wings, the butterfly made its way out of Teo's hand and into mine. I felt like it was looking straight at me, communicating something to me, though I didn't know what.

'What is it saying, Zoe?'

'I, I'm not sure.' To be honest, I hadn't really tried to listen. I think I was too scared to put in the effort. I mean, it was pretty hard to imagine that one might actually be able to hear the voice of a butterfly.

'Shhh, Zoe. Listen with your heart, not with your head. *Feel* what it is saying without thinking about it. You've made a big shift today, which means your heart is extremely tender and completely open right now. Please, relax and let it lead the way.'

His words were compelling, yet I still found it difficult to grasp what he meant.

'Feel what it's saying? Um, okay. Feel what it's saying...'

I sat in silence, looking at the purple and blue hues of the butterfly, and noticed a beautiful silver lining that traced along the edges of its wings with perfect continuity.

'Oh!' I gasped enthusiastically. 'There's a silver lining to what I'm going through?'

'Very good. What else?'

'Hmm...' I observed the slow, graceful pulses of its wings,

and watched how its antennas tapped my hand ever so lightly, seeking... searching... but for what? I had no idea, but it sure seemed like each movement came full of purpose.

'That it's okay for me to slow down and feel things out?'

'Wonderful, Zoe.'

And just like that, the butterfly flew out of my hand. It hovered at my face and I felt the light breeze from its delicate wings as it stared at me for just a moment before flitting away.

I tried to follow it with my eyes but it was already gone.

Chapter Twenty

'W here'd it go?'
'It fulfilled its purpose in that moment, and so it moved on.'

'What was its purpose?'

'To bring you a message.'

'What was the message?' I was puzzled.

'To listen to your heart for the answers you seek,' Teo's voice reassured me.

'Mmm...' I said, nodding in agreement. 'Okay, I think I understand now.'

But Teo must've gotten the impression that I was still confused, because he questioned me not two seconds later.

'Are you sure about that, Zoe?' he asked quietly, looking me straight in the eye.

'No. I mean, sort of. Well, I get the part about listening to my heart, but I *don't* get how the butterfly knew what to do.'

'I asked the butterfly for you, Zoe, because I knew you would have a difficult time sitting still enough in your surroundings without getting distracted by your concerns about the future.'

'Oh, sorry,' I felt slightly deflated by his comment, but I couldn't argue with it.

'Remember when you asked me earlier why you couldn't hear or see me?'

'Yes!' I said, perking up immediately, really wanting to know.

'The butterfly was your answer to that question.'

'Huh?' I was quick to respond. 'I don't get it.'

'What did you learn from that experience?'

'To slow down, to listen, to feel.'

'Yes, very good, Zoe. In order to see, or hear, or feel me, you must first call upon me, as you did, with your heart. This is the first step. But there is also a *second* step.'

'Seriously? I didn't know there were *any* steps!'

'Yes, Zoe, asking for help is only the first step.'

I felt a tinge of concern in what that meant, but Teo continued to clarify without a pause.

'Don't worry, Zoe. There is no special way of asking. You can say something out loud, you can say something in your mind, you can visualize God or an angel... anything that elevates your spirit.'

'Like the purple butterfly?' I interrupted.

'Yes, of course. Anything that will help you to get out of your head and into your heart will work. Even just thinking of me, you will know I'm there. There is no wrong way to ask for help, Zoe. Words are not necessary for us to hear your call, though humans do find it helpful to use words or say a prayer. Either way, whether it's a thought, a prayer, or a symbol... whatever *feels* good to you is the way to go. Simply invite me in with the simplicity of your pure intention. There is no need to complicate the matter with any kind of specific structure or form.'

'Simplicity of pure intention...

...simplicity of pure intention...

...simplicity of pure intention...'

It was a mouthful and I was having a hard time engraving it into my mind, so I thought of a phrase that would be easy for me to remember.

'Oh I know! Keep it simple to keep it real!' I blurted out with an air of triumph. I was pleased to get this one, for sure.

'Yes, perfect, Zoe. The first step is to make the call, yes?'

I nodded in agreement.

'And after you make the call, you must *listen* for that call to be answered. This is the second step. Yes?'

Again, he was looking at me, making sure that I was on the same page. I nodded my head, indicating yes. *So far so good*, I figured, wondering how long until the next round of confusion set in. Teo continued.

'Unfortunately, this second step is quite a challenge for most. This is often the time when people begin to lose faith. Instead, they could be strengthening their faith so as to receive miracle after miracle.'

Aaaaand the confusion was back.

'What do you mean?'

I was scrunching my nose slightly out of frustration. It was a lot to take in, as usual. Talk about mind...*blown*.

'Here's what happened, Zoe. You took the first step and called upon me. Well done. Absolutely well done. Many do not even make this first step. And in response to your call, I was immediately by your side, extending answers to you. However, you were unable to hear, or see, or feel those answers because your thoughts distracted you from receiving them.

In other words, calling for help signified an opening of your heart. But instead of maintaining an open heart – through having faith and patience that the Universe will heed your call – you immediately jumped back into your worried thoughts, returning the focus to your head. Doing that blocked you from receiving those messages of the heart.'

'Oh! Oh! Oh! So, I couldn't see the butterfly until you pointed it out to me because I was too distracted, even though it was always there?'

'Exactly.'

'So the answers are always there, even if we can't see, or hear, or feel, or know them?'

'Yes, wonderful, Zoe.'

'Okay, this makes sense. But a couple of things I still don't get. Why do you keep saying 'we'? And how did the butterfly have a message for me? It's just a butterfly. Isn't that kinda crazy talk to believe it could communicate with me?'

'Everything around you – no matter where you are, or what you are doing, or who you are talking to – is both a creation of *and* a message from God, regardless of its seeming form.'

'Um, hold on Teo, I'm not sure I understand what you mean when you say God. Do you mean like a guy in the sky, or...?'

This is a challenging word for many, Zoe. When I speak of God, I am referring to the energy of pure love. It is the source from which we are all made. It is your true essence, which means you have unlimited access to it. However, as I've mentioned before, you have become more accustomed to the habit of controlling your life, rather than allowing it to be guided by the divine power of love and light, available to all.

'So you're here to help me tap into that, er, essence... of, er, pure love?'

'Yes, Zoe. And when I say 'we', you can think of me as one of an unlimited number of angels... a messenger of God. As angels, we don't have bodies as such. We simply present ourselves to you in form because it is easier for humans to see us this way. In reality, we are extensions of God, the Universe, or Source

Energy, which are all words used to describe the same thing. Pure Love.

When people pray to God, or angels, or the Universe, or Jesus, or Buddha, or Jehovah – that is, whomever or whatever symbol represents their belief in a higher power – it means they are open to receiving help from beyond what they can 'see'. This is faith. And it is wonderful indeed! But humans often quickly become impatient when their call isn't answered within the time constraints they have placed upon it. In addition, they have often already decided what they want the answer to look like. So if the answer doesn't arrive in the form or timeframe they expect, they become upset.

And while we are *always* here in an instant, to answer your call and alleviate your pain, people do not see, hear, feel, or know our presence, because they try to control the outcome. Often, our messages are overlooked. You ask for help, but then you are afraid the answer will be different to what you want it to be. And even though the answer *is* often different, it's *always* much better than you could ever possibly imagine for yourself. Our answers are 100% pure love and perfection. They will make you feel better in the most profound of ways. However, it requires an act of faith to follow the signs. First you must let go of the need to control, and then trust in those answers you receive, as you follow them, one step at a time.'

'Oh, I think I get it. It's like that Rolling Stones song, when it goes: "You can't always get what you want, but [...] you get what you need".'

Teo began to laugh. 'Yes, it's very much like that, Zoe.'

'Okay, got it. So how do I get rid of those thoughts?'

'You must release the need to control the future by staying present in the moment. Instead of sitting here and planning and organizing what your life will look like in the next hour, or day, or next season, or next year, or 10 years from now, just be here now and enjoy your surroundings. Look at the trees and the sky with wonder, and have gratitude for the beauty of the moment.'

I let his words soak in.

'So, focus on feeling good, and don't worry about the future?'

'Yes.'

'But how am I supposed to get anything done if I do that?'

Teo's eyes sparkled as he smiled, and I swear it was like nothing else in the world mattered when I looked into them.

'Do your best not to worry about that right now, though I know it may feel difficult. This is the process of letting go, by giving yourself permission to lead more with your heart and less with your head. The details will work themselves out in miraculous ways, Zoe. All I want you to be concerned about is how you feel from moment to moment. Acknowledge your thoughts and actions. Then change them into a perspective that will accommodate the sensation of feeling good. Okay?'

'Ah yes. More positive self-talk. I remember. Yes, okay.'

We sat in silence, and my eyes glanced back over towards the mossy tree stump, but it was no longer there.

'Teo! The stump!' I turned to face him... but he too was gone. *Damn.*

A sense of abandonment rose within me, but then I reminded myself that just because I couldn't see him didn't mean he wasn't there. I clung to this thought for a few more minutes and noticed that it made me feel better; that the sense of abandonment, the scary feeling of aloneness, had dissipated.

It was late afternoon by the time I got home, and I was happy to see that Sophie had returned as well. She was out the back drinking wine with a girl I didn't recognize. Wait, was she... flirting? Whenever she tones down her naturally boisterous self, she's doing one of two things. One, giving a pep talk to her lifeguards; or two, trying not to scare off someone she likes.

Option *número dos*, obviously. So it made complete sense for me to grab a glass and venture out to interrupt their little soirée and see what was going on. I wanted some reprieve from all the crazy encounters I was having... and wine was by far the easiest way to get that.

'G'day Zozo!'

S clapped her hands in joy the moment she saw me slide open the door.

'This is Kiko! Kiko, this is my mate, Zoe!'

'Hey Kiko, nice to meet you!' I said, reaching over the table to shake her hand. She had a solid handshake, which, to me, was always a good sign of a strong character. At least, that's what my dad had taught me.

'Hey Zoe, so nice to finally meet you!' she replied smilingly.

Soph pulled out a chair, and as if by magic, my glass became half full. We sat in silence, sipping from our glasses, watching people do their thing on the beach; couples and their dogs, kids and their castles, joggers, surfers, and family feuds. It had been a long, strange, and beautiful day, and I was grateful to be where I was in that moment.

Yes, I decided. *This is what Teo meant.* I felt present. I felt... good.

Chapter Twenty-One

I slept amazingly well that night.

So well, in fact, that I didn't peel my eyes open until around 9am, insanely late considering my usual 6am wake-up call. Even so, I continued to lie in bed, relaxing and practicing what Teo had asked, being in the moment, and feeling good.

Now, I have to admit I still wasn't sure *exactly* how to conduct my day with this intention in mind, but my first thought was to figure out what I felt like doing. Sounds pretty basic, I know, but this turned out to be quite the mind game for me. There was so much going on in my head that it was hard to follow my heart. I mean, normally I would've planned my day the night before, and then woken up early, eager as a beaver to get a headstart on all that I needed to accomplish.

So even this moment, lying in bed and letting my mind wander into what would *feel good*? Weird.

Well, duh, the answer was surfing! I suppose it should've been obvious, but you know, since arriving home, I felt like I was having to repeatedly recognize that surfing was still my joy. Maybe a part of me was still scared that Derek *had* been right, that surfing *wasn't* what I wanted anymore, that I'd been too afraid to admit it. But no, it wasn't about my love for surfing *or* my love for competing. It was about *how* I was going about them. I had to change my approach. I had to match my thoughts with feelgood actions, just like Teo had said.

I got out of bed and hunted around for a bikini. I found one on the back of my shower door and put it on before cruising out to the back deck where my wetsuit was hanging in the sun. I knew Sophie was at work already, and I was kinda bummed she wasn't around to come play, but as I was grappling with my wetsuit, Seth came flying down the stairs, beaming with a happiness I knew only from the Smart family.

'G'day Zoe, how's it going?'

'Oh crap, hey!' I said as I fumbled around, trying to get my arms through the sleeves. 'You going out for a surf too?'

'You betcha!' he said with a youthful exuberance. 'Wanna come with? I'm just gonna walk up the beach to where it looks like the waves are breaking more consistently.'

I was excited to be my own boss again, to be able pick and choose the waves I wanted to catch, and not worry about the rest.

'Alright yeah, sounds good, Seth. You're off today?'

'Yeah, Zozo, taking it sleazy today,' he said with a smirk on his face.

I responded, 'Mmm-hmmm, I'm sure you are buddy.' But aside from surfing and skating, I actually had no idea what he was doing these days.

We waxed our boards and headed up the beach together.

'So what's new, Zoe? How's life as a pro surfer?'

Something I always liked about Seth was his interest in getting to know people. Even when we were younger and he was just a little grom, I remember that he always quietly observed what was going on around him, to the point we'd often forget he was there. (I mean, *who knows* what conversations of mine and Soph's he listened in on). He also had a knack for getting away with pretty much anything, most likely because he knew how to deal with the people around him, probably due to the fact he was so observant.

'Ah, it has its ups and downs, but it's pretty amazing. Sometimes it stresses me out, but I guess that's just part of learning how to play the game, right?'

I wasn't ready to divulge too much info, and wanted to keep the conversation easygoing.

'Yeah, that's kind of how I feel with skateboarding. I'm working on going pro too, you know?'

'You are? That's amazing. You must've come a long way since the last time I saw you skate then, ha ha!' I said as I looked over at him, jokingly poking him with my elbow.

'Aww c'mon, Zo, that was ages ago!'

'True. I should totally come to the park with you at some point. I haven't skated in forever. Maybe it'd be good for me.'

'Yeah cool, that'd be fun.'

About five minutes later we stuck our boards in the sand, put down our towels and gulped back some water in preparation for the session ahead. Seth appeared happy as he looked out at the ocean, and it was hard not to admire his beautiful, white smile. Such a warm soul, I thought. Then he looked straight at me, beaming with excitement before asking if I was ready.

'You know I am. Let's do this!'

We put on our leashes and headed to the edge of the ocean. Seth jumped in immediately and was already paddling out to the line-up, while I continued to gaze out at the ocean, taking my time.

I stood where the water washed against my ankles, closed my eyes and asked the angels for a fun session. I wanted to enjoy myself above all else, I felt, but it would be cool to learn something that would help me in competition as well. I thanked them – Teo especially – for their presence in my life. With that, I jumped on my board and paddled out after Seth.

The section we were going to surf was busy, as was to be expected. I took care paddling out, deciding that I wanted to feel out what kind of crowd I was working with before jumping into the middle of the pack (which, from the previous day's fiasco, you'll know can get rather feisty). I made my way over to Seth, who was hanging out away from the crowd too. This section of the beach had waves aplenty, so we had options, even though they're unlikely to form as well as those at the main peak. I sat up on my board once I was a few feet from Seth.

'You like to ease into the crowd, too?' I asked.

'Yeah, I kinda stick to the yummy corners over here. You have to wait for them, but they show up. I'm just not really into crowds. Too much ego over there, aye?'

'I hear ya,' I agreed.

A nice set rolled in and a mad scramble between the surfers sitting deepest ensued, with a guy in red boardies claiming the first wave. The second wave came in immediately behind the first and two people dropped in at the same time. The guy without right of way peeled off so the other guy could enjoy the wave that was rightfully his. The third wave rolled in but it was swinging wide, and everyone on the inside was too deep to catch it.

Seth turned towards it and paddled for position. A guy who was sitting deeper stupidly dropped in, but his position was shit and it shut him down, opening the wave up for Seth.

'Yeah, Seth!' I yelled as he dropped in. I watched the wave as it moved past me, and finally saw Seth's head as he reached the peak of the wave and fired off a damn sexy cutback before disappearing again. A few seconds later I saw him exit the wave in the distance with an enthusiastic fist pump.

Wow, he's so cute...

A couple more set waves came and went as I continued to wait patiently for my turn. Seth had caught his third wave by the time I finally saw a sweet peak starting to form right near me. It had my name on it. I turned and paddled hard to get myself into position, knowing that I needed to get closer inside if I wanted to catch it.

I looked left to make sure I wasn't going to drop in on anyone, and then went for it. I popped up quickly, riding high on the face of a gem of a wave, going right. And unlike yesterday it opened up beautifully in front of me! *Yesssss!* I carved a wide bottom turn, engaging my fins with strength and confidence to pick up some speed before driving up to the lip and going for a snap. I dug deep, shifting my weight to my heel and leaned hard, which happened to be right in front of Seth. I wanted to show off by spraying him, but instead I tripped on my rail and took a header.

'Argh,' I yelled out.

But then something cool happened! Instead of repeating my pattern of frustration, with the fear of screwing up like this during competition, I relaxed. I reminded myself that it *wasn't* during competition. It was here, now, while I was having fun surfing with Seth. And even if it *was* during competition, why should I let it bum me out? I shouldn't. I absolutely should *not* let this stop me from indulging in the sheer joy of surfing! So I popped up with a smile on my face, happy again in an instant, and all due to a simple shift in perspective. I glanced around to make sure the coast was clear of incoming waves. All good. The only waves were the ones being made from the sound of Seth laughing.

'Sorry mate! My bad!'

I started laughing. 'No worries! Besides, it's my bad. I shouldn't let you distract me so easily!'

Oops. I realize how this *could* be interpreted, but it was too late to retract the statement and... well, maybe I didn't care? And maybe... just maybe... it was even a little bit true?

I got back on my board and paddled to catch up to him. When I got there eventually, I was a little out of breath but also pretty excited.

'Your wave was sick, Seth! Nice one!'

'Thanks Z, yours too!'

We stayed out for a couple of hours. Seth caught a few nice ones sitting real deep, while I crept in ever so slightly, and only to the place that felt good in the moment. This experience had given me a better understanding of the fact that listening to my heart would help me to be in the moment, because I was honoring what felt good. Content with where I was and what I was doing, I had no need to distract myself with other thoughts.

Today, my heart had wanted: a nice long sleep-in; a fun and easygoing surf sesh; and some quality hangout time with Seth. And while it was all very unexpected, it turned out to be completely in the flow. And even though I still had *no idea* how this kind of day could benefit my career, I *did* know that I had to keep doing what Teo had said, and trust the process.

Walking back to the house after our session, Seth had a question about my bottom turn.

'Zo, how did you maintain your speed when driving up the face of the wave? I'm playing around with where I put my weight, but I'm still losing speed...'

'Oh, well, you've got to distribute your weight evenly at first, and then move the weight onto your toes when you start making the turn. If we're talking about your frontside... Wait. Hold this,' I said as I handed him my board. I widened my stance, pretending to be on my board, and began to demonstrate using hand and foot gestures, and body positioning.

'Ah, I get it. So then I have to push with my back foot as I come off the bottom?'

'Yep, you got it.'

He handed me my board back and we continued to walk.

'From what I saw,' I continued, 'you could definitely get a little lower on your board so keep those knees bent. But still, you looked pretty damn good. Also, you're really tall. Almost as tall as your dad?'

'Yeah.'

'Well, I'm not as tall as you, so you may have to take that into consideration as well, in terms of how much pressure you put on your board while maintaining your center of gravity. Know what I mean?'

'Yeah, totally. It's a lot like skateboarding, don't ya think?'

'Oh yeah, I hadn't thought about that, but yeah. Man, it's been a while since I've been on a skateboard.'

We made it to the back deck and he continued on up the stairs, yelling back down, 'Cool Z, see ya later. Thanks for the surf!'

'Later, Seth!' I yelled back, and I heard him disappear into the main house with a big *swoosh* of the sliding door.

Chapter Twenty-Two

After rinsing off, I had the grand idea to take myself out for lunch. *Why not?* I said to myself in the mirror, while plucking away at my eyebrows. I was already so freaking hungry, and there was a nice little Thai restaurant just a few blocks away that was calling my name.

I put on my jean shorts and a strange-looking pink silky tank top that flared out at the bottom. I checked myself out in the mirror and decided I liked what I saw. And then I did the unthinkable by my lazy tomboy standards, adding a gold bracelet and necklace to complete the look. One of the interesting aspects of being sponsored is the crazy amount of free clothes I get. And not to make anyone jelly or anything, but I'm often traveling with clothes I've never worn before, and it's always a neat surprise to see what I pull out of my suitcase, or on this occasion my wardrobe, for the first time in months.

I could always count on Taylor for some inspo, so I put in my earbuds and opened Pandora, clicking on the Taylor Swift station as I sauntered down the driveway. *Into The Woods* came on, and hit the spot instantly. I love Taylor as an artist. Her lyrics are so smart while super empowering. It was just what I needed.

The quaint little town of Lennox Head is literally two streets away from the Smarts' house. It gets crazy-busy during the summer months, attracting people from all over on vacation, as well as people from other parts of Australia who are looking for that coastal lifestyle vibe. Now that the town of Byron Bay had sprawled like it had, Lennox had become the next big pick.

All in all it's a pretty classy place, which serves the tourism industry well; a walking trail along the beach, shops, cafes, sunshine, beaches, epic surf, upmarket restaurants and then pubs on the main street, giving it pretty decent nightlife. I passed by the gelato shop, only a few doors down from the restaurant, and began to salivate. I had totally forgotten about their insane gelato, and it became evident that I'd need to save some room for dessert. But first, Thai.

The delicious aroma of curry that wafted through the air as I entered Mi Thai had me go from starving to famished in exactly 0.03 seconds. Luckily, it wasn't busy, so the lady was able to seat me immediately. I could see that she was already talking to me, but by the time I pulled out an earbud, I only caught:

'...indoor or outdoor?'

'Outside please,' I guessed.

She directed me to a table in the front by the street, and I sat down as she poured me a glass of water. When she tried to hand me the lunch special, I politely refused with a slight shake of my head and said, 'I already know what I want, actually.'

'Oh sure, go right ahead then.'

'I'll have the Pad thai, just veggies, and a Thai iced tea, with coconut milk, please.'

'Would you like tofu with that?'

'Um, no thanks.' (So not a fan of the tofu)

'Cheers,' the young waitress said, smiling as she walked away with the menu.

I leaned back in my chair and stared out onto the street, observing the passers-by. The ocean was right across the street, and stretched for miles; you can pretty much surf anywhere along this beach.

I zoned out, or rather zoned *into* lala land, and recalled how easily distracted I had become when Seth had hollered at me during our surf session. And how I'd wiped out as a result. Hmm, even though it was a fun session, it had raised some questions in my mind: how will doing what feels good in the moment further my career; how or why did I get so easily distracted while on the wave; and why couldn't I maintain focus and stay in the zone?

The waitress brought out my iced tea as I was pondering these questions. I took a sip of the sweet and delicious drink, and felt a little less stressed than I had the moment before. I continued to let my mind wander, remembering back to when surfing didn't have all of this other 'stuff' attached to it. I just surfed because I loved surfing. Maybe I needed to go back to the basics and ask myself some simple questions:

Do I still love surfing?

Yes, I love surfing, this has already been established.

Do I like competing?

Yes, I like competing. This, too, has already been established.

Okay, what do I like about competing?

I like getting to travel and surf new places around the world. I like that I get to surf lots of waves in competition with no crowds. I like competing with other awesome chicks who surprise and inspire me. I like getting sponsored, because who doesn't like free stuff and money to do what they love? And I like feeling a part of something bigger than myself, like in the way that being a pro surfer allows me to inspire others.

Cool. And I know I've asked myself these questions before, but c'mon! My life was like a rollercoaster of change right now. Second-guessing and questioning myself seemed to come along with the territory. I had to know with unwavering certainty that I was still eager to be a pro surfer.

The pad thai turned up and I dove into the noodles immediately. But the personal assessment continued.

Now that I know what I like about competing, what is it that I *don't* like about competing?

I don't like the pressure of disappointing my sponsors and myself if I don't compete well, especially if I don't compete to my ability. That really bums me out. I don't like feeling jealous or upset when I compare myself with any of my competitors. I don't like being obligated to do some of the things my sponsors ask of me, especially when it puts me in a bad mood because it's not what I want to be doing with my time.

I probably could've continued, but that was plenty to work with.

So knowing what I know now, why do I do it? And why do I want to continue to do it? Yes, into the good stuff!

I love inspiring other girls. Being on tour as a pro gives me the opportunity to broaden my reach in that pursuit. And even though I haven't actually given much attention to my fans in a meaningful way lately (due to being self-absorbed in my own drama), it's something I'd really like to put some effort into.

Wow! This realization was kind of a big deal, considering I'd avoided people on tour, shied away from interviews or given them minimal effort, and had pretty much abandoned Instagram etc. over the last few months. I had no idea I felt passionate about this! What else?

I admitted that I loved being skilled at a sport as well as being one of the best in my field. It required me to strengthen both my mind and my body, which meant a lot to me. I loved the ocean, its cleansing power, and the fact that it kept me (relatively) sane. Saner than I would be if I *didn't* surf, at least! And even though I'm an introvert, I did like meeting new people and traveling. In the end, it's always awesome to be good at something you love *and* get paid for it too!

Acknowledging all of this again made me feel so much better. I came back to my physical surroundings, looked down at my plate and noticed that I was only about halfway through my pad thai. I felt satisfied, so I finished my drink and decided to save the remaining noodles for the following day's lunch. Leftovers in one hand, phone in the other, and Taylor in my ears, I slowly made my way home, passing on the gelato for now.

Now that I'd cleared up any possible hesitations about continuing as a pro, the question still remained: why have I been getting distracted so easily and when did it start? I ventured through my memory bank, combing over my years on tour and reflecting on my biggest wins, my biggest losses, friends and rivals within the field of competitors, happy moments combined with sad ones, connecting with Derek, and then reconnecting with Derek...

I remembered starting to get distracted on the regular in the season after I won the world title. From then on, it felt like all eyes were on me to perform at the same high standard. Which I, of course, expected for myself as well.

And another telling moment was the first competition I'd bombed after Derek began coaching me. I was *so* embarrassed, frustrated, and sad that I had disappointed him. And *he* was sad and disappointed because I hadn't worked the strategy he'd given me. *That* was the moment I'd decided he knew better than I did, and that I'd better start doing what he wanted, if I was going to win. *He's my coach now, after all*, I remember thinking. It was right then and there that I'd made a new agreement with myself, one where I listened to others first, myself a distant second.

And then it hit me. The answer had suddenly become so damn obvious that I couldn't believe I hadn't pinpointed it earlier.

Ho-ly-crap. I haven't been surfing for me! That's why I get distracted so easily!

Surfing had become about what other people thought of me. I was no longer doing it for myself. I was doing it to please my coach, to satisfy my sponsors, and to maintain my position as a leader in the rankings. I thought back to the times I had competed poorly and realized that more often than not it was because I'd been stressing about either disappointing someone, or I was spending the heat worried about how my competitor was doing. The focus of my career had gone from having fun and enjoying the run into an experience based around the fear of failure.

Well, this would definitely explain why I was so easily distracted when Seth yelled out at me today. Man, I've become so hypersensitive about my external influences that I don't even know how to stay in the zone when I'm already *in* the zone!

Ho-ly-crap, ho-ly-crap, ho-ly-crap. Yep, that was *definitely* it.

I strolled around town for a bit, letting this new info sink in. When I eventually walked around to our street, I saw Sophie's car pulling into the driveway. She must have just finished her shift.

'S!' I yelled as I sprinted down the street, leftovers in hand. 'What's up, sista?'

'Zoelicious!!!' she belted out in her usual uninhibited manner.

'OMG, that's a new one!' I said laughing. 'How was your shift?'

'Nothing spesh, which is always good in my profession.'

'Right on, of course!'

I opened the door and we went inside, kicking our sandals off just inside the entrance.

'Hey, I have some leftover pad thai from lunch just now. You want it?'

'Oh yeah, that'd be sweet, I'm famished!'

She grabbed a fork from the kitchen and I handed her the box.

'What you been up to today, Zo?' she asked from her spot on the couch.

'Oh man, I have a lot of sorting out to do, but it's all good,' I replied, joining her.

I didn't feel like telling her about my big revelation. At least not yet. Nor that I had gone surfing with Seth. Besides, she was busy eating, so we just hung out and chatted nonsense.

Chapter Twenty-Three

That night I pulled out my 'everything book'. It was time to make a new plan, and just the thought of this excited me, because it had been years since I'd created my own schedule without having to compromise, conform, or sacrifice. It felt good to be on my own, I admitted.

I chucked the pen and notebook on the bed and hopped in. Pulling out my earbuds, I selected Pandora's Julia and Angus Stone channel, propped my pillows up against the wall, sat back, and closed my eyes.

What are my priorities? I asked myself as the music sang into my mind, soothing me with its sweet and mellow sounds. *What feels good to me?* I was imagining what my ideal day might look like, when just then I heard the lyric 'keep it simple, keep it real' from some random song I didn't recognize.

Huh? Keep it simple, keep it real? Oh yeah, that's what I came up with the other day in the park with Teo! Can it really be that easy? I wondered. At that very moment, the lyric repeated 'keep it simple, keep it real'.

It was quite possible I'd literally turned into a crazy person, but I couldn't shake the fact that it *really* felt like Teo was sending me a message through the song... a reminder. And whether or not this was actually true or something I'd made up, either way it was beyond my comprehension. The message spoke to me. And in my commitment to focus on what made me feel good, I *had* to accept that it was Teo communicating with me through the song.

Just because I can't see him doesn't mean he's not there! I reminded myself.

Alright then, keep it simple and keep it real, that became my guiding principle as I began to write:

Things that feel good:

1. *surfing*
2. *mind training – (meditation?)*
3. *body training – yoga, agility etc.*
4. *spending time with Teo*
5. *having fun with S and her fam*
6. *working harmoniously with my sponsors*
7. *connecting with fans and inspiring others (via social media?)*
8. *playtime – (skating?)*
9. *eating healthily for optimal energy and nutrition*
10. *quiet time and lots of rest*

I looked at my top 10 priorities scrawled on the page. I liked them. And the fact they would also be beneficial to my surfing career was a major bonus. It's funny, I was already doing a good chunk of these things, but now I was going to go about them differently. I wasn't sure *how*... but I had to trust, because Teo had taught me I needed to trust, and I trusted him.

I looked at the calendar on my phone to see how much time I had before the first competition of the season at Snapper Rocks. Just over two months. It wasn't a lot of time to get my act together, and I knew that the other women on tour would be well into pre-season training. Nope, not a lot of time, but where there's a will, there's a way.

Just as I put my pen down, I got a text from S. She was hanging with her family upstairs for an impromptu game of ping-pong, and told me to get my ass up there and help her win.

Perfect timing.

'2 secs! ' I replied, leaping out of bed.

As I bounded up the stairs, I heard a lot of commotion. S was yelling at her dad for cheating and Seth was throwing ping-pong balls at his head. Abby was over by the kitchen counter. Her paddle was on the counter and she was holding a glass of wine.

'Here, take this,' Abby said to me as she picked up her paddle from the counter with her free hand and handed it to me. 'I give up on these kooks!'

Abby, as usual, looked bright and sparkly even though she was dressed casually in some white pants and a turquoise singlet.

'Oh geez, it's been a while since I've played,' I said as I took the paddle from her. I turned around and Seth flashed me his sweet smile while S yelled at me to get my butt over there.

'Easy, S, easy!'

'She doesn't like to lose,' Peter replied with a serious tone, though I think he was doing it jokingly.

'Never have, never will... especially to you dorks!' she belted out as she tried to wrestle the paddle out of her dad's hand.

'I hadn't noticed!' I said sarcastically. To which Peter replied 'Ha! You're no different, Z!'

We were in hysterics. I was laughing so hard that tears were rolling down my face. Seth served the ball and I could barely see it because my sight was all blurry – but I still managed to hit it across the net as I was wiping my face with my other arm.

'Ha! Take *that*!'

We continued to duke it out and I even managed to score a few points, but I was really no match for Peter and Seth. They could hit 'em hard and fast, I tell ya.

'Sorry Soph, my reflexes are a bit slow at the moment!' I was laughing but I was also slightly frustrated.

'Awww, we need to practice. I can't stand when these guys beat me! I need you to pick up your game, hun!'

'I know it, S!'

'Good game, ladies,' Peter said triumphantly as he high-fived with Seth.

'Yeah, yeah, good game,' S mumbled, not meaning it at all.

Seth looked over at me and gave me a wink. I liked how it made me feel... S and I said goodnight and headed downstairs.

'Hey Soph, who's that girl you introduced me to the other night?'

'Um, that's Kiko, my mate from work,' she replied, playing it down.

'Do you have a crush on her?' I asked as we entered our place.

'I might...' she answered honestly. She wasn't shy about these things, but still, sometimes it took a minute to share a sentimental truth with others.

'Nice! Good on ya!' I replied with enthusiasm.

We both giggled and said g'night on our way into our rooms.

Part Three
Follow The Feelgood

Chapter Twenty-Four

I laid in bed and listened to S rumble around in the kitchen. '4:13am. Ugh.'

I tried to go back to sleep but my mind was already busy with organizing my day, and worrying how I would get everything done. Argh! It was no use. I gave up and decided to just get up and go say hi to Sophie before she left for her shift. I opened my door and trod slowly into the kitchen, giving myself a few extra quiet seconds to mentally prepare for S's early morning shenanigans.

'Morning Soph... Oh, er... Hi.'

I was startled. It wasn't Sophie. There was an awkward pause.

'Um, hey. Kiko, right?'

'Oh hey, Zoe.'

She was wearing a white t-shirt with a yellow and green pineapple on the front. I recognized it immediately.

'Is that Sophie's shirt?' I asked, pulling out a bar stool and leaning on the kitchen counter. It was the first thing that popped into my head, and I had to say something.

'It is! Pineapples are my fave, so I snagged it from her closet this morning, he he he!'

'Oh cool. I think I have one of those too. Or at least I did. I lose track. Super comfy, hey?' In truth, I'd given that shirt to Sophie. She ended up with a lot of my sponsored stuff, because I would get so much clothing that I couldn't possibly wear it all.

'Love it!' she said with enthusiasm as she fumbled around in the cupboards.

'Can I help you find something?'

'Yeah, I'm looking for the coffee.'

'Freezer. Keeps it fresh.'

'Aha! Thanks.'

I watched Kiko as she put the grinds and water into the coffee pot. Her long hair was straight and thick. She had chocolate brown eyes that matched the color of her hair, and the most beautiful, flawless, caramel-coloured skin that didn't display one blemish, which compared to my mishmash of tan lines was nothing short of amazing to me. For some reason, I felt kind of intimidated by her. She seemed extremely confident, like a force to be reckoned with. At least, this was my first impression.

She looked up at me once the coffee was brewing, 'So what's up with you? What are you doing up so early?'

'Ah I dunno, too much on my mind, I guess.' I turned my attention back to her, 'What about you?'

'We both have an early shift, but Sophie has us all doing a workout together before we start. It's a new team-building and endurance training thing she's trying out.'

'Oh no way! She's so awesome, isn't she?'

'The best, Zoe. For sure!'

Just then Sophie walked out of her room, all geared up and looking ready to get her workout on.

'Morning, lovely!' she practically yelled over at me.

'Easy S, easy, I'm only five feet away. I can hear you loud and clear!'

She walked over to the kitchen and took over so that Kiko could go get changed. As she shut the bedroom door behind her, I looked up at S from my stool, 'Um, I can see why you like her, Soph. Holy wow, she's beautiful!'

'Yeah, no kidding, right?'

'Is she as awesome as she is gorgeous?'

'You know it, dude!' And she high-fived me. *Ha!* Sometimes I feel like we're two bros, rather than two girlfriends.

As S got two travel mugs out of the cupboard and began to pour the coffee, I asked about the training.

'Yeah, Zo, it's a bit of an experiment, isn't it? I've no clue how it's going to turn out, but I wanted a way for us all to train and learn from one another at the same time.'

'What do you mean?' I asked, waking up with intrigue.

'Oh my God, Zo! I have *the best* idea. Come train with us!'

'Um, seriously?'

'Hell *yeah*, babe! You're a legend, Zozo! Everyone would *love* to have you join us.'

'Oh man!' I said. I wasn't sure if she was for real so I tried to shrug it off as I stood up from the bar stool.

'I'm serial, Z!'

'You're serial?'

We both started laughing and then Kiko came out, dressed and ready.

'Keeks, Zoe's going to train with us!'

'Nice one!'

It was an interesting idea, and one that only required a few seconds for my mind to process.

Well, it's not a bad idea, actually. I'll get to train with some new and interesting people, at the beach, and I'll probably learn a ton too. I was ready to start training again anyway, I suppose, but don't have a plan as of yet, which was one of the concerns keeping me up this morning.

And then I heard a whisper in my ear:

'Does it feel good?'

I looked around but nobody was there. This startled me, but only for a sec. *Was it Teo? It had to be. Of course, it was.* It eased my mind thinking this way. *Was it odd that these other-worldly experiences were my new normal? Ha!*

'Zo? Zoe? Zoeeee!' S was trying to bring me back from lala land.

'Oh, ugh...' I had to come back to earth and remember where I was and what we were talking about before responding. 'Yes! Yes, S, it feels great. I mean, sounds great, actually!'

'*Sa-weeeet!*' S exclaimed!

'Well, crap, I better get ready then.'

'You've got three minutes, Zoe baby,' S called after me as I ran past her.

I grabbed my workout clothes from the floor and threw them on. *Phew!* They were already a bit stinky, and even though I *was* put off by their moistness, I couldn't be bothered to find something else. I found my backpack, threw in my towel, bikini, phone, wallet, water, a handful of granola bars, some socks and runners – just whatever I could see lying around that I thought I might need – and bolted out of my bedroom.

I slipped on my flip-flops as Soph walked by me with my board. 'You could go surf afterwards, Z!' she suggested, not pausing for an answer. She made her way through the house and Kiko emerged from the kitchen with three delicious-smelling coffees. *Thank God!*

I shut the door behind me, wondering what the hell had just happened. Not 30 minutes ago, I'd been worrying about the day, and now I was off on a new adventure!

Thanks Teo, I thought to myself as I hopped in the back seat, acknowledging him for what *had* to be his doing.

Chapter Twenty-Five

Including Kiko, there were four lifeguards on shift and ready for training that morning. With me and Soph, that made six in total. Everyone was a wee bit groggy considering it was only 5:30 in the morning and the sun had barely risen over the horizon. S, on the other hand, had her metaphorical enthusiasm hat on, and was working hard to get everyone else as excited as she was.

'*Everyone!* This, as you likely already know, is the legendary Zoe Smith. She's going to train with us this morning, and hopefully for the next...' she paused and looked over at me, 'Zoe, when's your first event?'

'Ergh, about eight weeks I think?'

'Righto gang, so hopefully she'll stick around for the next eight weeks and we can kick her butt into shape, yeah?'

She was right. I *did* need my butt kicked into shape, and fast. Two months was not long, and I had *a lot* of work to do if I wanted to feel prepared for the season.

Two of the lifeguards were men, the other two women. They all looked over at me and smiled, and I was self-conscious as to whether or not they were stoked or bummed to have me

141

join them. But *since* I was there and it was already happening, and *since* I had to focus on positive self-talk, the only thing left to do was believe they were stoked.

We did our entire workout barefoot, jogging about a kilometer up the beach where we stopped and did a series of sit-ups, push-ups, and stretches before jogging back to the main lifeguard tower. There, S had us work in teams and do some agility training. I paired up with this guy named Tyler, an older blonde guy maybe in his mid-thirties, who was super fit. He was genuinely nice but also pushed me to my limits, given what I thought my capabilities were. I was able to keep up with everyone, but it wasn't easy. In fact, I was totally knackered by the end of it all, 90 minutes later.

'Alright guys, nice job!' Sophie congratulated us as we collapsed in the sand.

'As you know, my goal is that we learn from one another in these sessions, so I've put up a list of dates and times, and I want each one of you to sign up and lead us through training at *least* twice.'

One of the girls I hadn't met yet chimed in, 'What if we don't know how to train other people?'

S, with her always-positive mindset was quick to reply, 'It doesn't have to be something like we did this morning. You can show us anything *you* like to do. If yoga's your game, lead us in yoga. If it's swimming, or sprints, or dance... whatever you fancy. It's not a test, it's a team-building experiment. You are all exceptional *people*, not just *lifeguards*, and I want you to demonstrate what you've got. But if you want, I'm also okay if you want to team up with someone else for the first session. Got it?'

I leaned over to Tyler and said, 'Is she always this onto it? This...' I searched for the word to express how in awe I was of my friend, seeing her in this light.

'Yeah, I know, right? She's a legend.' Tyler said easily, not seeming winded at all. I was still ridiculously out of breath compared to everyone else.

'Right,' she continued, 'Take a break, hydrate, and eat something before your shift starts.'

As we both got up, Tyler asked, 'How do you know Sophie, anyway?'

I answered in breathless spurts.

'Oh we go... way back... actually. She was my... first... friend... when my dad and I moved here when I was 11. She... taught me how to surf, in fact!'

'Did she? Hey cool...'

I was still too out of breath to give him more of the story, so instead I passed the convo back over to him.

'When did you become a lifeguard?' I asked, while wiping the hair from my face. I had started out with a tight ponytail, but summer on the Goldy was hot and humid, so by the time our workout was finished, stray hairs were sticking to my sweaty face and neck.

'Well,' he began slowly, in a contemplative manner, 'I was 10 when I decided I wanted to be a lifeguard, right after I watched one save my dad's life when we were swimming at the beach.'

'Holy crap, what happened?' I said as I pulled the elastic out of my hair and tried shoving it into a bun. Tyler continued.

'Yeah, we were splashing around in the shore break, just a few feet out from the beach when he had a heart attack. I could tell that something was wrong because he just kind of froze and clutched his chest, but I had no idea what to do except yell and wave for help. I tried to grab onto him so that he didn't sink into the water, but he was just so much bigger than me that I was practically drowning myself. Luckily, two lifeguards got to us incredibly fast. It was amazing. Anyway, there's lots more to it, but you get the idea. They saved his life, and that day I decided I wanted to be able to do that for others. As soon as I turned 17, I got all my qualifications, took the test, and have been a lifeguard ever since.'

'Wow, that's an incredible story, and awesome that it inspired you to become a lifeguard. Thanks for sharing.'

'Yeah, no worries, Zoe. It was fun training with you!' and he walked off in the opposite direction.

'Thanks Tyler, I will!'

I headed back to the main building to grab my backpack and search for those energy bars. I noticed Sophie and Kiko, who were both standing at the side of the building not far from me, so I walked over to them. I handed one to Kiko, who smiled in thanks, and then I shoved one into S's sports bra while she was busy posting the sign-up sheets to the wall.

She snatched it out and thanked me, 'Now go get spanked for me!'

Chapter Twenty-Six

What's cool about Byron is that it's the location of one of my favorite surf breaks: Spanky's. Hence, S telling me to get spanked! With tired enthusiasm, I headed back to the car to drop off my stuff, change into my bikini, and hydrate. I fumbled around in my backpack, looking for a packet of emergen c to replenish my electrolytes. I always had packets of this stuff floating around in my bag, along with random tampons, coconut oil for my skin, and a much-needed leave-in conditioner for my post-surf hair.

'Ugh! Where is it?' I commented out loud. I continued to rummage for exactly five more seconds before giving up. Out of frustration, I leaned my head back on the headrest of the seat, closed my eyes, and tried to relax my mind.

'Be calm, Zoe. Be cool. This is so not a big deal,' I reminded myself, and began focusing on my breath. It took all of my concentration to pay attention to the sensation of the air as it entered my nostrils, and then left my body with the exhale.

My mind kept luring me away from my breath and latching onto a random assortment of thoughts instead. It became a game of mental tug-of-war, and it was beginning to drive me crazy.

What was I getting worked up for anyway? Never mind. Just breathe. Why is this irritating me? Argh! Breathe...

And then, another whisper floated into my ear:

'Be still the mind.'

It happened too fast for me to react with fear. Instead, the words were insanely soothing; in an instant, I felt superbly calm, and as before, no other sound could be heard. No loud cars driving by, no people conversing, no dogs barking or birds chirping. Heck, even the noisy thoughts scattering around my brain like a pinball machine had evaporated into nothingness. It was like being in a vortex. Or maybe one of those sensory deprivation tanks?

And then the whisper came again:

'Let the ocean move you.'

It was a strange yet exhilarating moment because it was completely out of my control, but also because all I felt was peace. And I'm sure you'd agree that feeling out of control doesn't usually elicit a sense of peace, now does it? Not in my experience.

But I knew there was nothing to fear because it was the sound of Teo's voice. By this point, I trusted him without question. In fact, this very moment solidified that trust. My eyes opened. I sat up and quickly looked to my left and then to my right, hoping that nobody was staring through my car window wondering if I was okay. Nope, all clear. And then the noisy streets of people and cars became obnoxiously loud once again.

The hustle and bustle of life, I thought with a sliver of disappointment as that sense of complete peace floated away. *Wait, what did he just say?* It was like a dream that's so vivid but one you forget as soon as you wake up. I had to jog my memory quickly before my own thoughts interfered and blocked the message. But it was already too late. I had no idea what Teo had whispered. *Sigh.*

It was starting to get pretty toasty in the car, so I chugged some water, stealthily put on my bikini, and hopped out to grab my board.

Spanky's is a left hand break, meaning that when you catch the wave you surf to the left. It works best at mid-to-high tide and is a hollow wave when the direction of the swell is right. On a more average day, it's a fun wave that carries a good deal of speed, which means you have to be quick on the takeoff to get into the wave without going over the falls, kind of like The Point at Lennox, but not so intense.

I walked towards the beach with my board under my arm, unsuccessfully racking my brain to remember what Teo had said. My frustration (or desperation) had somehow escalated to an all-time high, and before I knew what I was doing, I looked up at the sky and yelled, 'Teo! What did you say?'

Holy crap, I'm turning into a real nutter here! And not just because I was now talking to myself *out loud* in public, but because I was *also* talking to an angel!

As I walked past the main lifeguard building, a bright purple poster on the bulletin board grabbed my attention. It was a diagram to show people what to do when caught in a rip current. It gave two options:

1. Swim! - Swim parallel to the beach to escape them. Don't try to swim directly back to shore because you'll be swimming against the flow. Instead, get out of the rip by patiently swimming parallel to shore.

2. Float! – Give in and go with the flow. Most rips will circulate back to the beach, so relax, and let the ocean move you.

'Wait a minute. That's it! Let the ocean move you!' I squealed with a scary amount of enthusiasm, which attracted some quizzical stares from a group mingling nearby.

Instinctively and in true Zoe fashion, I stared at my feet and sprinted straight to the edge of the water.

'Let the ocean move you, let the ocean move you...' I kept repeating to myself over and over so as not to let it out of my slippery brain ever again.

Okay, I've got it on lockdown for sure this time! I looked up and mentally thanked Teo for the reminder.

'Let the ocean move you. I wonder what it means?'

I dug my feet into the sand and stared out at the wave about 30 feet from shore. From my count, there were 45 people out. Yeesh. It was a lot for that one peak. Nobody likes to fight for waves or deal with pecking orders, so the fewer people the better in my opinion. I put on my surf leash, tightened my pony-tail and launched into the ocean.

Paddling out, I noticed that my arms were sore and my legs were tired, a reiteration of the fact that the new workout had indeed kicked my ass. But at the same time, I felt a rising sense of energy with each duck dive. As the salt water washed over me, I became more and more rejuvenated, so by the time I joined the crowd in the line-up a few minutes later, I was feeling confident.

I felt a good vibe from the crowd, which was always a bonus, because sometimes you get a real douchebag or two who can kill the mood by being super aggressive and dropping in on people. I recognized the only other girl in the water but couldn't remember how, or what her name was. She smiled and waved when she saw me, so I smiled back, but turned quickly and paddled further outside on seeing a big set on the horizon. It was a clean-up set, coming in big and breaking further outside from the normal sets, which generally meant it would land exactly where people were sitting. So either, you have to paddle your ass off and try to get over the top of it before it breaks, try to duck dive it (which can be a challenge), or ditch and dive (ditch your board and dive under the wave).

Option one is ideal. Option two is great if it works. If it

doesn't, option three comes into play, where you get dragged and thrown about, as the wave pulls you towards shore. You'll have to take a few more on the head until the set is done too. In other words, a clean-up set takes people out, 'cleaning up' the takeoff zone, leaving unscathed the ones who were in a position to avoid it.

Luckily for me I was able to get out of the way without struggle. As the set passed, I looked to see who was left. Funnily enough, it was just me and – *oh, what's her name?* – the other female.

'Whew! That was a biggie!' she said with excitement.

'Totally! Has it been pretty consistent?' I asked.

'Not really, but every so often a big clean-up set like that comes through, so you gotta watch out, hey.'

'Right on, right on,' I said nonchalantly.

'So how's things on tour?' she was super bubbly, and I still couldn't place her.

'New season starts in a couple of months.' I said casually. 'Remind me. How do I know you?'

'Oh, you don't really know me, but my sister is on tour as well, so I sometimes travel with her.'

'Who's your sister?'

'Bailey Wells. And I'm Bridget.'

Ah yes, Bailey, the rookie who won my heat in Maui.

'Oh cool Bridget, nice to meet you. Okay, now I remember seeing you two together. Awesome. How's Bailey doing?'

'She's great, actually! She's up in Indo right now, filming an ad for one of her sponsors. Um, can't remember which one.'

'No way! That's awesome!' I pretended to be happy for her, but the truth is, I was jealous. *Hmm, I'm going to have to work on that*, I thought, wondering what reason I had for feeling this way.

We scrambled to get into position for the next set coming in.

I was feeling feisty so I dropped into the wave real deep, popping up seamlessly and grabbing rail as I sped down the line. About 8 feet ahead, I noticed someone about to be in my way, so I went for a hard cutback to avoid running into him. Instead, I caught my edge and wiped out. At least we didn't collide.

I got back on my board quickly and hurriedly paddled out to position, eager for another wave. I couldn't see Bridget, but no matter. I needed to focus on surfing, not talking. I took a few smaller waves over the next 30 minutes and felt pretty warmed up. I stared out towards the horizon in between waves and repeated my new mantra over and over:

'Let the ocean move you.'

I was doing my best to follow its lead by paying close attention to the current and how I had to keep paddling to stay in position.

'Let the ocean move you...'

Hmm... I decided to let myself drift with the current to experiment with the mantra. Slowly but surely, I drifted about five meters away from the crowd. There was nobody over here, which is not surprising, since Spanky's is a more predictable and consistent wave. Nonetheless, I waited patiently, continuing to listen to the ocean's movements and doing my best to follow the mantra. Well, at least follow my *interpretation* of what it meant.

As I drifted, something in the distance caught my attention. It looked like a random set coming in from a different swell direction. *Weird*, I thought. But as I watched it move, it seemed to be lining up in my favor. It wasn't huge, but it was definitely beginning to form in front of me.

'No way!' I exclaimed out loud. I paddled into position. I still wasn't sure if it was a left or a right until I saw it about to peak in the middle. 'Damn!' It looked good both ways, but from where I was positioned I had to go right. It was such a sweet peeler, glassy and clean. It opened up beautifully as I sailed down the line, enjoying the opportunity to play with the whole face of the wave. I completed a nice, wide bottom turn, then came up and did a big hack, releasing my fin and making some spray before going back down and up again for a floater. The wave continued and I continued with it. It was beautiful and perfect. I peeled off the top feeling stoked.

Let the ocean move you, I thought again.

I paddled back out quickly, and caught another wave immediately, this time going left. I focused again on letting the ocean move me by feeling for a graceful flow. The wave was moving at just the right pace: not too fast and not too slow. It made my connection to it feel natural, effortless even. Instead of trying to carve out big moves and hacks forcefully, I focused on letting the wave tell me where to go and what to do.

In competition, there's a list of moves I will ideally want to do to maximize points. But the reality is I can only do what the wave will allow, which is dictated by its shape, its speed, and a number of other factors like wind and tide etc. It's easy to rush through moves, forcing the flow, instead following it. It's like trying to find the balance between your head and your heart. The wave is the heart, but it's super easy to let your head get in the way and push through what you want to happen.

'This is what I've been missing! I need to work with the rhythm of the wave. More heart, less head. Okay, I think I've got the message!'

For the next hour, I tuned in with the waves as if we were one. A few people had paddled over after they saw my rides, but I didn't let it disrupt my focus. Instead, I kept my mind on the ocean and let go of everything else. In surfing, just as in life, there are days when all the right elements line up in your favor. And *this* was one of those days...

I could barely contain my excitement as I rinsed off in the outdoor shower before heading back to the car.

S had entrusted me with her fancy vehicle, which was really a horrible idea because I don't drive all that often. In any case, she had insisted I take it, and that she'd get a ride home from someone else. (Though I'm pretty sure she was referring to Kiko.) How could I argue with that?

I dug my key out of my wetsuit, chucked my board in the back, hopped in and drove home, my smile wide with enthusiasm, starving as usual.

Chapter Twenty-Seven

For the next week or so I worked out almost every day with the lifeguards, and it turned out to be an amazingly easy way for me to get to know new people without having to socialize per se. Plus, it taught me new ways to train my mind and body.

For example: Stacy, a tall lean brunette, was into beach volleyball. In her workout, she had us warm up with a bunch of super exhausting sprints before working in pairs at the beach volleyball nets to do some cool team-building stuff. In one of the pair exercises, one person would serve the ball while yelling out an easy math equation. Then, the other person had to yell out the answer while also returning the ball. It was surprisingly difficult at first, but it was also amazing to see how quickly we were able to adapt and progress.

Another lifeguard named Tess was into chess, so she taught us the importance of thinking ahead, and how to out-maneuver others. She had us do this crazy fun game in the carpark. She showed us a printed plan of the car park, on which she had numbered each space randomly. After giving us only a brief minute to look at the sheet, she put it away. Our job was to remember what each parking space was numbered, and then, as she called out one of the numbers, we had to run to its corresponding spot. It was harder than it sounds – not just remembering which number went with which spot, but because I'd end up following someone else's lead *even though* I knew the answer on my own. Interestingly, I began to trust myself slowly over the course of the game.

I led the group in a session as well, and took them surfing! They varied in levels, but it didn't matter because I made sure we were all helping one another out. And before we jumped in the water, I gave them a brief talk on mindset and how to stay calm in moments of fear. The session reminded me of the importance of working together as a team, and the joy I feel from helping others to overcome their fears. It was a humbling experience that gave me perspective.

Yet my favorite morning was Kiko's workout. She led us in a tai chi session and I can't even begin to tell you how *ah-may-zing* it was!

Tai chi is considered by many as a martial art, but unlike the fast pace and high impact characteristics of other martial arts like karate or taekwondo, the movements of tai chi are typically slow with no impact. It incorporates elements like breathing, self-defense, meditation, and hand forms. And I found it *very* difficult to maintain focus.

The slow movements made me antsy. I had to fight off a strong urge to ditch class and dive into the ocean. I didn't, but only because I wouldn't want to embarrass myself. I tried to come up with another exit strategy. Pee break? Faint? Leg cramp? As I pondered alternatives, something strange happened. I zoned out completely and became fully immersed in the rhythm of the movements. I didn't even realize I was doing them! In fact, apparently I wasn't thinking about time or surfing or anything at all. When the session was over, it felt like only a minute had passed! I felt wonderfully calm, which I made sure to mention to Kiko.

'Good on ya, mate, that's fab! It's all about coordination and relaxation, rather than muscular tension, so you got it!' Her voice was confident.

'Is that why you made us run up and down the beach first? To get us all revved up?'

'Yeah, I wanted you to feel a real contrast. Well, I wanted you to get a good sweat going too!' she said, laughing. 'Do you ever meditate, Zoe?'

'Um not really, no. I guess not.'

'Well, tai chi is a form of meditation, which means it'll help to clear your mind of thoughts so that you can focus on the moment. Anyway, I gotta jet, Z. I see someone I need to talk to. Catch you later!'

'Right on, Kiko,' I said. But she was already sprinting off towards whoever it was.

My session in the water that day was perfection, and I'm pretty sure I owe it to the tai chi. My mind was calm, so my thoughts didn't interrupt the great task of listening to the ocean. It made it a lot easier to *feel* where the waves were going to line up, which allowed me to focus on technique. Specifically, maintaining speed and linking maneuvers without a break in the action, which is important in terms of pleasing the judges.

Listening and feeling had been my two biggest lessons over the last couple of weeks, and they were definitely having a positive impact on my surfing, not to mention the anxiety I'd been feeling over the last year or so, which had weakened its grasp. That's not to say it wasn't there, because it was, but now it didn't have such a tight grip.

At home later that day, I spent some quiet time in my room. Sitting on my bed cross-legged, I leaned against the wall, closed my eyes and focused on my breath, the way Kiko had taught us that morning. I continued to focus on my breath as best I could. Sometimes my thoughts would take over and I'd imagine myself at the next comp, or think about how I missed my dad, and Derek, or something random like a movie I'd seen. After a while, when I noticed it happening, I'd come back to my breath.

And then, while in the middle of my meditation with my eyes still closed, I saw a vision of Teo standing at my bedroom window.

'Zoe,' he smiled and radiated gloriousness as usual. 'The key factor to success is time spent in stillness. The greatest healing work can occur when you take a moment to get out of the mindless chatter of your thoughts, and listen to what your heart has to say. It's easy to think you don't have time for it, especially when your mind is fully occupied by the doings of the world, but Zoe, none of those external distractions is more important than listening to the guidance of your true Self.

If you wish to increase your level of productivity in the world, learn to extend your time spent in stillness. I promise you will have more focus and determination because your direction will become crystal clear. Rather than squeezing more and more tasks into the day, resulting in a frantic mind and a tired body, you will be able to relax into an amazing flow of prioritized events that will connect the dots for you in just the right way. And without having to plan everything out, you'll be more flexible with last-minute changes. You'll feel more energized and be more productive at the same time.

This is why it is so important to start by spending at least *some* time in stillness, Zoe. After all, over time, a little will amount to a lot.'

Judging by the way he stared at me, he seemed to be finished speaking.

'I totally get it, Teo! I feel like that's exactly what I've been experiencing. The last couple of weeks have been so interesting, and I didn't plan any of them out. It's like the right people were inviting me to do the right things, at the right time. I've been training in new ways and meeting new people. And most importantly, feeling better in the water.'

'Yes, you are finding your groove again, Zoe. Good job!'

He smiled just as a bright ray of light came shining in from the window behind him. It gleamed straight through him and shone onto me. Or rather, *into* me. I felt warmth in my heart and calm in my mind. The light shone brighter and brighter while Teo became more and more of a shadow. Until, eventually, he was gone.

I opened my eyes and looked towards the window, but of course he wasn't there. I picked up my phone to check the time. It was 4:17pm. It had only been about 15 minutes since I had closed my eyes.

Even if it was only in my mind, I still got to see Teo today. *Icing on the cake*, I thought happily, as I took to heart what he had said.

Chapter Twenty-Eight

'Holy crap!'

I woke up way late the next morning. It was 7:33am and I had missed the lifeguard workout. Ugh man, my body was sore!

'Have. To. Get. Up.' I moaned with grogginess.

I rolled over to the side of the bed and laid on my stomach, thinking about getting up. *It's the smart thing to do*, I decided. But sometimes, what you think is the *smart* thing to do, isn't actually the *right* thing to do. Today, my body told me that the *right* thing to do was close my eyes and go back to sleep. So I did, and I didn't even twitch an eye again until 9:15am, when I awoke, this time feeling rested.

I made a cuppa and headed to the back porch with my new book *Thinking Body, Dancing Mind*. It was Kiko's favorite, and she had lent me her copy after our tai chi chat the other day. Apparently it was a book that could bust me into the next levels of sports performance. It incorporated a lot of eastern philosophy, which I was relatively unfamiliar with, but since I loved the tai chi workout so much, Kiko figured I could benefit from the teachings of this book, both in my life and my career. I trusted Kiko, so I was totally open to it.

I opened the book to a random page near the beginning:

"TaoSport warriors create inner and outer goals and strive to develop the skills to accomplish them – without seeking to destroy their competitors. The TaoAthlete:

1. is individualistic;
2. has courage to risk failure, learn from setbacks, and forge ahead;
3. possesses a multidimensional approach to competition;
4. focuses on how the game is placed (process) as opposed to outcomes (product);
5. uses the event to gain greater self-realization;
6. trains the mind to see through the complexity of outer trappings of athletics into its essence;
7. knows his or her vulnerabilities and trains to strengthen them;
8. creates balance, moderation, and simplicity when possible;
9. sees competitions as partners who facilitate improvement;
10. sees success as one part of the process of sports;
11. understands that performance is a rollercoaster and has the patience to ride the ups and downs;
12. blends with forces so as not to create counterforce;
13. has vision, and dreams things into possibilities; and
14. enjoys sport for the pleasure it gives."

I liked everything about this list, including the sound of being a TaoSport warrior – cool! Plus, just the simple act of reading this list made me feel better. More expansive, more open to the possibilities of personal growth through surfing. It resonated with me deeply.

As I took my last sip of coffee, I heard the familiar *swoosh* of the upstairs sliding door as it opened. I heard heavy footsteps above me and shortly felt sand falling through the cracks of the upper deck onto my head.

'Wowzers! Hello?' I called up.

'Zoeeee!' Next thing I knew, Seth was leaning over the deck railing, peering down at me. He had a baseball cap on which made it hard for me to see his face, except that his smile was gleaming in the sun. 'What're you up to? I thought you were deep in training with my sis and her lifeys. He he he!'

'So funny, Seth,' I said sarcastically. 'Yeah, I kinda slept in this morning. What are you up to?'

'I'm going to the skate park. My mate asked if I could teach some of his rugrats a few things. He has a class three times a week and he thought it'd be fun if I came as a guest instructor.'

'No way, that's awesome. Do you know what you're teaching?'

'Aye, sort of. Not sure. Hey, do you wanna come? You can have a giggle at my expense!' he said with a chuckle.

I laughed and paused for a second, pretending to contemplate the decision, but I couldn't deny the fact that my heart was saying yes.

'Um yeah! I could do with a good laugh!'

'Sweet. Meet you out front in 10.'

Swoosh, swoosh, and he was back inside.

Gathering my stuff, I felt excited and nervous. Skateboarding had been my thing back in Colorado, but I hadn't done it much since I'd left the U.S. many years ago. Maybe it reminded me of my mom too much; she was the one who'd always taken me to the park. Now we barely talked. I felt sad all of a sudden, and started to second-guess whether I should go.

'Z, you ready?' Seth was calling from outside.

C'mon Zoe, you can do this, no turning back now, I thought.

'Okay, just gimme a sec,' I yelled back, quickly filling my water. Shutting the door behind me, I realized something kinda important. *Oh crap.*

'Seth! I don't have a skateboard!'

'Ye of little faith! I'm way ahead of ya!' he said, holding up two boards. As he shut the boot, I noticed a black bumper sticker with 'Follow The Feelgood' written in bold, white letters.

'Follow the feelgood, huh? What's that supposed to mean?' I said curiously as we both hopped into the car.

'Seriously, Z? Isn't it self-explanatory?' He gave me a squinty-eyed half-frown as he turned the ignition, like I was being stupid. 'Zo, you've got to let loose a little bit!' He smiled at me and then looked back as he reversed out of the driveway and onto the road.

'Well, maybe,' I said somewhat defensively. 'I just like to stay focused, I guess.'

'I hear ya, Z, but focus can be full of fun too, you know.'

'Hmm. Well, I *have* been working on that these last few weeks.'

'Really? You've been working on letting loose?' And he wasn't baiting me this time. He seemed genuinely to not have noticed. I grunted and slouched into my seat, embarrassed at the obvious contradiction in what I'd said.

'Hey, don't worry,' Seth said as he looked over at me and smiled kindly. And then he patted my thigh and added, 'Today is all about fun and feeling good, okay?'

I sat back up and took in his authentically sweet vibe, admiring him for it.

'Damn, Seth. When did you turn into a cute lil' smartypants?'

We both laughed and I felt lighter already. Seth turned up the radio and we listened to music the rest of the way to the park.

Chapter Twenty-Nine

'No way!' I said with excitement as we turned into the park a few minutes later.

'What's up?' Seth said, looking over at me quizzically.

'I didn't realize we were going to *this* park! I don't know why. I guess I wasn't thinking about it, but I love this park. I was just here the other day.'

'See? You're feeling good already!' he said happily.

'Are you going to taunt me with this 'feelgood' thing the whole time, Seth?' I was joking, and actually enjoying the kind attention he was giving, even if it included a little sarcasm.

'No, of course not! Soon I'll be too busy embarrassing myself to be able to give you all the attention, so I have to get it in now!'

'Well, maybe it'll give me a chance to take the piss out of you instead!' I used the Aussie term for 'poking fun', making an effort to act casual.

We got out of the car and noticed his friend was already there with about six kids between 9 and 13 years old, judging by the size of them. Seth handed me his extra board and I made my way to the flatter stretches of the park away from the crowd to warm up. Luckily, Seth had an extra set of elbow and knee pads too, and a helmet, which made me very happy and slightly less nervous. My mom had always made me wear protective gear, and it had saved me from bumps, bruises and broken bones on a number of occasions. Falling onto concrete sucked, I remembered. It hurt like hell, *and* it was way too easy to break a bone. Not to mention the fact that it would be super reckless of me not to protect myself. As a professional athlete, I needed to take extra special care of my body at all times.

I weaved around the park, getting comfortable with the board under my feet, trying to find my groove again. After about 20 minutes of playing around on my own, I felt confident enough to join the others, so I skated my way over to the group of kids Seth was teaching, and stopped next to his friend.

'Hey! I'm Zoe!'

'Oh hey! Oh... hi! Yeah, of course, I know who you are! I'm Zach.'

'Nice to meet you, Zach!' I said as we shook hands.

I looked him in the eye, and got the sense he was nervous about something. He kept looking away while we were talking, but maybe he was just keeping an eye on the kids. I wasn't so in-tune with the whole kid thing, but nonetheless tried to keep the conversation going.

'Pretty cool that you teach these kids,' I said. 'Do you like it?'

'Yeah absolutely, I love it. They are good lil' whippers, aye?' He kept looking over at them, and I decided that, yes, he was making sure that Seth was fine on his own with the groms.

'So how do you know Seth?'

'Just from skating. He's got a real nice rhythm when he skates, and he's friendly with everyone, so I thought the kids would be stoked to learn from someone like him. I don't even care what he teaches, really. I just figured whatever he has to say will be helpful. We're no experts here, aye? Just having fun and learning along the way.'

We went back to watching Seth getting the kids to work on some ramp stuff. He looked back at me and called me over with a big swing of his arm. I skated up to him, throwing a 'see ya' over my shoulder at Zach. It was a bit weird joining in with the kids, seeing as I was much older than them. But hey, I was here to feel good, right? Seth and I both laughed in unison after watching their confusion with my participation.

'Guys, this is Zoe. And for any surfers among you, she's a professional, and she totally kicks butt. So make sure you get her autograph later too!'

A few of the kids gasped as they seemed to recognize me.

'Oh geez, Seth, now the pressure's on!'

'Ha ha! No pressure, no pressure. Only fun! What's our goal, guys?' Seth asked with enthusiasm.

'Fun!' they all yelled back.

'And how are we all doing?'

'Awesome!' they all yelled back again.

'See Z, no pressure, only fun!'

'Wow, you are so damn proud of yourself, aren't you?' I joked.

'Is there any other way to be?' Seth shot back.

'Ugh! Good point!'

Actually, it was a brilliant point. And a brilliant concept. With it now etched into my brain, I skated down the ramp, joining in with the flow. The kids were just so cute too. They were friendly and adorable and they stuck to me like glue. I felt like I'd taken a happy pill; they lifted my spirits immensely. My skating wasn't half-bad either! In fact, it may have been their fun-loving attitude that helped loosen me up. I couldn't believe it.

It's like that tree metaphor. The one about how tree

branches are made to bend with the wind. If they were stiff, they'd snap off with any breeze. Something like that anyway. And that's how it went. The more relaxed I was, the more fun I had, and the more confident I felt, which made me relax more. Geez, I really had gotten highly strung!

Seth demonstrated a few moves on the ramp, and Zach wasn't joking. He had a nice rhythm. He stayed low and did a lot of footwork. He was relaxed in a way that allowed him to shift his weight and maneuver his board effortlessly. Watching him closely worked well for me because I learn best by emulating what I'm shown. It's like I can tap into the person's vibe and connect with their rhythm. In fact, I'd say it's exactly how I got so good so quickly at surfing. Oddly enough, I learned the most from watching surf videos. I'd watch the same clips over and over again, and connect with the styles of certain surfers.

Wow, I need to start doing that again! It was a nice little reminder.

By the end of the hour, the kids were sooo happy! And the parents, who were all hanging out on the sidelines together, came forward and thanked Seth and Zach for a great lesson. They took pictures of their children with Seth, and then with me, and we all had a hoot hamming it up! And when a bunch of the kids asked for my autograph, I told them to make sure they got Seth's too, because he was for sure going to be a pro soon enough.

'Way to pass the buck, Zo,' Seth said with a smirk on his face as he scribbled his signature on the pieces of paper the kids were handing him.

'Ha ha, you know it!' I said happily, feeling like I finally got one on him.

We chucked our gear in the back of his car and drove off.

'So hungry, oh God!' I said as we pulled out of the park.

'Yeah, let's feed.'

'Sweet, okay, but I'm buying.' It was the least I could do.

'Right on, mate! I'll take it. Thanks!'

He took me to a cafe near the beach by our house. It was pretty busy, obviously a popular choice. It had a Hawaiian theme, which made sense, since the name of the place was Aloha Vibes. We ordered at the counter and sat down.

I was curious to learn more about Seth, which I suppose is why I offered to take him to lunch. His easy going confident nature intrigued me, and I was starting to view him less as Sophie's little bro, and more as an individual worth getting to know.

'Seth, you were amazing with those kids. They loved you!'

'Yeah, it was pretty fun, hey?' Seth replied in a nonchalant manner. He was playing it cool, or maybe he was just modest. Either way, he was doing a good job of under-acknowledging his talents.

I continued, 'So, are you really wanting to turn pro?'

'Yeah, for sure. I just can't imagine what else I would want to do with my time. Plus I really want to travel. I haven't been many places yet.'

And then, looking up at me, he asked, 'Is it amazing to travel around like you do?'

'Yeah, pretty much! I mean, it's great to check out places around the world with epic surf spots. Plus, I just love to spend time by the ocean – and being on the WSL means spending *a lot* of time hanging out in between heats.'

'What about the different cultures?' he asked with curiosity.

'It's been great to see how other people live, for sure. On the downside, I don't always get to explore the sights of places I travel to, because I'm preoccupied with the competition. And then once the event is finished, or I'm eliminated, whichever comes first, I'm off to the next. So it can get kind of tiring at times.'

'Yeah, but still, Zoe, it must be pretty cool.'

The waitress brought out our drinks.

'Iced vanilla latte with whip?'

'That's me, thanks!' I said, excited to take that first delectable sip.

She reached across the table to put my refreshment down in front of me, then placed a green smoothie in front of Seth and let us know that our food would be out shortly. Before getting sidetracked by my drink, I turned my attention back to Seth.

'Seriously though, Seth, you really are smooth on that skateboard. It's almost like you're floating. How do you do it?'

'Um, dunno really. I just try to stay relaxed the whole time. As soon as I get tense, I remember to relax. And the more consistently I can be relaxed, the easier it is to follow the feelgood.'

And again he smiled, that sweet smile, a smile that would eventually come to be known as 'the smile that soothes the soul'. I cupped my head with my hands, shaking my head in disbelief and wondered aloud, 'Who is this guy?'

Just then the waitress arrived back with our food.

'Chicken cranberry wrap?'

'Yes please!' I was freaking hungry by now.

'And here's your tofu scramble burrito with a side of avocado.' She placed it down in front of Seth, handed us some napkins, and told us to enjoy, before walking away.

'Are you veggo then?' I asked

'Sort of. I mean, I eat meat on occasion, but less and less. My goal is to be vegan, but it's a bit of a slow transition as I learn how to do it properly. Plus, meat production is horrible for the environment, and if it's not organic, it's actually really harmful on the body...' he trailed off, looking somewhat embarrassed.

'No, it's cool that you're super healthy. I want to be healthier, but I'm not very good at it. It's hard to be picky because I travel so much, you know? Sometimes the options just aren't there.'

'Well, we can't have that now, can we? I've seen you with the hangries and it's not a pretty sight!'

I wish I'd had a chip or something to throw at him, but I didn't, so my best evil glance had to do.

'Ugh, Zozo, if that was your mean face, I'd say you failed miserably.' He winked at me. And I blushed.

Chapter Thirty

Seth dropped me off at home and headed off to a mate's house. There was no denying that it had been a pretty remarkable day. I got to hang out with Seth and learn about his world, participate in a fun skate class with a bunch of groms, who were just so freaking cute and that's saying a lot coming from me. Most importantly, though, I'd enjoyed being back on a skateboard again, despite the painful memories associated with it.

I flopped down on the living room sofa, but left my dirty feet dangling over the edge so as not to muck up the couch. I stared up at the ceiling. My blank canvas. As my mind began to wander, it took me back to the Colorado days of my childhood, when I was maybe 7 or 8 years old, and when skating was a huge part of my happiness. I would spend hours at the park while my mom waited patiently for me to become too exhausted to skate anymore.

The cool part of skating when you're little is that there's less fear of getting hurt, which equals more room for adventure and risk-taking. This can create a ton of joy when playing with friends.

I loved those moments with my mom at the skatepark, but thinking of them also made me feel sad from the fact that she'd left us. *How could she do that to us?* I wondered. *How does someone just up and leave their family?* As an adult, now I realized that it wasn't because she didn't love me, but at the time, all I knew was I no longer had her around. And it was hard. I missed her all the time. I was confused too. There are moments in a child's life when nothing can replace a mother's touch. It's innate. It didn't matter how awesome my dad was (and he was awesome for sure), there was always a void, a hole where my mom was supposed to be, supposed to be there for me, her daughter.

When someone you love leaves you, it's hard to not take it personally – so I spent years wondering what I had done wrong that had made her want to go. But over that time (and with countless hours of therapy), I learned that what she did had nothing to do with me personally, and everything to do with *herself.* And whether her reasons were fair or unfair, well, that wasn't going to change the fact that she had left.

The experience taught me that I never wanted to end up like her; that is, spending years living a life I didn't love, only to wake up one day and decide to bail on it all. Yet ironically, I *had* been questioning lately what I'd been doing this past year. And not just in a few random moments here and there. I'd been poised to throw my whole career away, so many times I can't even count. And my attitude showed it.

Wow. Is this all that life is? Are we all just lost and confused? Are we all blindly stumbling around in the dark, desperate to survive?

I could feel a headache coming on. *Dammit Z, you're stuck in your head!* I said to myself disapprovingly as I leapt off of the couch in one quick movement. I grabbed S's yoga mat from the corner of the living room and walked out the back door and onto the beach to find a spot to do some stretches. My body was feeling rather stiff after skating all morning, and I needed to move this energy out. As I put the mat down, I heard someone yelling at me from the house. I looked back and saw Abby on the upper deck, waving her hands at me.

'Zoe! Come up here if you're going to do some yoga. I need to practice too!' By the sound of her voice and the erratic waving, I got the impression she was excited about it. I, on the other hand, am the worst yogi ever! I'll do anything to avoid getting on my mat. For me, yoga has more to do with a few random seated postures and then savasana. In fact, this is how I would sum up yoga: *blah blah blah... savasana!*

'Okay cool!' I yelled back to her, wondering what this yoga session was going to entail. *My mind was resisting the potentially long session, but I knew my body would thank me for it afterwards. So in this instance, doing what felt good meant sucking it up and following Abby's lead.* I picked up my mat and shook it out, then jogged the few meters back to the house and up the stairs to the top deck.

'Hi Abby,' I said with a smile as I entered the house.

She gave me a hug to welcome me. 'Zoe, lovely to see you! Having a nice day?'

'Yeah, it's been awesome. I went to the skate park with Seth actually. He's incredible!'

'So I hear! Of course he doesn't want us to go watch him. That would be too embarrassing. But he does show us videos every once in a while.'

'Yeah, I was really impressed.' I stopped, unsure of how much info to divulge. Abby was cool with Seth's choices, but I didn't think it was my place to tell her the specifics of what Seth was up to.'

I put my mat next to Abby's and felt obliged to let her know that I wasn't much of a yogi.

'When I say I'm *doing yoga*, what I really mean is I'll do a bunch of downward dogs, pigeon, and a few other random poses. I don't have much of a routine about it. I'm just stoked to get any sort of stretching in.'

'Oh that's fine. Actually it's perfect because I want to practice my teaching skills. Do you mind if I lead you in a short series that I've been working on?'

'That sounds perfect. Thanks!' In absolute truth, I most liked the fact that she'd said 'short' series.

About 20 minutes later we were done, and my body was feeling *much* better. The tension in my back seemed to have disappeared, as had my headache.

'That was great, Abby! Way better than what I would've done on my own, that's for sure!' I got up slowly as Abby handed me a glass of water.

'Here, it's got lemon, cayenne and honey in it. Really good for your digestion, and even better if you drink it first thing in the morning, before you do anything else.'

'Cayenne?' I wasn't sure I liked the sound of this concoction.

'It's just a tiny bit. Try it and see.'

I took a tiny sip and then gave myself a moment to taste it.

'Not bad!'

'It's a lot better than drinking coffee first thing in the morning.' I think she was trying to hint at something.

'Oh geez, I don't know about that!' I replied in disbelief. I *loved* my morning coffee.

'I promise. It was hard for me at first too, but now I'm so used to it – and it's made a huge difference in my life. I'm more alert and clear and stable. Without the caffeine crashes.'

'Yeah, early afternoons are tough for me. I'm always so tired.'

'If you do this instead of coffee, it'll change your life. Just think about it, okay?' I could tell she was pretty serious about this request.

'Okay, sure, I'll give it a try. Thanks for taking such good care of me. It means a lot. Your whole family is... just... well, I don't know how I'd be doing if I wasn't here with you guys right now.'

'You're family, sweetie, and you always will be. We love when you're here and we only want the best for you.'

'I know. You guys are the best!'

She hugged me tight and I felt a tear glide down my face. I had had such a nostalgic day, going skating and then thinking about my mom, the direction of my life, all of it. The moment made me realize just how much Abby had been like a mother to me over the years, ever since we moved here when I was still a girl.

Chapter Thirty-One

I was on a mission to figure shit out.

Okay, so if I want to feel good all the time, I think it comes down to: what am I not doing that I want to be doing and what am I doing that I'd rather not be doing?

It was going to take a process of elimination, I decided. I pulled out my 'everything book', had a look at my list of priorities, then rated how I was doing on each one on a scale of 1-10, 1 being failing miserably and needing an immediate change, 10 being totally rockin' it. Here's what I came up with:

1. *surfing and surf training* – 5
2. *mind training* – 3
3. *body training* – 9
4. *talking with Teo* – 6
5. *having fun with S and the family* – 7
6. *working harmoniously with my sponsors* – 3
7. *connecting with fans and inspiring others via social media* – 2
8. *skating/playtime* – 5
9. *eating healthily for optimal energy and nutrition* – 1

10. *quiet time – 4*

I felt pretty good about the progress I'd made on some of my priorities, but there was still a ton of room for improvement. I decided it would be best to focus on the areas that were desperate for my attention, i.e. anything rated less than a 5 out of 10. Of course, these were the areas I'd not given much energy to at all, because it was easier to avoid anything that would require extra diligence and willpower to change in ways I wouldn't necessarily like.

Luckily, I had Teo on my side, and knowing that he was watching over me was a bit of an incentive to get my butt in gear. And if he could see me living at my highest potential, then I had to do my best to fulfill my role completely. Right?

Okay, here goes. I decided to start with *eating healthily for optimal energy and nutrition.*

It shouldn't take much to move this from a 1 rating up to a 6 or 7, I decided optimistically as I got up to make a cup of coffee. Why don't I make three healthy changes in my diet, by replacing something that lowers my energy with something that increases it?

I opened the freezer door to pull out the coffee tin, but as I did so, it fell out on its own, dropping to the floor. The plastic lid shattered as it hit the tiles and dumped the grinds all over the floor.

'Dammit!' I complained out loud. *How the heck...?*

Grabbing the broom from beside the fridge I began to sweep. I was glad the grinds were dry and easy to sweep, at least, instead of a wet, sloppy mess.

'G'day Zozo!' Sophie sang as she and Kiko walked through the open doorway, bags in tow. She stopped in her tracks when she saw me crouched on the floor, sweeping the grinds into the dustpan.

'Yikes, what's going on here?'

'Ugh, a little coffee explosion. Can we add coffee to the grocery list please?'

'No worries, hun. We have a new plan anyway!'

'Uh-oh, another new plan?' Ever since we were at school together, S had a tendency to come up with a *lot* of new plans. She loved to think up creative ideas about anything and everything, so I usually just rolled with the idea until she came up with a new one. This was how Sophie's excited mind worked.

'This is a *for real* plan!' she insisted, as she proceeded to unload the reusable canvas shopping bags.

'What's all this?' I queried, dumping the grinds out of the dustpan and into the organic waste box.

'Mum's specialty: cayenne, honey, and a shit ton of lemons. Apparently this is what she's been drinking instead of coffee for the last couple of months, and she *suggests* we do the same. She says she feels amazing.'

'OMG!' I cried ecstatically, as I put the broom away. I wondered about the possibilities of Teo instigating the coffee spillage. *Was it truly a coincidence?*

'Wow, didn't think *you'd* be so thrilled about giving up coffee, Zoe,' Kiko said, though not unkindly.

'Ha! I think I'm just reacting to the strangely perfect timing of it all. I just dumped all of our coffee on the floor by accident, but also I'm trying to choose some ways to improve my health and nutrition. Maybe this is a sign?'

'Well then, a sign it is! Water, lemon, and cayenne replaces coffee from now on. Right?' Kiko tried to get us all in agreement.

'Yep, guess so,' I said with hesitation. I mean, I liked the *idea* of it, but...

'Hell yeah, ladies! Keeks, Zozo, you both ready for this?'

Kiko looked over at S, trying to communicate via a scrunched face something like *that's not my name.* S winked at her, not apologizing for what she'd said, or for being herself for that matter.

'So what else are you planning to do?' Kiko asked, changing the subject.

'I dunno, this all literally came to me about a minute before you walked in the door. But...' I paused, tilted my head up and looked at the ceiling, thinking about what else I could do. After a moment or two of Sophie noisily putting the stuff away, I came up with an idea.

'I could do better with eating more *real* food instead of so many energy and granola bars. I'm just super lazy about it, though. Especially breakfast, because we have to get up so early for our workouts, and then I usually go surfing right afterwards. By the time I'm done, I'm starving and end up eating whatever I can get my hands on!'

Kiko was quick to respond, 'I usually make smoothies before I work out, so we could do that? I know how to make them real tasty *and* super healthy. I can show you, if you like.'

S and I nodded enthusiastically, but of course S couldn't stop there.

'Better yet, why don't you just spend the night, and you can make 'em for us, eh Kiki?' She winked at her again, this time raising her eyebrows and making a sexual innuendo gesture.

Kiko rolled her eyes, 'Guys, try to stay on track here, hey?'

But we were all laughing with S, who just wouldn't let up with her ridiculousness. Once we calmed down, Kiko suggested that she do a bit of both. 'I'll make them and teach you how to make your own.'

'Sounds great, Kiko. Thanks!'

'Yeah, thanks babe!' S said as she grabbed Kiko and gave her an affectionate peck on the lips. Kiko pulled away after a couple of seconds, seeming to be a bit shy with the PDA.

'Okay,' I continued. 'Any thoughts on meals? Usually, I eat

my main meal mid-afternoon because I'm just so damn hungry. Plus, I hate going to bed too full because then I don't sleep well. So something light. What do you think?'

'Salads!' Sophie said. 'We could take turns making salads, you and I. You know, my mum's got some killer recipes, and I'm sure she'd love to participate.'

'Yeah, love it.' Any excuse to spend more time with Abby, if you asked me.

'Cool,' S replied. 'We'll talk to mum later and sort it out. And what do you guys say we do a big shop tomorrow? I don't know what you're up to, Zozo, but we've got the day off, so we were gonna sleep in and then no plans. Maybe shop late morning?'

'Yeah, I love it!' I said again. 'This is all so awesome!'

We all high-fived one another, and just like that, I had the potential to boost my food and nutrition up the scale. After all, anything was an improvement on a 1!

Chapter Thirty-Two

Abby, of course, was thrilled to be invited into our little health kick, not only for the nutritional aspect, but also because it meant spending more time with her daughter and her daughter's girlfriend. I think she liked seeing how happy Sophie was. I mean, we know S is pretty much always happy, but this was different. It was cool to see her with such an awesome chick by her side.

I woke up early the next day, anxious to keep working on my list. I got up and made my hot water, lemon and cayenne concoction before sitting down at the counter to address the next life area.

Connect with fans and inspire others via social media jumped out at me.

Hmm, well, I definitely haven't given my fans the attention they deserve, at least not since social media fell off my radar. But social media was a great way to connect with them, and I had no doubt they wanted to see what I'd been up to.

Maybe I just need to be honest from now on, and share the good with the bad? It scared me, but in a good way. Plus, you can't have the highs without the lows, so this felt like the most authentic way to create long-term consistency. *I'll have to be smart about how I do this, if I want to inspire them with those lows.*

I thought for a minute about how I could get back in the game with Instagram. Obviously beginning on a low was not the way to go. Not after all this time. *Ooh! I should post a photo from the skate park. It's a perfect and fun way to start. Yaasss! This is legit awesomeness!*

I posted a super silly photo that made me smile. While I continued to scroll around my feed, Kiko came out of Sophie's room and closed the door quietly behind her. She had on a pair of Thai-style fisherman pants and a pink singlet, and was tying her dark hair up into a bun. She looked up afterwards and gasped when she saw me at the counter. 'Oh sorry, Zoe!' she said in a whisper. 'I didn't expect to see anyone out here already.'

'No, no, it's all good. I just couldn't sleep any longer. What are you doing up?'

'I want to do some tai chi while the world outside is still quiet, and before Soph gets up and starts bouncing off the walls!'

'Ha! I get it. Hey, do you think I could join you?' The words just flew out of my mouth before I even had a chance to realize what I was saying. 'I loved the class you taught with the life-guards that morning and I had such a good surf session afterwards.'

'Yeah, of course! I was gonna do it on the beach.'

'Sweet. Thanks! I'm gonna change real quick and then I'll meet you out there,' I said as I hopped off the bar stool and bounced into my room.

I put on some yoga tights, then changed out of my t-shirt into a random navy singlet that was lying on the floor. As I walked out back, Kiko was on the beach and had already started.

I left a few feet of distance between us, and began to follow her flow. Slow, steady, purposeful movements. The first 10 minutes were pretty challenging. My mind was busy so my body had a hard time working slowly. Initially, my pace was rushed, but as we continued, I found myself easing into the rhythm of tai chi. *Focus on the moment*, I reminded myself over and over again, while noticing how challenging that was.

We were done about 30 minutes later.

'Kiko, you are one beautiful being!'

Kiko smiled, accepting my compliment gracefully with a delicate 'thank you'. Picking up her water bottle, she asked, 'You know how I mentioned tai chi was a kind of meditation? Have you thought any more about trying meditation since the other day?'

'No. Well, I keep wanting to, but then I never get around to it.'

'Look, you're more than welcome to do tai chi with me whenever you like.'

'I'd love that, thanks! I feel so much better from it, but in a way that's hard to describe. How did you get introduced to it?' Kiko fascinated me and I was curious about this girl making my friend even happier than I'd ever seen her.

'Oh, I learned from my grandparents, actually, on my dad's side. When they were younger, they spent many years traveling, exploring the world with just their backpacks while picking up odd jobs and work-trade options along the way. At one point, they were in China, and some guy they were volunteering with was really into it. He invited them to do a class and apparently they were hooked instantly, so they made it a daily practice from then on. And when they finally came home, they opened up their own studio here. Needless to say, the whole family has been raised with it. I guess you could say it's sort of in our blood.'

'Wow, so you're like a ninja!' I said enthusiastically – and not joking at all. She was a unique individual, and the more I got to know her, the more I wanted to learn from her.

'How have you benefited from it? I mean, can you see the difference when you *don't* do it?' I figured she'd been doing it for so long she may not be able to tell.

'OMG I *totally* know what it's like to not do it! There were a couple of years, a while back, when I completely rejected it from my life. My parents call it my *teenage rebellion years.* Ha ha!'

'Ha ha! Awesome. You're such a rebel!' We were both laughing as she continued.

'Well they're probably right, but no matter what the reason was, at that time I just didn't want to be told what to do. I didn't care about the benefits of tai chi. I didn't care to be in the same room with my family. I just didn't care at all. So I ditched it for quite a while, like a couple of years. And I was definitely a different person. More agro, more controlling, moodier. It was a lot harder to feel peace because I was reacting to the little things in daily life, like traffic, or an awkward conversation, or when things didn't go my way. I'm sure there were emotional growing pains of being a teenager thrown in there too, but still...

And after a while of rebelling against my family and, to be honest, against my 'self', I reached a... tipping point, I guess you could say. During that time, I was dealing with bulimia, and well, I ended up in the hospital...'

'Oh wow, Kiko...' I didn't know what else to say.

'Yeah, it was a wake-up call, that's for sure. My body was shutting down, and it forced me to decide: do I want to live or do I want to die? And that's when I decided I had to change the way I was going about my life. So the first thing I did was join up with my family again. And being with my family took me back to tai chi and lots of other things. Immediately, I became happier. Like a peaceful happy, just a sort of feeling of content, even though I was still unsure of my life path.'

'And now?'

'Well, I still don't know my life path! But I *do* like what I'm doing, and who I'm with, and how I feel, so I'm just going to keep doing that right now.'

We walked back to the house and I made my way to the kitchen to make Kiko's cayenne drink. I made one for Soph too, since I could hear rustling from her room, as Kiko and I chatted away.

'G'day guys!' Sophie swung open the door and came bouncing out.

'S, do you just wake up excited?' Of course, I already knew the answer to this.

'You betcha, Zozo! The attitude's gratitude, right babe?!'

She looked at us, and gave her signature wink. I couldn't help but admire her ability to set things straight. Kiko chimed in, asking when we wanted to go shopping, but I wasn't feeling motivated for it. I hated shopping. I got irritated standing in crowds, driving in traffic, waiting in line, etc.

'Actually,' I said, coming to grips with myself, 'do you guys mind if I stay back? I'm working on this thing, and I feel all zen from tai chi, and I think it would be a good time to sort out a few things.'

'Yeah, no worries.' Kiko said easily, without hesitation.

'You guys did tai chi without me?' Sophie pouted, acting fake-hurt. We knew she was kidding, because tai chi so wasn't her vibe. After a moment of playing her little facade, she straightened up and with an air of confidence said, 'Of course, chica, no worries. Get your shit together and we'll grab everything we need for food, okay?'

About an hour later, after a delicious smoothie lesson from

Kiko, the two of them left for the store and I sat back down at the counter with my list.

Well, well, what do you know? I was looking at priority number 2 – mind training – which I'd given a 3 rating. I crossed out the 3 and bumped it up to a 5. *If I practice tai chi or meditation of some sort three times a week, I think I'll be able to bump it up to at least a 7. Here's hoping.*

Since that one had been easy, I decided none of the priorities list should feel difficult. Nothing about anything should feel difficult for that matter! *Geez, why do we make things so painful for ourselves?*

I felt wildly excited with this revelation, and decided to roll with it. I put down my pen and slipped on my bikini instead.

Chapter Thirty-Three

The conditions were onshore. It was a soupy mess out there. Generally speaking, this is far from the ideal scenario for surfers. The wind was blowing onto the beach, which forces the waves to fold, closing them out. *Bleugh!* But as a pro, I have to be prepared to surf in any condition, so it's always been a habit of mine to go out and practice no matter what. The plus side of surfing in crappy conditions was that it wouldn't be as crowded. Bonus!

I battled my way through the wind, duck diving through like a million waves. (Okay, okay, more like 15!) I made it to the line-up after about 10 minutes. *Whew!* I thought to myself as I finally got to sit up on my board and stretch out my shoulders. The trouble with choppy conditions is that everything feels hectic. Imagine running on a track versus running cross-country. One is a clear, predictable course on a smooth surface, and the other is full of twists and turns and obstacles on uneven ground.

I took a few minutes to catch my breath before looking around to see if I recognized any of the other four people out here. Nope. But I did make eye contact with a couple of them, exchanging friendly nods. See, when it's crowded, everyone is a bit more ego and agro; people ignore one another because we're all in this kind of dogfight over the waves. But in conditions like these, when there's only a handful of people out, it becomes an encouraging community. Weird.

I paddled for a wave that wasn't awesome-looking, but if you waited around for the perfect wave in this slop, you'd be waiting all day. Needless to say, that would get boring and frustrating, or I'd wind up cold and pissed off. Instead, I would have to take what waves came and do what I could with them. It was a smart approach, and I knew for sure that I'd won a few comps because I was able to dominate in less-than-ideal conditions. Not all of the venues had the best breaking waves. Huntington Beach, for example, could be really *meh*, but it was a great spot to attract a huge crowd. And that was good for the progression of the sport on a marketing level.

Luckily, I enjoyed surfing on days like this. It was a different experience, with a real sense of solitude that came with it – like jogging in the rain.

Speaking of rain, about 10 minutes and two mediocre waves later, it started to pour. And I mean raining buckets! It was pelting so hard I could barely see what was going on around me! Everything went gray and dark, and it was loud, with fat rain droplets plummeting into the water. I sat on my board waiting for the thick of the rain to pass and zoned out. I was busy entertaining myself with an existential conversation around the infinite possibilities of the Universe, when I saw a peculiar movement out of the corner of my eye. My initial reaction was 'shark', so I lifted my legs out of the water quickly and laid down on my board. Was this the right thing to do? I dunno. What I *did* know was that I wasn't going to let my limbs become shark bait. If it was coming at me, it was gonna have to work for it.

But as the movement got nearer, I saw it was a person. The rain was too thick to decipher anything until it was right in front of me. I sat back up with a sense of relief. I mean, this was the ocean and you had to respect that anything could happen at any time. Just because I was a surfer didn't mean I wasn't scared of sharks. At the same time, I'd learned that there was nothing helpful in worrying about potential dangers out of my control. I could take whatever necessary precautions were available to me, but in the end, nature was nature.

The other surfer paddled towards me.

'Hey!' I yelled out. 'It's crazy out here!' I was feeling slightly alone and isolated, so it was nice to have someone close by.

'OMG, Zoe? Hi!' she yelled back. But the wind was too loud to decipher the girl's voice.

'Huh? Who is it?' I asked, but as she got within three feet of me, I could finally see it was Bailey. And even though I should've been thrilled to see a familiar face, I felt a strong surge of rage towards the rookie who'd kicked my ass. I put it down to jealousy. I couldn't let that show now though, could I?

'Bailey! Holy crap! Hi!' I said with a smile, masking my irritation. Why was I so damn irritated? She paddled up to me and we hugged.

'It's good to see ya, mate. Have you been out here long?'

'Eh, probably about an hour,' I estimated.

'I was paddling out when it started dumping buckets, but I didn't feel like going in.'

'Yeah, I decided to wait it out and see what happens, but this is pretty intense,' I replied.

We paddled around looking for something to catch, but it was just so sloppy out there. I paddled for waves that looked like they had potential but then closed-out on me way sooner than I had expected, so I kept getting caught up in the whitewater. And then I'd have to work my ass off, exhaustingly duck-diving wave after wave until I made it back out again. I did manage to carve out a few nice turns on a couple of okay waves, and even though the waves were patchy, I did what I could nonetheless.

After a while, I started to shiver and noticed that my arms were covered in goosebumps. I was getting cold and had thoughts about going in. I hated feeling cold.

'Look!' Bailey said as she pointed towards the horizon. I turned to look behind me, and there, not too far in the distance, was a break in the clouds.

'Sweet!' I said optimistically. 'I was just about to succumb to the weather and head in, but it looks like it's clearing up!'

The weather improved quickly, and after about five minutes, the visibility became clear again. The current was strong, and we hadn't noticed it had pulled us about 10 or 15 feet out to sea. We paddled back to the line-up, which warmed me up slightly, though my muscles felt tired and crampy.

Back in position, we zoned back into surfing. It was still raining, but it was more like a light shower, and the sky had turned from a dark charcoal to a light gray. The sun was working hard to come out to play, and I had the feeling that the waves were about to clean up as well. And they did. Bailey and I started scrambling to catch as many waves as we could because we knew it wouldn't be long before it became ridiculously crowded as usual. I tried to stay in the moment and not think about others showing up. Right now, with us two and just a few others in the water, there were plenty of waves for everyone. It was like a dream. We were all just cycling through the waves, one after another. And with Bailey in the water, I couldn't help but tap into my competitive mindset. It was good. I felt strong.

Bailey was surfing with confidence, too. She was fantastic at using as much of the wave as possible – always moving, always working, and always on point. I wanted to be happy for her, but... I still felt jealous.

The crowd moved in pretty quickly once the conditions

improved. In about 45 minutes, there were 20 or so people in the line-up. I was ready to go in, and so was my shriveled skin. Bailey seemed keen to call it a day too, so we both caught a wave together and rode it into shore. The sun was now beaming, and it would've been hard to believe that it was stormy chaos less than an hour earlier.

'Nice, Zoe!' Bailey said with a big smile as we walked up the beach and stopped where she'd dumped her bag.

'Yeah, Bailey, that was fantastic!' I answered, adding, 'Hey, where do you live?' I was working hard to be friendly. But why did it feel like work? What was bothering me?

'Oh, I'm just over in Ballina. What about you?'

'I'm staying just over there,' I said, pointing towards the house.

'No way! That's prime, hey! How'd you score that?'

'Oh, it's my best friend's place. She and her family have kinda taken me in. It's pretty sweet, for sure. Do you want to come over?'

It came out of nowhere, I swear to God. I had zero intention of spending more time with her, let alone inviting her in. I honestly had no idea what the heck had just happened.

'Um...' she paused, looking at her watch. 'Yeah sure, I've got about an hour, then I've got to pick up my lil' sis.' She picked up her bag and we headed towards the house, with me still wondering what on earth I was thinking.

Chapter Thirty-Four

'Wow Zoe, this is amazing. I can't believe your house is right on the ocean!'

'Yeah, it's epic. I'm so lucky. You can hang your towel and bikini up here after you change, if you like,' I said, pointing to the outdoor clothesline.

'Right, thanks.' We went inside and I ran to my room to change, scrambling around to find a clean shirt and pair of shorts in what had become a typically messy space.

When did I become so messy? I wondered as I threw on a singlet and made a mental note to clean my room before I went to bed.

'Make yourself comfortable, Bailey,' I said, as I came back into the kitchen. 'Mi casa su casa.'

'Hey cool, and you can call me Bails,' she said, sitting down at the counter.

'I met your sister in the water the other day, actually. Bridget, right?' I asked.

'Oh yeah, she mentioned. She's a good lil' sis. Good surfer too!'

'She said you were in Indo for one of your sponsors?' I

quizzed Bailey, as I opened the fridge, looking for something to offer her.

'Right on, yeah, I was filming an ad for Foxy.'

'Wow, you're so lucky!' I said as I pulled out the container with the leftover smoothie from this morning. I poured what was left into two glasses, each glass filling about halfway. As I had my back turned, I hadn't noticed Bailey was peering down at my list that I'd left open on the kitchen bench.

'Hey Zoe, what are you working on?' she asked, pointing to my notebook as I handed her one of the glasses.

'Oh crap! Um, yeah, forgot that was there.' I grabbed the book, closing it and putting it aside, feeling a little like my privacy had been invaded.

'Sorry, Zoe, I should have minded my own business.' She took a sip of smoothie and seemed to like it. 'Oh man, delish! Did you make it?'

'Yeah, it's got lots of yummy goodness in it.'

A couple of awkward moments went by as we drank our smoothies in silence.

'Um, I hope I'm not being too nosy by asking again, but I'm really curious to know what you're working on.'

I took another sip and thought quickly about what I wanted to say. I didn't know her very well, and I'd learned to be cautious with sharing personal info with fellow competitors, because it could end up being used against you. Mental scare tactics and all that.

'Um, well, I guess you could say I'm re-evaluating some things.'

Could she tell that I was purposefully not offering much information? I don't know, but after another few moments more of awkward silence, she made another attempt to get the conversation ball rolling:

'I'm just asking because I made some big changes last year,

and I believe it's totally what helped me to place so high in the rankings and re-qualify for this season, which, as a rookie, was quite a relief. So anyway, I noticed that maybe you're doing something similar?'

'Um, well yeah, actually...'

I paused again. *How do I know I can trust her?* I wanted to talk openly with someone who might actually understand what I'm going through but...

'So, I've been on a bit of a hiatus since the end of last season. Derek and I broke up. Wait, do you really want to hear this stuff?'

'Yes, I really do...'

'Okay, well...' and unexpectedly, I let loose, 'it's just been strange the last couple of seasons. I haven't felt like myself. I realized recently that I've lost control of how I'm living my life. I haven't been happy and I haven't been competing well. So one of the things I want to do is re-evaluate my sponsors. I feel like I need to figure out who I want to work with and why. And even who I *don't* want to work with anymore and why *not*. Anyway, that's what I was planning to do today.'

'Oh mate, yeah, I totally get that.'

'Really? So what did you do?'

'Well, joining the Foxy team was what really changed the game for me, not just because they are awesome, but because I had to drop a couple of other sponsors in order to work with them in the capacity they were asking of me. So I had to thin the crowd, if you know what I mean?'

'Yeah, actually, I was a bit jealous when your sis told me you were in Indo on a film trip. I want to do more of that kind of stuff. So you like working with them?'

'I *love* working with them.'

'What do you mean?' I needed more info.

'Well, prior to joining the Foxy team, I had a couple of

sponsors who put a lot of demands on me, which would've been fine if I'd liked what they wanted me to do, but I didn't! I realized that they were both trying to mold me into a certain image for their brand, but that image wasn't me at all. So in the end, I felt like I had become stuck in a job that was making me miserable. It just wasn't working for me – so I broke those contracts.'

'What about what you were getting from them? How did you manage to move forward?'

'Well, leaving was scary for sure, I'm not gonna deny that. I didn't know if what I was doing was a smart decision, but my coach backed me on it, so I just went ahead and did what I needed to do for me. It felt like a big leap of faith, but I was lucky and it all worked out. Better than I could have imagined, actually.'

'So how did you end up with Foxy?'

'Yeah, so after I left the other sponsors, I felt free again. I was elated, at least at first. Then I went through a phase of being scared shitless that I had made a big mistake. But I won the next competition, the Cascais Pro, and that's when their team manager approached me and I ended up working out a contract with them.'

'How are they different from your other sponsors?'

Bailey nodded her head as she put down her empty smoothie glass.

'Yeah, mate, total game changer. The Foxy team feels more like family. Plus...'

She was interrupted when Sophie and Kiko walked in the door, carrying a few big bags of groceries.

'*Hey gorgeous ones!*' Sophie shouted through to us, as she chucked the bags on the hallway floor. She smiled at Bailey and I introduced them without a pause.

'Bailey, this is Sophie and Kiko.'

'Hey, nice to meet you both,' she smiled at them before looking down at her watch and realizing what time it was.

'Crap, I gotta go get my sis. Thanks for the smoothie and the chat, Zoe. Let's do this again?'

'Yeah, for sure.'

'Later, B!' S was already over-familiar with our visitor. And Bailey grabbed her stuff on her way back to the beach.

I took my book and headed to my room, eager to straighten out everything going round in my head. For one, people imagine that the career of a professional surfer is a dream life. We make money doing what we love, get free stuff, travel the world, hang out with cool people, become famous, etc. And while all of that's true to an extent, life isn't always rainbows and coconuts. It's full of obligations and itineraries, jetlag, time away from friends and family, dealing with injury. And let's not forget the pressure. An athlete is a product, an image used to generate sales for a company (or three), and that means additional expectation to perform. To win...

We all start young in this industry – and it's *a lot* for a young person to handle. What separates the top-seeded athletes from everyone else has a lot to do with their ability to manage themselves through the ups and downs of it all. It takes time and experience to practice this level of awareness. Without it, it's too easy to get lost in the chaos. I've seen it happen and it's not a pretty sight.

During my time on tour, I'd witnessed a handful of both men and women practically drowning in their desperation for self-validation via external gratification. Their self-worth became dependent upon winning competitions, making money, maintaining the big sponsorships, getting recognized, and relishing the fame. Everything became personal, meaning when all was going well they were on top of the world, but when things weren't going so well they were a complete wreck, at which point the industry chewed them up and spat them out before they had a chance to turn it around and prove otherwise. It could all get very ugly.

Even though I had clearly seen it happening to others, I hadn't seen it in myself...until now. Ugh! I'd fallen into the trap of despair and it was time to reverse the process – and fast – before I got spat out unwillingly and lost everything in the process.

This was my *life*, for God's sake, and I needed to decide which of my sponsors were able to support me in a way that would strengthen my sense of Self, not weaken it.

I listed them off on a piece of paper and acknowledged how I felt as I wrote down each name. It was crazy cool! And the funny thing is I wasn't at all surprised by which ones did and didn't feel aligned. I speculated that some people would think that I'd lost the plot to leave good sponsorship deals, but I didn't care, and I didn't have room to second-guess myself based on other peoples' supposed opinion. I mean geez, Teo had been teaching me to go with my gut instincts; if I was going to listen to anyone at this point, it was going to be my guardian angel, right?

So here we go again, I thought to myself. First Derek, then Greg, now my sponsors. It dawned on me that our lives were filled with different kinds of relationships. Some romantic, some business, some friendship, but they *all* need the same thing in order to survive. A connection. And not just *any* connection. It had to be the kind of connection that inspired and motivated us to work together in harmony. A mutual connection.

This realization helped me understand my jealousy towards Bails as well. I was approaching the situation as if she'd taken away something from me when she beat me at Honolua. If I wanted to create a more positive connection with her, though, I had to come from a different perspective. I remembered back to the page I'd read of *Thinking Body Dancing Mind*. Something on that list was crossing my mind now as I thought about seeing relationships in a new light:

see competitors as partners who facilitate movement

Hmmm. It was a simple shift in my mindset, yet it gave me so much clarity and confidence.

I won't bore you with the details of 'breaking up' with my sponsors. Long story short, I spent the rest of the afternoon on the phone taking care of business. There was a bit of back and forth, as I tried to explain 'why', and in the end it worked out. I'm not going to say it was easy, because it was frankly nerve-wracking, but I did it and I was proud of myself. I let go of two out of my four sponsors, keeping my main source of income, which was my wetsuit/clothing sponsor, and my board shaper sponsor. This left space for a couple of new ones, just in case something appealing came my way.

I was relieved. *So* relieved. I'd made some major decisions in the last couple of months, and somehow, after I got off the phone, I felt almost whole again. *Is that strange?*

'Ladies, how about a road trip?' S announced the moment I opened my bedroom door. She made her way to the kitchen and sliced up some lime wedges. She pulled three shot glasses from the cupboard and slammed them on the counter. Did I mention she wasn't the type to be discreet? S wasn't going to let anyone ignore her.

'Well, you sure got my attention!' I made my way to one of the bar stools and turned to see if Kiko had a spark of interest in her eyes. Kiko was lounging on the couch, and looked up from the magazine she was reading.

'Sure, why not?' she replied.

'Where did you have in mind?' I asked hesitantly. I mean, I

was just getting into a new rhythm here, and time was ticking towards the start of the season. 'And what about all of our training and smoothies and salads and shit?' I was going to need some convincing.

'Gotta live life, Zozo!' she said boldly. I was getting the sense that this invitation was non-negotiable. 'Besides I've got a room for two nights at a hotel in Surfers, so I say we make it a bit of a staycation. C'mon, we're just driving up the coast for a weekend. Stop being such downers!'

'No way! How'd you score the hotel room?' Kiko put the magazine down and met us at the counter.

'Well, it's a slight work trip for me. I have a lifeguard manager meeting, but was thinking of making it a mini retreat for the weekend. Plenty of time for fun, hey! What do ya think, Zo?'

Of course, it wasn't really a question. But even if it was, the answer was the same.

'I'm in, ladies! But only on one condition. Dancing must be involved!'

'Yeeeewwww!' they shrieked simultaneously.

'Ha ha! I'll take that as a yes,' I replied.

But S was already pulling Patty Sils (Patron Silver) from the cupboard and pouring us tequila shots.

'Cheers!' we chorused, throwing them back.

Chapter Thirty-Five

I slept soundly that night, which was a surprise considering I'd let go of two sponsors (and the cash that came with them) that very day. I had expected to be awake, nervous and uncertain of my decision. But then again, tequila has a nice way of relaxing the mind, now, doesn't it?

I woke up feeling rejuvenated, and decided to go for a jog along the beach. It had been a while since I'd gone for a run on my own, now that I was working out with the lifeguards, so I was excited to cruise at my own pace to my own music.

It was unexpectedly serene. I felt calm, which was weird. *When am I going to start freaking out about dropping those sponsors?* I wondered. As I walked the last hundred meters or so back to the house, I noticed Kiko on the beach doing her morning tai chi and I joined in quietly, following her movements until she was done.

We walked back to the house silently, pausing to rinse off the sand from our feet under the outdoor shower. As we did, Seth came flying down the stairs.

'G'day guys!' He was smiling a big, bright smile. 'How ya...'

He tripped on the second-to-last step and stumbled his way to the bottom, recovering beautifully with the help of the handrail.

'Hey Seth! Nice skateboarding reflex!' I wasn't about to let him get away with that without making a comment, because both he and Sophie would have had at me in a second if it were me tripping down the stairs. He smirked and shrugged his shoulders ever-so-innocently, then followed us inside. S was already up, making our morning smoothies.

'G'day, lil' bro! Like some smoothie?'

Seth accepted and I was happy to receive my share too, but not before taking the opportunity to tease her.

'Geez S, one minute you're pouring tequila and the next it's smoothies!'

'Oh you just wait till tonight, Zozo!' She winked at me as usual.

'What are you up to tonight?' Seth asked.

'Oh just heading up the coast for a lil' playtime,' S replied innocently.

I chimed in, 'Well, also because S has a lifeguard thing there. So we're gonna cruise together and have a little staycation.'

'Nice!' Seth replied. 'Hey Zo, did you know they have a bunch of really good skate parks in the area?'

I shook my head. 'No idea.'

'Yeah, mate, you should check 'em out. I'll get that board for you.'

'Cool thanks, maybe I'll get the chance.' But to be honest, I didn't expect to be venturing to a skatepark on my own.

'Thanks for the smoothie, sis. That was tasty!' Seth placed the empty glass back on the counter and stood to leave but Sophie had other ideas.

'Hey, why don't you meet us up there tomorrow? We're

gonna hit the clubs, and I'm sure there'll be lots of pretty ladies there, hey?!'

We laughed, but Seth didn't care. Besides, he probably knew the ladies loved him. Maybe he was even proud of it.

'I'll see how it goes,' he replied. 'I have to teach in the morning, but I'll be done around 11, so yeah, could be good times...'

'You teaching those same kids?' I asked curiously.

'Yep, another guest session. I guess they had fun with me the last time so Zach asked me to do another one.'

He made his way towards the door. 'Righto, I'll see you in a bit.' And off he went.

We loaded our surfboards and bags, and hit the road ourselves around noon. The Gold Coast of Australia was absolutely stunning, and sometimes I forgot how lucky I was to have ended up living here. This time, though, I took in the breathtaking beauty of the hinterland and glimpses of the ocean as we followed the road to Surfers Paradise. I always felt a sense of freedom that came with being back in Oz – not just in the vastness of the continent and its unique landmarks like Uluru – but in the people, their outlook on life and how they took care of one another. Wherever I went, there always seemed to be someone willing to welcome me into their world, their home. Sophie's family for one.

'Earth to Zozo.'

'Huh?' I snapped myself out of it. S was trying to get my attention in the back seat, but I hadn't heard her.

'Sorry, I must've zoned out. What is it?'

'Mate, you scare me sometimes. It's like you're off in a different world.'

'Yeah, I know. I am. I can't help it. It just happens. But don't worry, S, I always come back eventually.'

Kiko was giggling in the front passenger seat.

'You two! Honestly!'

Kiko had tried to sit in the back seat before we left but I refused to let her. It seemed to me that she should sit next to her girlfriend. Plus, I didn't want to feel like I *had* to talk to anyone. It was much easier to chill in the back.

'We were just wondering if you brought snacks.'

'You know it!' I reached into my backpack and pulled out some chocolate almonds.

'Will this do?' I said as I leaned forward and dangled the bag in between their seats.

'OMG, Zoelicious!' S screeched.

I handed the bag to Kiko and sat back to zone out again.

We made it to the Hilton in about 90 minutes. It was a modern, four-and-a-half-star hotel only a block from the beach. *The Australian Lifeguard Service probably gets a deal on hotels everywhere*, I thought to myself. *Either way... sweet!* Kiko and I were pretty excited to check out the room, so we went ahead while S chatted with the front desk person, trying to figure out when and where she was supposed to meet people.

'Let's go, S!'

She sprinted to catch up with us, still texting on her phone, and we all headed up several floors to see where we'd be staying. The room was epic. I had been wondering if it would be a tight fit for the three of us, but it was totally spacious! There were two queen beds, a cool living area, and a kitchenette. We even had an ocean view with balcony.

'Damn S, you must be a bigwig to get this room, hey?' Kiko was looking around, mesmerized.

'I dunno, Keeks, I think they're just taking care of us. But we'll take it!'

Looking out at the ocean from the balcony I could see some lines rolling in. There were waves. They looked small, but it was kinda hard to tell from the 24th floor.

Surfacing

'Ladies, I'm going surfing. Anyone else?'

'Yeah, let's do it!' I've got a couple of hours before the first meeting tonight. Kiko, you in?

'Um, well, you guys know I don't really know how to surf, right? I mean, I'm kind of a beginner.'

'No way, more like beginnermediate!' S said.

'Okay yeah, well anyway...'

'No worries, Kiko, we got your back!' I tried to reassure her, like she always did for me.

The waves were small but fun. It was mostly beach break anyway. Despite being called 'Surfers Paradise', it was anything but paradise to a more seasoned surfer. But hey, we were all hanging out together having a laugh, so it didn't matter.

'Kiko, what's this crap talk about not being able to surf well? You're doing great!' I was happily surprised to see her catch waves pretty easily, and even though she wiped out a lot, she still went for it.

'Well, I can't surf like you guys!' she beamed back.

'Well, we can't tai chi like you either!' I said in reply. 'Why don't you come over here? You need to sit deeper.'

'Ugh...' I heard her mumble.

'No worries, hun, it's all good.' I said, realizing she felt uncomfortable putting herself in a more aggressive position. 'S will block the wave and I'll tell you where to line-up.' She looked over at S who gave her the thumbs up, and then started paddling towards me.

'Perfect,' I said when she got to me. 'Okay sit here and watch how the waves are coming in. See how they're moving towards us at an angle?'

Kiko nodded and I continued. 'Okay, you want to watch them closely so that you can position yourself in the right spot. The conditions are pretty predictable right now, so look for the pattern and trust what you see. It's like in tai chi. There's a rhythm you follow, right? Well, it's the same thing, but with surfing you have to adapt to a rhythm that's constantly changing. Does that make sense?'

'Yeah, I guess. But how do you find a rhythm in something that's always changing?'

'Well, yeah, good question. Change is part of the rhythm. You have to be attentive to how the ocean moves and fluctuates and pulses. Anyway, don't worry about it so much. The waves are small so you can pretty much catch whatever you want and just go for it. I just figured that while we're here together, I might as well try to get you some sweet ones, right?'

S and I caught tons of 'party waves' together, goofing around and cutting one another off, being silly and having a good giggle at each other's expense. After a while, Sophie and Kiko decided to go in, but I stuck it out for another 45 minutes or so, wanting to work these shitty waves and practice inside moves.

'Working' the inside means being able to maintain speed, do carves, and as many cutbacks as possible without losing momentum or falling off the back of what are generally small waves. It takes a lot of skill to do this, especially when the face of the wave shifts as you go down the line. Our competition in Brazil has similar conditions, and it's an area where I could definitely use more practice, so I seized the opportunity.

Unfortunately, it wasn't an encouraging experience. I wiped out. *A lot!* Even though I felt focused, I kept tripping on my rails, losing balance, and generally being awkward. It wasn't good. With the first competition of the season just down the coast at Snapper Rocks, where there's an amazing inside section, there was much work to be done.

I got out of the water, trying not to let the frustration get to me, and reminded myself that this was the weekend of fun. It wasn't the time to get down on myself – no matter what. Instead, I had to listen, listen, listen, just like Teo had said.

As it turned out, Sophie's 'meeting' was a social, happy-hour event on the deck of the hotel pool. She texted me and Kiko, 'Bitches! Already done with the meeting. Now socializing at the pool deck. Come!'

I was back in the hotel room with Kiko, and it took no effort to convince us to join her. *Duh.* We wasted not 10 minutes getting to the pool. And when we entered the deck, about 30 people, casually dressed, were mingling.

Almost instantly, Kiko spotted S on the other side of the pool, and we headed over. The atmosphere was incredible. There were lights in all the right places. With the palm trees, setting sun, and fit, tanned, good-looking lifeguards littering the area, let's just say it was worth the effort of a little lip-gloss.

Sophie looked at Kiko lovingly before closing her eyes and planting a kiss on her mouth. The sparkle in Sophie's eyes was something I had never seen from her before. It was obvious to me she was in love. Still not A-OK with the PDA, Kiko pulled away, but this time she giggled ever so slightly, acknowledging Sophie's sentiments. It was sweet.

I left them to it, and headed over to the bar to get a cocktail and hunt down a snack. Of course, I was hungry.

'How you going? What can I get for you?'

'Hi, Corona please, ta.'

He stuck a lime into the neck of the bottle, and placed it on the bar in front of me, smiling. With chubby cheeks, deep dimples and big lips, he was awkwardly cute, I decided, even though his brow was dabbed with sweat and his white, short-sleeved collared shirt was looking rather damp.

I grabbed a handful of nuts from a bowl left out on the bar top, turned around, and leaned back to people-watch. I'm not big into small talk, so I was happy to hang back and watch the action from the sidelines. It was quite a scene. As I looked at the lifeguard crowd, I couldn't help but wonder, *are they all living the life of their dreams?*

They certainly seemed happy. Then again, you never know what someone is truly feeling on the inside, no matter how they present themselves on the outside. I mean I must seem happy a lot of the time, but deep down, I had a lot of crap to sort out – crap that contributed to a fair amount of personal disharmony, even though most people wouldn't know it by looking at or talking to me. I didn't notice her approaching, but the next thing I knew, S was standing in front of me.

'Helloooooo! Zozo? Zoooeeeee!'

'Oh crap, hey!'

'Where were you just now?!'

'I dunno, S, just off in lala land again. How's things?'

'Really great. Let's go get dinner. We're starving!'

'Oh thank God!' I downed that last mouthful of Corona, turned around and put the bottle on the bar, acknowledging the bartender with a smile.

'Have a good one!' He said with a charming grin.

'Where are we going?' I asked as we met up with Kiko by the elevator.

'Just down the street. Apparently there's a choice Mexican restaurant called Cheeky's Taqueria with the best margaritas. What do you think?'

'Oh hell yeah, I'm in!' Honestly, I was ready to eat anything by then. But Mexican couldn't have been better.

The restaurant was more like a cantina where you order at the cashier, take your number, find a table and they bring you your food when it's ready. It's casual dining. And man, this place was popular! We had to get in line to order our food, while Kiko sat down at a table to reserve it for us. After putting in the order, S joined Kiko at the table with a free plate of homemade corn chips and salsa, while I sauntered over to the bar and showed the bartender the receipt with our drinks order.

'A pitcher of margarita, please.'

'On the rocks or blended?' she asked.

'Um, on the rocks I think.'

This place was packed, but they seemed to keep things moving fast. *They must have it dialed in*, I thought to myself. Carrying the pitcher and three glasses while weaving around people to get to our table was interesting, but I handled it like a champ. The only time I spilled any of the margarita was when I was pouring it into the glasses.

'Easy, Zozo, easy!' Sophie cried out as margarita dribbled down the pitcher.

'It's the stupid ass spout! It's not me, I swear!' But as I laughed I was spilling even more.

The drinks were delicious, and we discussed the weekend agenda until the food came. S still had a big day of meetings the following day, so we decided that tomorrow night would be our big night out, and we'd keep tonight low key. This suited me just fine, since when our food came, the portions were huge! Though the food was amazing and I was starving, I couldn't even eat half of my meal. I had a fish burrito, which I swear was the size of a melon. It was covered in sour cream and filled with the goodness of local barramundi, beans, and rice. It was exactly what I needed to satiate the hunger.

We all needed takeaway boxes, and as we walked outside into the warm air of Surfers, it was insanely congested with people wandering the lit up streets lined with bars and restaurants. I'd say it's a cross between Disney World and Vegas. It was the perfect kind of chaos us party goers were looking for!

Back at the hotel, S and Kiko hopped into their bed and I got in the other, the one closest to the door. We flipped the channels, eventually settling on some romantic comedy from the

80s called *Can't Buy Me Love*. It was hilariously cheesy. But hey, a chick flick is a chick flick. Hard not to love, right?

I heard S snoring not long into the movie, so I assumed they were both asleep. I spent a little time wondering, wandering in lala land, thinking of Teo and hoping I'd see him again soon. I must have drifted off soon after...

Chapter Thirty-Six

I snuck out for an early run the next morning, before the others were up. I ran about 5km up the beach before turning around to make my way back.

The beach was quieter than the night before, but there were still plenty of people getting in their morning workout like me, or walking their dog with coffee in hand. Then of course, there were the late night stragglers who'd passed out on the beach, now stumbling around, slowly getting their bearings.

I stretched as I cooled down after my jog, then decided to do a little meditation to finish off. I was feeling anxious about the start of the season coming up in only four weeks, and didn't want that to get in the way of enjoying myself this weekend. Even though I didn't really know how to meditate, what I *did* know was what Teo had told me: I needed to have patience.

I dropped my ass onto the sand, crossed my legs, sat up straight and closed my eyes. I focused on my breath. It was not an easy task. My mind ran wild with thoughts of anything and everything. I came back to my breath whenever I noticed I was distracted, but it would only be a few seconds before my mind wandered off again. After what felt like 35 minutes, I opened my eyes and looked at my watch. Only 13 minutes had passed. *Damn!* I thought to myself. Well, that was as much as I could handle right now. I *did* feel calmer, at least.

Brekkie was included with the room so I met the girls at the hotel restaurant for an insane buffet of everything tropical and delicious, including waffles. Since S was busy for most of the day, Kiko and I hung out together and it was pretty cool to get to know her a bit more. She had many talents. After leading me in a post-breakfast tai chi session, she explained its fundamentals while we were walking towards the beach to go surfing.

'Have you started reading that book I gave you?' she asked.

'Yeah right, *Thinking Body, Dancing Mind*. I've read like a page or two and already found it helpful.'

'Perfect. It'll explain things way better than I can. And it's a really great read for athletes as well, sort of like sports psychology.'

'Yeah, I'm excited to dig into more of it.'

I gave her as much instruction as I could while we were in the surf, which was helpful for me as well. It's always good to be reminded of the basics because they don't become any less important as your skills improve. In fact, the basics are crucial in terms of upping your game. If you think about it, you need that solid foundation to build upon, otherwise it's like building a house of cards: it's bound to collapse.

Kiko got out of the water and I stayed for a few more waves to give myself some undivided attention. With all this socializing, I needed some alone time. Plus, I knew I'd feel better about our big night out if I put in a good practice session first.

There was a guy in the water who ripped! He was an older gentleman on a longboard, and his style was so dynamic! He walked up and down his board, making sharp turns with such fluidity! It was amazing considering the length of board he was riding. I watched him catch wave after wave, even though there were tons of people in the water. It seemed like he knew this place like the back of his hand. I couldn't help but watch him, even doing that trick where I tried tapping into his rhythm – feeling the ocean as he felt it. I know that may sound weird, but getting in sync with someone or something happens naturally when you give it focus. Imagine a basketball team that moves as if the team members are one unit. Together, they're in the zone. Now imagine world-renowned basketball player LeBron James, who operates at such a high level that he can read his teammates effortlessly, commanding a collective flow that allows for those epic passes and shots.

Feeling the connection to the wave via this dude was beneficial as I could translate the feeling into my own rhythm and style. As I've mentioned, I used to do this all the time when I was first learning to surf, from watching videos. I'd watch a clip of someone, and tap into their vibe, feeling their movements, even though it was on a screen and I wasn't in the water at the time. It felt like I was experiencing what it would be like to perform at my highest potential, but through others. Then, when I'd get *into* the water, I'd surf heaps better. Somehow my body had adapted to this new rhythm, with new muscle memory, even though I hadn't physically practiced yet.

After my surf session, I went to the room to rinse off and change. Grabbing my most recent copy of *Surfer Magazine*, my Mexican leftovers and some other bathing essentials, I headed to the pool to chill. It was not overwhelmingly busy, and I managed to find a lounge chair under a shade umbrella, where I could eat my lunch. I was eager to get into it and didn't care that it was cold from the mini bar fridge. I'm not picky that way. And I didn't even mind using the highly ineffective plastic knife and fork. It was yummy just the same, and I enjoyed every bite until it was gone.

Whipping off my shirt, I laid back on the lounge chair in my bikini, mumbling to myself about how nice this all was. Settling in, I flipped through the pages of *Surfer*, landing on a Foxy Sunglasses ad featuring Bailey.

Good for her, I thought.

My eyes began to feel heavy, so I rested the mag on my stomach and let my eyelids close, dozing off almost immediately.

Wait! Where am I?

I had a familiar feeling about this place but still felt confused. I turned around, and as I did, my question was answered. I was back in Colorado at my old skate park – the place I had spent much of my time as a kid. The air was fresh. It felt like autumn. I loved that time of year in Boulder, not just for the cool climate, but because it also meant that winter was near – and soon I would be on my snowboard! I inhaled deeply, reliving the past. And boy did it feel real, because I also *felt* the cool air. I looked down at my bare arms and noticed goosebumps.

Why am I here? I wondered.

I lifted my head and looked towards the skate ramp about 50 feet away. I noticed someone on it. At first glance it was hard to recognize the small figure, but as I let my eyes focus in on the little person I realized it was me! But it was the me from about 14 years ago, when I was 9. I was wearing the same ripped jeans, and pink and lime green t-shirt that I always wore at that time. I was obsessed with that outfit for some reason, and never wanted to wear anything else. It used to drive my mom crazy when I'd hide the items from her at night, so that she couldn't wash them.

I watched myself on the ramp – skating back and forth, back and forth, getting comfortable with my stance and searching for the perfect momentum – a speed and rhythm that was necessary to keep me moving – up and down, up and down. Little me was laughing, loving the feeling of wheels under my feet.

From where I was watching, I was drawn to look in the other direction, and there she was... my mom. She was on the sidelines of the ramp, smiling and clapping her hands while yelling at me to keep going. She looked so young. *I* looked so young!

I was admiring the scene as it played out in front of me, remembering how happy I was. But then my 'feelgood' moment somehow turned into feeling bad. Sadness washed over me. It felt *horribly* depressing. Instead of experiencing joy from my past, I was confused and anxious.

My throat tightened. I couldn't breathe properly as I choked on my tears. And now all of these questions popped into my mind. *How could she leave us like that? How could she leave me? What did I do wrong?*

The sadness turned to hatred and anger. It felt like my blood was boiling and my skin was on fire. I wanted to lash out and punch someone. I was *so* angry! And right when I was about to run over to my mom and explode on her, I couldn't. Because I was no longer on the ground. I was sitting high up in a tree nearby, looking down at the skatepark. *What?* It was the same scene, only now I was watching older me watch little me with my mom, who was still on the sidelines cheering me on.

From up here in the tree, I no longer felt angry or sad. It was weird. The fire in my eyes and the pain in my heart was completely gone. I felt... what was it? *Peace?*

Yet, it didn't feel like it was coming from me. It felt like there was a presence with me, or like someone had sprinkled fairy dust all over me, to protect me from myself.

Next I knew, there came a flash of light. Instinctively, I looked towards it, and there he was... Teo.

'Teo. What...?' I was trying to speak but I couldn't get my words out.

And again I felt that relaxed state, instead of being afraid. This time I felt more curious than confused.

'Why am I here?'

'Look at your mom,' he said calmly. 'Do you see how happy she is to be with you?'

'Yes.' I was staring at her and couldn't deny it.

'Can you feel how much she loves you?'

I took a moment to watch her. Her excitement was real. Her smile was genuine. It had to be. I *felt* that it was, even though part of me wanted to fight the truth.

'Yes,' I answered.

'Do you know how much she still loves you?'

I wanted to say no, but the word literally wouldn't come out of my mouth. I tried again but the same thing happened. It was like when you try to scream but nothing comes out. Weird.

I shifted my gaze from my mom to Teo. He was staring at me intensely, almost as though he was looking *through* me, and diving deep into my soul. There was a gentle fierceness to this moment. I was being shown a dark place within my mind, but the light was shining onto it, exposing it and releasing it. I couldn't move. I felt frozen in time, even though the scene of my youth continued to play on below me. Eventually, the 'no' I'd originally wanted to say was gone.

The scene turned to my mom. She was in our old house, the one we all lived in before she left. She was sitting alone at the dining room table, crying, elbows on the table, head resting in her hands. She was so sad, and I'd never seen that side of her before. I only remembered her as being a happy and cheerful mom.

'Whether it's your mother, your best friend, a competitor or a complete stranger, remember that everyone is struggling in some way, including yourself. It may not always be obvious, but it's important to know that everyone is doing the best that they can at the time, even if it doesn't look like much to you.'

'I... I didn't know my mom was struggling.' And I honestly hadn't. This new understanding shifted my perspective.

'Zoe, it was not easy for your mom to do what she did. She was dealing with her own demons, and came to a turning point that led her in a different direction. There's much more to the story than what you or even your dad know, and certainly more than you witnessed, just as there is much more to *your* story than others may know or understand. Do you see?'

I stayed quiet for a few moments to let his words sink in before I was ready to speak.

'Well, I thought I had dealt with all of this, but I guess there's still a lot of anger and sadness around her leaving. I just didn't realize it.'

'Yes, Zoe, and that's why there's always a part of you that holds back. In friendships, in competition, whatever you give your attention to, you maintain a protective layer that prevents you from giving it your all.'

'I hold back?' I wasn't sure I was ready to hear this. I always considered myself to be someone who was all in, all the time.

'Yes.' he replied simply. Factually.

'So now what?' I asked openly. I was looking at him attentively.

'Now it's time to forgive the past, to let go of the negative emotions that are holding you back from feeling the freedom you search for in everything you do. That freedom comes from within, Zoe. You can't find freedom *in* anything, but you can bring it *to* everything. With your thoughts, your words, your actions, your choices and decisions.'

I admit that I *liked* what he was saying. I liked the *idea* of what he was saying, but...

He whispered into my ear, 'Let compassion lead the way.'

Just then I felt a sense of peace wash over me again. Teo was undoubtedly working his magic on me. And again, time stood still and I was motionless as I felt love for my mom, for my dad, and even for myself. I felt love for what they'd been through. I felt that peace again, extending to my mom as the pain left my body, my mind, and my heart. My body felt like it had disappeared, and all that was left was a vibration of millions of cells that emanated Pure Love. Peace. Harmony.

'Zoooeeee, Zoooeeee! Wake up, mate!'

It was Seth.

I bolted upright and opened my eyes, and was momentarily blinded by the sun. I felt I'd been sucked into a time warp and spat back into real time, and as a result, I was totally disoriented. I needed to get my bearings. I scanned my surroundings: lounger, pool, hotel, surfing... 'Okay, okay,' I muttered to myself as I came back into my body and its whereabouts. My magazine had fallen off when I'd sat up so abruptly, so I leaned over to pick it up and placed it calmly back on the edge of the lounger, gathering myself.

'Are you okay, Zoe?' he asked, sounding somewhat concerned.

'Ugh... Oh, yeah. Hey, Seth!' I smiled awkwardly, trying to hide my embarrassment. And I tell ya, it's a good thing I had my sunnies on, otherwise he would've known for sure I was not okay. At least in the sense that I'd just experienced something that left me feeling raw and sensitive.

'I, ugh, fell asleep.'

'Yeah, I can see that,' he said as he sat down on the lounger beside me.

'Hey, wait, you made it!' I said, perking up, now that I remembered he'd driven up to meet us for the rest of the weekend.

'Yep, sure did. And now I'm ready for a dip in the pool. Care to join?' he said playfully as he took off his sunnies.

'Um...' I was hesitant for no logical reason. But as he proceeded to take off his shirt, the answer became quite obvious. I stood up, slapped his abs and jumped into the pool without saying a word, letting the water wake me up and bring me back into the moment.

Chapter Thirty-Seven

The 'big night out' certainly *was* a big night out, at least by my standards. Seth had gone to visit a friend for pre-party drinks and was planning to meet up with us at the club later. This gave us a little extra girl time to get ready. And we all scrubbed up quite nicely if I do say so myself! I may even venture to say that both S and I went through something of a transformation, thanks to Kiko, who was even more striking than usual.

S and I hardly ever go out of our way to dress up. I dunno, the whole makeup and outfit thing just takes up too much time if you ask me. And honestly, I just can't be bothered! But tonight we had Kiko on our side, and apparently 'personal stylist' is one more thing to add to her already long list of talents, because her work was impressive.

While S and I both refused to don heels, we did succumb to some fancier-than-normal outfits: me, a short blue-green dress, Soph, a little black skirt with loose top. We completed our overhaul with mascara and lipstick. Kiko was in a tight-fitted red dress with high black peep-toe pumps. Her hair was shining like stars on a dark night, and as she waltzed around the hotel room looking confident in her skin, it was hard not to admire her.

A few minutes before it was time to leave the hotel, S pulled out some tequila from the mini bar and grabbed tumblers from the kitchenette.

'Ready to do some gratitude shots, ladies?'

'Huh?'

'Just get over here!' she said as she poured the potent golden liquid into glasses.

Kiko and I followed her out onto the balcony.

'Seriously?' Kiko said. 'Do we have *any* lime or salt, or do you just expect us to deal with this straight up?'

'Hang on, hang on!' S said as she went back into the room and then re-emerged a minute later with a lime, a salt packet, and a pretty basic-looking knife. I sliced through the lime and made three rather rudimentary wedges, while S opened the salt sachet and dabbed some on the back of one hand for each of us in turn.

'Alright ladies, this is a gratitude shot. We drink to what we're grateful for. I'll go first. I'm grateful for you ladies, for joining me on this trip, and for loving me for exactly who I am, and not for who you want me to be!'

She looked at me. Then once again, I noticed that sweet sparkle in her eye as her gaze landed upon Kiko.

'Well,' Kiko began, 'I'm grateful for getting an awesome surf lesson from a famous pro,' she said as she looked over and gave me a wink. 'And I'm grateful for all the sleepovers and smoothies and salads at casa de Sophie – an amazing place on the beach, to which I'd never have been privy, if I hadn't met you, S!'

She was laughing, but S and I knew what she truly meant.

It was my turn. 'Um, well, I'm grateful for having friends like you two. Whether old or new, you've both brought me back to life, back to my Self, and I don't know what I'd be doing right now if it wasn't for you. Thank you!' I said as I bowed my head.

'Cheers!' We clinked glasses before throwing back the tequila. It was a sweet way to get the evening started.

Sophie wasn't the type of person to sit still for long, and after being stuck in meetings for most of the day, she was eager to get her groove on. Add a little tequila into the mix, and you can bet she was her usual boisterous self, but dialed up a few notches. Yeah... that! Kiko, on the other hand, was as poised as ever. She carried herself so elegantly no matter what she was doing. Tonight was no exception.

We ventured to a bar on the main strip of Surfers Paradise that had been recommended to S at the cocktail party the night before. It wasn't too busy yet, and we were just there to warm up, so to speak. I enjoyed watching the scene while snacking on some appetizers. Sophie and Kiko were babbling on about something but I wasn't paying much attention to them. Instead, I reflected on the experience I'd had with Teo during my nap at the pool earlier that afternoon. I was still very much in awe of the encounter and hadn't had any time to process it. I felt lighter, more peaceful, and more at ease towards my mom, like much of my pain had been healed because I had a new perspective that made it easier to forgive her for what she did. It wasn't all about me, I realized.

We sauntered on to the club at about 11:00pm. S was a few drinks in by now, so Kiko was busy making sure she didn't get too obnoxious in public. We stood in line at the club with a dozen or so others. I looked back at Kiko with despair, 'I honestly don't understand why clubs have to open so late. Why won't they let us dance earlier on in the night?'

The girls laughed at my comment, but I wasn't even joking! I mean, I *love* dancing, and I'd go clubbing every week if it didn't also mean staying up all night.

We moved quickly through the short line, paid the $10 cover fee and were greeted with pink and purple lights bouncing off plain concrete walls, giving the intimate club something of a modern appeal. With a capacity of maybe 500 people, the little dance floor was already packed with people moving to the DJ's beats.

'We're gonna get some water,' Kiko shouted over the music to me as she and Soph headed to the bar. I stood by the wall, listening to the music and watching people dance. The DJ was good, I decided. I could feel my mind relaxing with each passing minute, as my body slowly felt for the groove until my rhythm finally connected with the beat. It was mostly house music, with some soul in the mix. My kind of vibe. Lost in the music, I felt *fabulous*. I was way past due for a night out on the town!

So there I was, dancing away in my own little world, among the crowd crammed onto the dance floor, sweat flinging everywhere. Occasionally, I'd have a look around to observe the people around me. I saw them as freedom-seekers. *What were they thinking? What were they going through? What brought them here tonight?* Each and every one of us had a completely different story, but right here, right now, we were sharing this experience together. It was a nice crowd. Everyone was here to *feel good*.

I did a little spin, a 180 on the dance floor to get a new view of my surroundings, and there he was in front of me: Seth. We smiled as our eyes met.

'Hey you! How's it going?'

I smiled so big I surprised even myself, and I dare say my heart skipped a beat. He was lookin fiiine! He had on a black collared shirt and jeans, and his blonde messy hair was a bit wet with sweat. *Very sexy.*

'Heeyyy! Isn't this place great?!' I couldn't think of what to say.

'Yeah, the DJ is a local chick who plays here every weekend. She's really good, hey!'

'So good. Oh my God! I haven't danced in ages. It's been way too long!'

We continued to dance, weaving around one another and finding a nice sync. It felt effortless with him. I dunno, sometimes it's hard to connect with someone on the dance floor, and other times it's no trouble at all. This was the easy kind. The song waned and moved into something else.

'I need to get a drink,' I said to him as I grabbed his shirt and tugged it so that he'd follow me to the bar.

Sophie and Kiko were still there, talking to a couple of other people.

'Little bro, little bro!' Sophie shrieked when she saw Seth, raising her bottle of water and tapping it on his forehead as she said, 'Cheers!'

'Hey sis, hey Kiko!' He said, nodding his head as he acknowledged them.

'You want anything?' I asked him.

'Yeah, a beer, please.'

I had to wait a few minutes before I could get the bartender's attention and order a couple of *cervezas*.

'You want anything?' I asked Kiko who was standing next to me.

'All good here, ta.'

I paid the dude and reached over to hand one of the bottles to Seth who was talking to his sister.

'So, Zoe, I couldn't help but notice you and Seth on the dance floor.'

I was a bit surprised at the words that came out of Kiko's mouth, and felt a bit defensive. I didn't say anything in response, so she continued.

'Are you into him?'

She was super straight-faced as she made the suggestion, keeping her voice down. Nonetheless, I looked around nervously, hoping nobody had overheard her.

'Um, I don't know? I kinda think so? I guess?'

I suppose I had secretly known it already (and you're probably rolling your eyes at the obviousness of it all), but this was the first time I was being asked to admit it.

'Well, it's obvious that he's totally into you, Zoe, in case you hadn't noticed.' Kiko was not wasting any time getting to the heart of the matter.

'You think so? Oh man, Kiko, I dunno. I mean, he's my best friend's *little* brother!' And there it was: Fear. Doubt. Guilt.

'Never mind all that for a sec,' she said. 'Are you into him or not?'

I paused, not knowing what to say, or not ready to say it. I took a deep breath, letting my eyes wander over to Seth. I paused briefly when my lungs were full, and then exhaled, letting out a big sigh.

'Fuck!' I said as I tilted my head back and rolled my eyes as I finally allowed myself to feel what I really felt.

'Yeah. I'm into him.'

I looked back at Kiko, wondering what she was thinking. She stared at me blankly, and I could only assume that she didn't approve. But then, her straight face turned into a wide, smiley grin before she spoke.

'Nice! Your best friend's little bro, way to pick 'em!'

Okay, that's a better response, I thought, which lightened things up and made me feel more comfortable to talk about it, now that the cat was out of the bag.

'Ugh! C'mon! What should I do? I've known him since we were both little, and I'm like family to these guys. It could ruin everything!'

'Oh now, don't you think you're being a bit dramatic, Zoe?' Kiko was obviously highly entertained by this.

'I don't know! I just... I mean... who knows if this is anything anyway? Is it worth the potential risk of upsetting Sophie *and* her parents?'

'Chica, there's no need to get all bent out of shape about this right now. Nothing's even happened, has it?'

'No, no, of course not!'

'Then just enjoy the moment and see where it leads you. You're getting all caught up in the future and it's pulling you out of the beauty of the present moment! Look at him!' We both looked over at him. 'He's cute, he likes you, you like him, we're all out having fun. Just be here right now!'

She was enthusiastic about the whole situation, which helped me to think that maybe she was right.

'Damn, you're like a guru or something.' I replied. Everything she said seemed so aligned with Teo. It made me wonder, so I had to ask.

'Hey, do you know anyone by the name of Teo?'

'Huh? Who?' She looked sincerely confused.

'Never mind, never mind, you just sound a lot like this guy I know.'

We tried to join in on the conversation with Seth and Sophie, but it only lasted about a minute before we all headed back to the dance floor.

'How ya feeling, Sophie?' I yelled at her over the music while the DJ kicked it up a notch.

'Fabulous!' She held up her water, pointed at it and winked. 'Right on!'

And we danced our asses off for most of the night, having an unreal time.

Chapter Thirty-Eight

Sorry to disappoint, but I didn't make out with Seth that night. Still, doesn't a little flirtation, fun conversation and the knowledge of our mutual attraction count for something? I was feeling a bit groggy after our late night out, so we didn't make it to breakfast until around 10:30am the next morning. Luckily it was Sunday brunch, so we hadn't missed out. I'd only had two tequila shots, one beer, and the rest of the time just water, so I was feeling fine. Just tired, and as usual, hungry.

Seth had ended up spending the night at his friend's place, but he joined up with us for brunch where we all had a good laugh going over the previous evening's shenanigans. With his mouth still full of toast, Seth looked over at me and said, 'Hey Zo, I'm hitting this really cool skate park before heading home. Wanna come with? I brought an extra board for Justin...'

'Huh? Who's Justin?'

'Just in case!' And the laughing fits began again.

'For reals, Zo, let's do it!' he encouraged me.

'Okay, sounds fun!'

'That sounds perfect, Zoe,' Kiko chimed in with a smile,

'because we have to check out soon anyway. Plus, I need to get back to help my family later this afternoon with a tai chi event, so better you won't have to rush on my account.'

'Gettin' your skate on, Zozo?' S said with a hungover husky-sounding voice, which she still managed to make sarcastic.

'It's called cross-training!' Seth said with a grin. 'Gotta get our girl in top-notch shape before the big comp!'

Kiko and I looked over at each other, rolling our eyes simultaneously at the silly siblings.

It was 12:30pm when Seth and I rolled into the skate park. Neither of us had much to say in the car, or maybe we had plenty to say, but just didn't know how. Anyway, we listened to some tunes on the radio and blasted the A/C because the sun was shining and we were about to be outside during the hottest part of the day.

'Hey, are we meeting anyone here or is it just us?' I asked him as we arrived and he handed me his extra skateboard from the back seat.

'Not sure. I told my mate, the one I stayed with last night, so he may show up with a couple of guys, but you never know on a Sunday after a big night, hey.'

We skated around the park on our boards, just warming up and getting into the groove. It was fun to skate around the other people who were milling about. Most of them were youngsters in their teens, goofing around, either on the half-pipe or on the pavement and in the carpark. I followed Seth's lead as he pointed out certain things about the park; it was obviously a familiar place to him.

'Back when I was younger I tripped over there', he said, pointing to a small ramp, 'and wiped out and broke my arm. And over there, see where that tree is?' He indicated some greenery at the back of the park.

'Yeah, I see it.'

'Well, I climbed that tree one night because a party was going on and a bunch of guys got real sloppy drunk. A fight broke out and the cops came, so I bolted from the scene, climbed the tree and watched the entire thing from up there!' He was laughing pretty hard by the time he finished.

'Did you cause another fight, mate?' But I knew that wasn't his thing. Even when we were little he was never a punk-ass kind of guy. He was always a bit more on the shy side.

'Nah, I'm a lover not a fighter, Zoe. You know that!' And he winked at me.

'Mmm-hmm, sure you are! Are we all warmed up now?' Before I finished my sentence, I took off on my board, heading towards the pipe.

We were there for a couple of hours, and I spent a lot of the time watching Seth's movements, then working on a few moves with him giving me pointers. Actually, he gave me a good amount of coaching, and the way he taught was impressive, so clear, but also making sure to only give a couple of tips at a time so I could practice those specifically, before moving on.

His friend never did show up, but Seth didn't seem to care, and it didn't make much difference to me either way. He made quick friends with the younger kids, after giving one of them a tip that made a huge difference, like immediately. You can imagine how stoked that kid was. The next thing we knew, the friend of that kid was hanging around Seth looking for pointers as well. Of course Seth happily obliged, and well, now *everyone* was happy.

There was only one other girl there beside me. She was a lot younger, about 8, and it turns out she was the little sister of one of the kids Seth was helping. While Seth was doing his thing with the two boys, she and I took turns on the pipe, cheering each other on and working on keeping good form rather than pulling out big tricks.

When the dad arrived to pick the little ones up, he seemed cautious at first, probably wondering who these adults were with his kids. But when they showed such enthusiasm to introduce us to him, he realized we were being helpful, not harmful, so he let down his guard.

'Dad, Dad!' The boy was pulling Seth over to his dad to introduce them to one another, and the girl, following her big brother's lead, did the same with me.

'G'day mate, Seth said. 'I'm Seth, and this is Zoe.'

'G'day,' he greeted us. 'I'm Bob.' And as he looked over at me to shake my hand, he had a look of shock on his face.

'Wait, are you Zoe Smith?'

'Uh, yes, I am,' I said, smiling kindly as our hands met.

And then he looked at his kids. 'Kids! Do you know who this is? Zoe is a professional surfer.' He glanced back at me, 'Hey, could we get a picture with you?'

'Sure thing, of course!'

He seemed pretty excited now, and pulled out his phone as he told the kids how lucky they were to play with me today. I pulled out my phone so Seth could take a pic of us all, before we all said our happy goodbyes.

We were hot and sweaty, so it was a relief to be back on the road, heading home. I found my water bottle and handed it to Seth after taking a swig myself.

'Well, this sure is becoming a habit, isn't it?' he said jokingly, after taking a big chug of water.

I shrugged my shoulders, not really sure how to reply, but then ended up saying, 'Yeah, getting recognized kinda comes with the territory. But the same goes for you, you know, working with kids so easily. Plus I have a feeling you're going to experience the whole autograph thing soon enough.'

'Hey?' he said quizzically. 'What do you mean?'

'Well, you're a phenomenal skater and you're an amazing teacher. I think it could be easy for you to go far in this industry, if that's what you want. Both times I've come to the park with you, you're like an instant hit with the kids you teach. Now if you ask me, that's a pretty great way to start a fan base. Add some competition into that, and I don't think it would be too hard for you to turn pro.'

'You think?'

'Pretty much. I know how it goes by now, you know. But it does help to be in the right place at the right time, too.'

'Well, how do you make *that* happen?'

I thought for a minute or two before speaking.

'Mmm, I think it just comes from doing the things you want to be doing, instead of forcing yourself to do things you think you *should* be doing. Like, allow things to come to you – and then it *seems* like luck, or magic, or serendipity, or whatever, but really it's just because you're in the flow of being true to you.' I was surprised at the words that came out of my mouth, but Seth didn't seem surprised at all. In fact, he seemed to totally understand them.

'So it's like, do what feels good and the rest will follow?'

'Yes, I guess so.' To be honest, I was still a bit surprised at what I had said.

'Good point, very good advice.'

'But Seth,' I continued, 'you already do that. In fact, *you've* been teaching *me* to do all of that! Before I got here this summer, I hadn't really been doing what feels good. I forgot all about it, in fact! I got caught up in what everybody else wanted me to be doing, and let me tell you, it's not a fun place to be. My state of mind has been shit.'

'But you still love surfing, don't you?'

'Yeah, I love surfing. It was everything revolving around my career that made surfing less enjoyable. And once that was happening, I began to question everything, *including* my love of surfing. It's a slippery slope, I'm realizing.'

'Wow, Zoe, I had no idea you were going through such a difficult time. Sorry to hear that.'

'Yeah, it hasn't been awesome, but luckily S and you and your family came to the rescue. Maybe a bit unknowingly, but still. It's been perfect, magical really, in how the timing of it all happened. And really these last six weeks have been helping me to slowly come back to me. It's been a lot of letting go. Plus, I've needed time to gather the right kind of support to allow that to happen. And the Smart family has been the right kind of smart!' I glanced over and shot him a smile with my eyes. He returned the favor.

'Well, I'm glad to be of service, Zoe.' And with that, his nearest hand left the steering wheel, and he calmly reached over and gently wrapped my hand in his. I felt safe, and warm. Loved, even. The kindness I felt within his grasp made my heart instantly soften, and it allowed me to relax and be totally open to whatever could happen next.

We drove in silence for most of the rest of the way back, but I believe we had some beautiful conversations of the heart. I understand now that words are often highly overrated. The ride went more quickly than I wanted it to, and before I knew it, we were back in our driveway. We paused after he turned the engine off, sitting there, both of us hanging on to the moment a little while longer, knowing that the energy would shift as soon as we opened the vehicle doors. But it had to be done. I got out, grabbed my bag from the back seat, and watched as Seth walked around the car to talk to me.

'Well, Zoe, thanks for playing with me today. You are a gem of a person, and I hope we can spend more time together before you head back on tour. What do you think?'

'Well, yeah, I'd love that!' I was smiling big, but was also feeling shy. And then he pulled me in close and wrapped his arms around me. Instinctively, my arms went around his waist as my head rested on his chest. I could smell the scent of his sweat and I liked it. After a moment or two, or three, I looked up at him to give him a smile, and as I did, our eyes locked, and he planted his sweet lips on mine. His kiss felt calm and confident. There didn't seem to be any concern at all that he was kissing his sister's best friend in the driveway of his family home. It helped me feel more okay about it too; that none of that stuff mattered. Who knows? Maybe it didn't. Maybe it wouldn't.

So I kissed him back, and it was divine...

Chapter Thirty-Nine

Falling asleep the night of The Kiss, I was elated. I felt like a teenager who'd snuck out of the house to make out with my new boyfriend at the scenic lookout (AKA the make-out place). And even though Seth wasn't my boyfriend, well, you get what I mean, right?

Spending time with Seth was the icing on the cake of a fabulous weekend. Actually no, it was the cherry on top. The icing was spending time with the best two ladies around, and the cake was the Goldy itself, a beautiful stretch of coastline, one of my favorites in Oz.

The first event was fast approaching and it was time to put all of my focus on surfing. I shifted into high gear, where the next two weeks were a mixture of sleep, train, eat, surf, tai chi, meditate, skate, and a few other preparatory bits and pieces. Of course, I still had fun with the Smart fam, and spent some enjoyably innocent quality time with Seth. But then again, I knew it wasn't smart – he he! – to lose myself in the excitement of a boy crush. So for the most part, I was able to manage myself and direct my attention towards competition. I also spent most of my surfing sessions at Snapper, to re-familiarize myself with its features.

It was pretty awesome how my list of priorities had been set into motion over the last couple of months in a way that felt natural. After letting go of an awful lot in my life (like Derek, and Greg, and sponsors, and a whole bunch of my own inner crap), new opportunities and experiences came to me, things that felt oh-so good. I was eating better (at least a bit) with the smoothies and salads. I trained with the lifeguards. Kiko led me in tai chi. Seth took me skating. And I did my own brief little meditations when I woke up and before I went to bed, incorporating some of the visualizations I was learning in the book Kiko had me reading.

I thought about Derek often, but what had started out as a depressing hole in my heart, was slowly becoming less of a hole and more of just heart. I wasn't totally fine, but I was better.

The remaining sponsors in my life were legendary. I got some new boards, as well as some new gear, but more importantly were the great phone conversations and emails from my team managers, who knew exactly where I was at and what I'd been going through over the summer. Why? Because I'd finally told them the truth. Instead of wondering what was up with me, and questioning why I'd dropped off the scene unexpectedly, they were able to give me what I needed most: support. I'm sure it was helpful that I'd been a solid member of the team for many years, but I still appreciated their words of encouragement, and their confidence in my ability to pull through.

In fact, I was feeling supported by everyone surrounding me. Come to think of it, maybe that was the key to success I'd been missing. You have to *choose* to be in the presence of people who lift you up, not bring you down, which means you have to be aware of who those people are. You can't just expect everyone to treat you in the most favorable way; you have to be okay with picking and choosing, allowing people to come and go easily in your life. Like the breath. It comes in, it goes out. We don't get attached to holding onto the oxygen in our lungs after we inhale, and we don't pine for it as we exhale. You take it in, and then you let it go. The inhale and exhale must work together, simultaneously. You can't have one without the other.

Wait, where did that come from? I had never even thought of the breath analogy before. *Oh, is that you, Teo?*

I felt a warm, tingling sensation all over my body, and knew that it was confirmation from him. I was getting much better at trusting his presence whether I could see him or not, which helped me to focus on my other senses. Feeling him, hearing him, and just knowing he was there strengthened my ability to maintain a positive mindset.

As for surfing, was I up to par? I'm not sure I felt 100%. But I *was* feeling more relaxed in the surf than I had in a long time, which made it heaps easier to work *with* the wave – connecting with its rhythm and adjusting to its subtle shifts, which was crucial in competition. So as long as I could remember to stay loose and relaxed, all would be well.

I noticed how my attitude had changed over the summer; I was less uptight and fearful of failing. Instead excitement had replaced the fear – excitement to bring a new attitude to the game, a renewed love for surfing. With the help of Teo and everyone else, it was like I had shed layers of fear, layers upon layers that had slowly thickened into a cloud of negativity and doubt. Releasing those layers had been the real work for me over the off-season, and I had to recognize this as I moved forward. I also knew that when I was back in the scene and watching all the girls rip, it would be easy to fall back into my old patterns and old mindset; I had to be conscientious with my thoughts and intentions.

In terms of my skill level, well, I hadn't exactly been

working on my technique, nor had I been perfecting new moves, so I could definitely be at a disadvantage in that area since all the ladies were stepping up the level of competition. You have to be well-rounded these days, and then exceptional to make the top rankings.

The nature of a surfing competition is that it can be long and drawn out, simply due to the fact that you're relying on the elements of nature to bring in a good swell during the dates of competition. On a day the competition is called 'on', you're pretty much at the site all day, and you're not even sure if you're going to end up surfing. You may be all dressed and warmed up, and then they put the next heat on hold to wait for better conditions. It could be later that same day, or maybe it's not until the next day, or even a week later. On the other hand, the conditions may be so good that they plow through as many rounds as possible all at once.

I explain all of this to show the added element of uncertainty. You have to have a strong, consistent frame of mind throughout the two-week holding period. Not to mention managing your energy levels rather than letting the excitement drain you – especially important if you do well in the first few rounds, because there's still a lot of work to do to make it through to Finals.

When it comes to mindset, tennis is an amazing sport to watch, because you can witness the wide range of emotions each player goes through over the course of a match. And if you ask me, the number one trait the top-ranked players have in common is their superhero mindset. Think about Serena Williams. Whether she's up a set or down a set, she never gives up. Even if there's a triple match point in favor of her opponent. And often, these number one players, like Serena, or Roger Federer, or Novak Djokovic, make the most fucking insane comebacks! They don't let fatigue get to them, they know how to manage their emotions, and they certainly don't let lack of preparedness become a factor. They train hard, mentally *and* physically – moving through fear, doubt, injury, jetlag, doing their best to stay calm and centered amidst the inevitable ups and downs that come with winning and losing. Their focus is unparalleled.

Now, in the past, surfing wasn't as hardcore as it is now. People didn't train in the gym or maintain a specific diet. No, they surfed, and socialized, and partied a little bit... *ahem, maybe a lot*. And while it's still like that to a certain extent, the level of competition has become way more fierce. And the chicks these days? Wow, they are super athletic and skilled. It takes a lot more effort, drive, and consistency to win a competition now than ever before.

These were the thoughts turning over in my head the night before the first event of the season.

Yeesh! Even after being a part of the WSL for the last eight years, I was still a ball of nerves getting to sleep that night. Everything in my life felt different to me now than it had at the end of last season, and I didn't know how that was going to translate into the professional surfing scene. I hung out on my bed, reading a chapter from *Thinking Body, Dancing Mind* when Seth texted me.

'You up?'

'Yup, what u doing?'

'Just wanted to let you know I'm thinking about you, and I'm excited to be your sidekick tomorrow!'

'Aww, you're the best. Thanks!'

'Sending you hugs and a big fat kiss!'

'Kisses right back atcha!' I replied.

I put down my book, set the alarm on my phone, laid down and closed my eyes. Kiko taught me a technique where, if you can't sleep, you meditate lying down by having awareness of the sensations in your body. It's a way to get out of your head, I guess, and since my mind was chattering pretty loudly, I decided to give it a shot. It was hard to stay focused on my body because my thoughts of the next day kept distracting my mind. It was frustrating. I'd focus one moment, and then be gone like two seconds later, obsessing over something about the competition.

I persevered. And I kept coming back to my body, over and over again, until eventually, I fell asleep.

Chapter Forty

The day began early. I was up at 4am to make sure I had enough time to head out to Snapper and get in a warm-up session before the competition started. The forecast was looking good, so the event would most likely be on. I'd already packed my necessary snacks, clothes, bikinis, boards, wax and other gear the night before, so I didn't have to run around panicking in the morning or worry about leaving something behind. S and Kiko were already up and making our smoothies by the time I made my way to the kitchen.

'What are you guys doing up so early?'

'Babe, we had to see you off this morning!' S never missed an opportunity to give me support, especially when she knew I needed it most.

'Yeah, sorry we're gonna miss the first day, Zoe.' Kiko said, pouring my smoothie in a reusable cup to take with me.

'Aww, you guys are so sweet. Thanks so much!'

As Kiko handed me the smoothie, Seth came in through the sliding door with a backpack.

'Zo, are you ready to do this or what?' His hair was all

disheveled and he seemed a bit out of sorts as he tripped on the leg of a dining room chair on his way to greet us.

'Ooh, ouch!' he grumbled as he stubbed his toe, but he shook it off quickly as if nothing had happened. Maybe still too sleepy to react. Kiko filled up another portable cup and handed it to him.

'Can you handle this or shall I give it to Zoe to hang onto for you?'

'Gimme that!' he said, trying to bring out sarcasm in his voice but still coming across as the sweetest guy ever. The ladies gave me a hug, and Seth and I went out the front door to his car.

'Are you sure you don't mind taking me this early?'

'C'mon Zoe, you know I want to!' he said with eagerness.

Surf events are kinda like going to an outdoor festival. It's completely amazing to me how the beach transforms. There's the competitor area, the VIP area, a lounge area with snacks and drinks, plus our locker rooms with our jerseys (AKA a rash guard with our name and number that we wear during our heat). I got a VIP pass for Seth so that he could watch in the lounge area with the family members, friends and girl/boyfriends of other competitors.

'Pretty sweet!' he commented as we walked in. We both had our backpacks on, plus a board under each arm. Four total, all four mine! We'd left Seth's board in the car in the parking lot, where we had changed after our warm-up session. The waves were fun and clean, and it was nice to be in the water with someone who had such light-hearted energy. Unknowingly, he helped calm my nerves.

Walking around the competitor's area felt surreal. There's a camaraderie that comes from getting to know one another as you travel from one event to the next, which is comforting on one hand. But then on the other hand, some of the people I 'knew' still felt like strangers.

On top of that, I hadn't spoken with *anyone* during the off-season except for Bailey, so I had no idea what the ladies had been up to. It made me feel insecure about being out of the loop, in case there was some major news I was oblivious about; this felt especially true when it came to my fellow Aussies. But when I started to see some familiar faces, my fear was instantly dissolved by their friendliness.

'Zoe!' Tanya called out.

'Aloha, Zoe!' said Cindy.

'What's up, Zoe! Haven't seen you in a while!' Ruth said with a big smile as she walked by.

'Ah, Zoe! *Salut!*' Julie said in her usual bubbly manner.

Everyone is so friendly, I thought to myself reassuringly.

'You good, Z?' Seth joined my side once I'd dropped my stuff in my locker room.

'I am now! I guess I was a little unsure about how the others would respond to me, since I wasn't in the best of moods last time I saw them. But yeah, it feels good. I'm good! How about you?'

'It's alright, hey! I love VIP!' he said with enthusiasm and charm as he gently put his arm around my shoulder, kissed me on the cheek and nudged me to walk out to the deck to check on the conditions.

'Looks pretty nice, hey. I hope it holds.'

There wasn't much else to focus on, except for maintaining a strong mindset. I wasn't about to start worrying about what the other girls could or couldn't do. All *I* had control over was my own ability to perform my absolute best.

I headed to the locker room as the competition got under-way. I was in the third heat, which didn't leave much time to get ready, seeing that each was only 30 minutes. Luckily the water had warmed up over the summer, so I didn't have to deal with putting on a wetsuit anymore. Just my bikini, the lotion on my face, and making sure I had my jersey on. You get to pick your own number, and I've had the same number for years: #33. It felt good having it on my back again. After a series of warm-up stretches, I headed back over to Seth who was still sitting outside on the deck, watching the second heat.

'How's it going?' I asked.

'The sets are looking good. Not too long of a lull in between sets, so you should have plenty of waves to choose from. The tide's coming in, so it'll pick up a bit too.'

'Thanks for being here, Seth, it means a lot,' I said, flashing him a smile before making my way to the beach.

There were three of us in the water: me, Tanya, and Ruth. It was a non-elimination round, meaning nobody would get cut. Instead, the person who won this heat would get to skip Round Two (an elimination round) and head straight to Round Three. It was the first goal of the comp that we all aimed to achieve.

Typically, Tanya played smart, and I'd been in plenty of heats with her before, averaging five wins to her seven, so I knew to expect her to take care of herself and be on top of her game. As for Ruth, she wasn't the most consistent competitor, but when she was on, she was *on*. She may not have performed to her potential over previous years, but it wouldn't be smart to discount her ability to come in strong. She was an extremely skilled and fearless surfer with nothing to lose, and these factors could put her at an advantage.

In a nutshell, here's how the judging system works: your worst scores are thrown away, keeping the best two, and there's no wave limit which means you can catch as many waves as you want.

Also, in order to get high-scoring rides you have to:

1. pick a good wave

2. make the most of it (do turns, cutbacks, and other maneuvers)
3. complete it (finish without wiping out)

And since each wave was different, it took *a lot* of skill to pick the right wave at the right time *and* be in the right position to catch it. Another element to consider was gaining priority, which basically meant getting pole position. Having priority gives you pick of the best wave. Once you took your wave, priority would change. Confused yet? All I'm saying is there were plenty of technicalities to deal with in the water, and strategy was key.

Unfortunately, I choked in Round One. Or rather, Julie slayed. She dominated the heat, without question. Ruth had a few nice ones, but neither of us could match her full round-house cutback.

Moving onto Round Two and I was still a bit of a mess, struggling to maintain any sort of consistency. There were plenty of waves to catch, which was a bonus, but I kept screwing up on them. I fell off the back of one, tripped on my rail on another. It did not impress the judges one bit, and my low scores – a 6.51 and a 6.97 – demonstrated just that. Luckily, however, Erica couldn't quite seem to pull it together either. I say 'luckily' because normally she would rip! So we both kinda sucked; I just happened to suck a little bit less than her in those 30 minutes.

Fuck! I thought to myself. *That's what happens when I'm focused on proving myself to others. Okay, Zoe, time to let it go and focus on the next heat.*

Round Three was a success! I didn't catch *a lot* of waves, but I did pick the *right* waves, which gave me the opportunity to find my rhythm, carve out some critical turns and bash away at the pocket. Carly, one of my opponents, ended up on the wrong side of priority, meaning her waves didn't have enough 'meat' on them to get anything significant done. Anna, on the other hand, chased down some high scoring waves in the excellent range, but it wasn't enough to beat my 8.13 and 8.25.

It was imperative I keep my head in the game, because I was now headed to the Quarterfinals against Emily, who has multiple World Championship titles and therefore knew exactly what it took to win. She had a particular style and set of skills that have proven to be a powerful combination, so I would have to be 'on' if I wanted to come out on top.

'Right on, Z, you got this!' Seth whispered in my ear when he gave me a hug right before I made my way to the beach from the competitor's area. His presence was soothing. His smile, and his light-hearted energy helped me stay present and relaxed, instead of nervous.

Em was on fire! Snapper was a local spot for her as she lived in the area, so she knew this feature like the back of her hand. She gouged through every bump in the wave, scoring some excellent points right off the bat, putting her in the lead and me into a combo situation. I needed to replace both of my scores... two new waves, each scoring over an 8.27! It was a tense situation, but I refused to give in to the pressure! Instead, I maintained my focus by embracing one of the principles of a TaoSports athlete – enjoying the challenge that Emily had given me to showcase my talent.

I got this! I said to myself. But there was a lull in between sets where neither of us were able to catch anything for a good chunk of time. *Oh no!* With only five minutes remaining, I had to step up my game. I snuck to the inside section and found a sweet one while under priority. I took it almost all the way into shore: *snap, snap, snap!* I was just hammering down the line, using every piece of the wave until there was nothing left of it. *Yes! An 8.67.*

I was paddling my ass off to get back out there with only two minutes left when another gem of a wave lined up right in front of me! Emily still had priority, but she was sitting too far outside to play defense. I knew this would be my last chance, so I went for it... and got barrelled! I saw it starting to form down the line and had to race to catch up to it. I could see it was going to be a tight fit, but I was in the zone! I stomped on my back foot and put on the brakes, tucking myself in with perfect timing, riding deep before digging in my rail to pick up speed before flying out of the pit unscathed.

One word for getting barrelled: divine.

Even with an 8.67 and a 9.25, I had only narrowly beaten Emily. Still, it was enough to advance me to the Semifinals! Em, of course, was gracious and friendly as we got out of the water. I have no doubt that she was bummed, but her good sportsmanship reminded me yet again that professional surfing isn't all about the results.

The men were up now, which meant I wouldn't be surfing again that day. Seth and I hung out, enjoying each other's company, while I reacquainted myself with the others on tour. *Socializing*, if you will. And Seth was stoked to meet the likes of Jay Jay, Nelly, and Rick, watching heats and getting the feel for the 'scene'.

It was a great day, not just for the surfing, but also in re-aligning myself with the people on tour in a positive way. They were my surfing family, not just the competition. And this *attitude* helped me relax, loosen up, and have fun!

Chapter Forty-One

Two days later and it was Finals day. There were still two heats left in the Quarterfinals, so I was able to watch the action and get a good sense of the conditions without expending any energy. Bailey was in one of those heats and had won – and now, we were seated together!

The Semi Finals were on, and Bails and I were in the water. It turned windy and hectic at the start of our heat, but I was confident I could manage myself in these conditions because of all the time I'd spent practicing in shitty waves for this purpose. Bailey had been very active during her Quarterfinal heat less than an hour ago, and as a result she was looking sluggish. Regardless, I focused on myself and maintained priority so that I could pick the most ideal waves. It was a smart strategy that paid off. Bails, unfortunately for her, wasn't able to find one that would give her enough scoring potential to catch up to me, and even though my rides were only in the low 8-point range, it was still enough to win the heat. *Yes!!*

I felt stronger and stronger as I progressed through the event, gaining confidence in my ability to make a comeback. And now, *I had made it to the Finals!*

Bails, of course, was thrilled as ever. A Semifinal finish at the first event of the season in just her second year on tour was incredible.

'Right on, Zoe!' Bailey said as she high-fived me. 'You were on fire!'

'Thanks!' I was so excited. It felt like a sweet victory, beating Bailey. It wasn't so much about *beating* Bailey (though I admit it felt good), but more about surfing to my ability, and having the confidence to execute my rides with precision.

After an hour break, they called the Finals *on!* Tanya and I were in the water, both ready to charge. She hadn't made it to Finals often over the last couple of years, but then again, neither had I.

We both held steady, maintaining momentum throughout the entire heat without losing steam. I could hear the excitement from the large crowd of people watching from shore as we battled it out. Tanya laid into a massive arc on one of her flawless rides, impressing the judges and scoring her an 8.95. I answered back with a drawn-out layback carve before coming back up and attacking the lip. It landed me an 8.99. We went back and forth like this, slashing out turns and even getting barrelled. Surfing in Finals at uncrowded Snapper Rocks with killer conditions was insane!

Tanya took the lead from our last exchange, and now there was only one minute left on the clock. The pressure was there, trying to grab my attention like the itch of a mosquito bite. But I didn't scratch. No way! My head was in the game... I had priority, and needed to find a wave ASAP. I scanned the horizon and noticed a set in the distance. I paddled frantically to get into position, praying for the wave to catch up to me in time. I felt its surge from behind, but still needed to get in one more stroke before I could...

Bzzzzzzz... The buzzer went off. Time was up and the heat was over. Tanya took the win.

Argh, bummer! I gave myself a brief moment to mourn the loss, and then quickly pulled things back into perspective. I paddled over to 'T' and gave her a hug.

'Great job, T, congrats!'

'Thanks, Zoe, thanks so much!' She was beaming with joy, and I can honestly say I was happy for her. I mean, I could stay bummed and angry and negative or whatever, or I could share in her happiness. The choice was mine, I'd come to learn, and option two was decidedly the one that *felt good*. Of course, my first *choice* is always to win, but if that doesn't happen, why not just share in my opponent's victory? Besides, the purpose of my competitor was to help me improve my game and develop my mind, right?

I surfed into shore, signed some autographs and got my photo taken with a bunch of younguns before seeing Sophie's parents waving at me from on the beach. Greg was with them. I walked over and gave them each a big, wet hug, thanking them for being here.

'Greg! I had no idea you were here! Where've you been hiding?' He was looking much better than the last time I'd seen him. A little less intense, a little less weight, and a lot more spark.

'Of course I'm here, Zoe. I watched the whole thing! I didn't want to distract you with my presence, just in case, so I just kept to myself over there,' he said as he pointed down the beach.

'Aww, well, I'm really glad you're here. Thank you so much for your support. And again, I'm really sorry about bailing on you. I know you had the best of intentions.'

'No worries, Zoe,' he said gently. 'I understand now why you did what you needed to do for you, because I have to say, you looked great out there. Calm, confident, powerful. It even looked like you were having fun!'

We embraced goodbye, and I walked over to Damo for my post-heat interview

'Zoe, you looked fantastic out there! You had the crowd pretty excited! Have you gotten your mojo back?'

'Thanks! Yeah, well I came to grips with a lot of things during the off-season, hey.'

'What did you learn or do?'

'Well, I had the right kind of support from the right kind of people. They helped me come back to having fun and doing things in a way that feels good. I dunno, kinda weird I guess, but it worked for me!'

'Does it feel good to be back on tour this year? Are you going after another title?'

I giggled, 'That'd be ace, yeah! Of course the title is on my mind for sure, yeah. But right now I'm focusing on one heat at a time, and learning how to stay present in the moment. If that takes me to a world title, well yeah... that'd be tops!'

'Right on, Zoe,' Damo wrapped things up, 'Congrats on starting off the tour with a second place finish. It's great to see you back in the game!'

I smiled at the camera and gave a thumbs up before heading up the steps into the VIP area, where I was greeted immediately by Kiko, Sophie, and Seth who all smothered me in hugs.

'Zoe, you were so great out there. You did the best you could, hey?' Sophie was beaming.

'No worries, babe. I'm stoked!'

It was so awesome to have my entourage there for the awards ceremony. And even though I placed second, I felt like a winner.

I was proud. I was grateful. I was happy.

After a celebratory night out of dinner and dancing with

Tanya, Ruth, Bailey, Erica, Julie, and a bunch of the others, I came home pretty late. Still feeling awake and buzzed with excitement, I decided to take a few moments to write in my 'everything book' and acknowledge how I felt.

When I was done, I closed my eyes and thought back to the first time I met Teo, on the plane on my way here almost three months earlier, and all that had happened since then. So much release, so much letting go, so much moving on. It had been a lot of work (and still was), but now I know it had all been worth it, and Teo had made it so much easier. He had been a huge blessing.

'It has been my pleasure, Zoe.'

I opened my eyes as soon as I heard his voice, and there he was.

'Teo!' I whispered loudly.

He was sitting next to me on my bed, and I leaned over to give him a hug. I couldn't help but cry. I didn't know what it was, but every time I was in his embrace, I just felt so relieved, so safe, so cared for in a way that comforted me to the depths of my being.

'That's the feeling of Pure Love, Zoe.'

'I love you, Teo.'

'I love you, Zoe. And congratulations on your performance. I'm very proud of how well you listened to the waves and maintained your center. You had such composure. You were graceful with all your competitors.'

'Thank you,' I said softly, feeling like a little child who had just won over her father's approval.

'It was noticed, and it will be rewarded. I believe you can expect to receive a couple of calls from some potential sponsors.'

'Really?'

'Of course. Remember, you are always rewarded for your

efforts, so maintain the 'right' kind of effort, and blessings will always come to you with ease.'

'How will I know who to work with?'

'Be clear with how you want to feel, and how you want to work with others. There will always be plenty of opportunities so never worry that you have to say yes if it doesn't feel right. Trust your gut, Zoe. It will take you far.'

'Okay, I will.' But then, all of a sudden, I felt sad. 'Wait, Teo, it sounds like you're saying goodbye. You're not leaving, are you?'

'No, Zoe, of course not. I am always with you, in your heart.'

'But...?'

'You will see less of me in form, Zoe. It's time for you to move on, without 'needing' me.'

'But I just...'

'The human mind develops a craving that turns into attachment, and you must know that you don't need me in the way you think you do. Don't worry, Zoe, you'll see me from time to time. You'll see my face in the clouds, in a flower, in the eyes of your loved ones. I'm everywhere, Zoe, you just have to focus on love, and know with certainty that our connection is always perfectly intact.'

I hugged him again, my face wet with tears.

'Thank you so much, Teo. I love you so much. Thank you, thank you, thank you.'

I felt his warm embrace as he gently caressed my head, my face buried in the nape of his neck. And then, just like that, he was gone. I opened my eyes just to be sure. Yes, it was true. He was gone.

I laid back in bed, and before I had a chance to feel a sense of loss at his departure, I was asleep.

Chapter Forty-Two

I sat out on the deck the next morning, relaxing with a cup of hot water and lemon, and with Soph.

'Are you excited to go back on tour?' she asked. This was my last day here, and I was set to head south the next morning to Western Australia where the next comp was being held.

'Yes and no,' I replied. 'I mean, there's pros and cons to everything, including being a pro surfer. And one of the cons is being away from home, and from family and friends for so long. Staying here has been a miracle for me S. It really brought me back to life, and I have you to thank for it.'

'Aww, c'mon.'

'No I'm serious, S, I don't know what I would've done these past couple of months if I wasn't here. You guys are all amazing. And I have to say, Kiko is a keeper. You guys are sweet together, and she's a solid person. I'm really happy for you!'

'Thanks, Z. Yeah, I'm quite stoked she's into a nutter like me, hey!'

We sat in silence for a bit, until she said something I wasn't expecting in the least, 'You know, Z, if you like my bro, you should go for it.'

I spat out my water as the words came out of her mouth and I looked over at her with wide eyes. I saw that she was grinning.

'Umm... er...' was all I could mutter.

'Seriously, babe, Kiko told me. And besides, my bro has had a crush on you for the longest time. You seriously have no idea! I saw how you guys were dancing and hanging out when we were up the coast. I may not have let on, but c'mon, I'm not blind!'

I put my cup down, not sure what to say.

'So, are you into him or what?'

'Umm, well...'

'Just spit it out, Zozo. Don't think about it so hard!'

'Well, yeah, I am into him! But he's your little brother!'

'So?'

'Well, there's a slight weirdness to it, don't you think? I mean, what would your parents think?'

'Awww, c'mon. You're not seriously going to let that get in the way, are you? You know my parents are liberal about these things! They're not trying to get in the way of love, hun.'

'Love?!' I kinda blurted out the word, questioning how this crush between Seth and me had somehow escalated into love.

'I dunno about that...' I said, and as my words trailed off, I started wondering again about love, and thinking back to my break-up with Derek, which was not so very long ago.

'Well, hun, whatever it is, I see a spark. And you're awesome, and my bro is awesome, and I say go for it!'

I looked at Sophie beaming with honesty. I swear she doesn't let anything get in her way. People can't block her, and she never limits herself as to what she wants out of life. It's astounding. As she smiled at me, I got up from my chair and leaned over to give her a hug.

'You simply are the best, Sophie. Thank you so much!'

'*You're* the best. I'm stoked for you to be here. Now, what do you say we go for a surf?'

'Yes!'

We gathered the whole gang and surfed for a while just out the front of the house. The waves were small and fun, and accommodated all of us: Peter, Abby, Seth, Kiko, Sophie and me. Kiko had improved a lot, I might add. The rest of the day was a mixture of hanging out, packing, organizing, figuring out logistics and more. Before I knew it, evening was upon us.

'Ladies!' Peter yelled from the upstairs deck. 'Get your butts up here!'

Even though we'd had plenty of family dinners, this one felt surreal. Almost like a time warp. I thought back to that first dinner on the night I'd arrived. Man, it felt so long ago yet also like it was just yesterday. So much had happened in between. This time, though, Kiko was with us. I loved how much the Smarts had made her a part of the family already, just like they had with me.

'Zoe! Stop spacing out! What are you doing over there?'

Dammit! S had caught me again. I snapped myself out of it, and realized I was standing just inside the sliding door, in a kind of a trance, while everyone else was milling around the kitchen.

'Wowzers!' I mumbled to myself as I walked further inside the house. 'I was just admiring the scene!'

'Get over here, sweetie,' Abby said as she grabbed my arm and pulled me in to give me a hug. 'We are going to miss you, Zoe!'

She had the calming scent of lavender on her. Mixed in with her sweetness, it was a soothing combination.

'Yes, Zoe, you are always welcome here.' It was Peter's voice now, but I couldn't see him because he was behind me, and I was sandwiched in their hugs.

A few moments later when Abby loosened her grip, I was

able to have a nice conversation with both her and Peter, thanking them profusely for including me in their family, and for supporting me, not just in allowing me to stay there, but by their words of wisdom, their kindness, and their ability to demonstrate what it means to care for family.

'You both have taught me so much, and I hope one day to have the kind of relationship that you two seem to have. Plus, you've raised some pretty amazing kids, a bit crazy, mind you, but amazing just the same!'

We sat at the table. Now that S had her girlfriend by her side, I sat with Seth on the other, and the parents were placed at each end. Once we were all settled into our chairs, I raised my glass to make a toast.

'To Abby, for helping me to eat better and breathe more deeply. To Peter, for demonstrating both strength and gentleness at the same time. To Seth, for teaching me to do what feels good. And of course, to Sophie, for always having my back and bringing laughter into *every*thing. Kiko, thanks for teaching me tai chi, meditation – and for your all-round poise. Thank you, everyone, for being in my life at a time when I really needed you – albeit unknowingly. It's been quite a journey these last few months, and you all helped me to see the light at the end of the tunnel when I couldn't see it for myself. I love you, and I'm going to miss you. But hey, just make sure my room is ready again at the end of the season, alright?'

'You betcha!' S said. 'And I'd like to add to this little sentimental moment that it sure is going to be a bit more boring around the house without you to pick on, Zozo. I guess I'll just have to start getting on Kiki here! Right Keeks?'

She was nudging Kiko with her arm, hamming things up as usual, to which we all raised our glasses and harmoniously rang out, 'Cheers!'

The evening continued as such, with lots of yummy food

and chit-chat, finishing off with a feisty game of ping-pong. I might as well add that there was some flirtation between Seth and me. It was a slight, almost shy flirtation, considering family was all around us, but sitting next to him at dinner allowed for the occasional shoulder brush, foot touch, flirtatious gaze, and giddiness.

After saying my goodbyes to Peter and Abby, who I probably wouldn't see in the morning, the four of us went downstairs and hung out for a bit until Sophie had to drive Kiko home because she had to work early in the tai chi studio.

Seth and I sat side by side on the deck, staring out at the darkness.

'Shall we venture out for a walk?' Seth said gently as he looked my way. His hair was blowing in the light breeze, so he had to shake his head slightly to get the hair out of his eyes. It was a sexy move, even if unintentional... I'm not sure it was though.

'Yes, please,' I said quickly, realizing that there was nothing more holding me back after Sophie's approval. We walked onto the sand, heading closer to the water.

'I'm going to miss you, Zoe,' Seth said, as he looked towards me with that beautiful, glowing smile.

I looked over at him, smiling. 'Thank you for being such a genuine person, Seth. Guys like you are hard to come by. I'm going to miss you too.'

We continued to walk up the beach in silence, but my thoughts were busy. Seth had become an amazing confidante and friend. I felt like we'd developed a connection that had allowed us to motivate and inspire one another to move forward in our goals and aspirations. The attraction was there the whole time, now that I thought about it and admitted it to myself, but we had let our relationship develop first. That's what had made the experience between us even more yummy.

'I have a pressie for you,' he said as he stopped to face me, pulling something out of his shirt pocket.

'Really?' I said, surprised, feeling nervous all of a sudden.

'It's just a small reminder to help keep you on track while you're away on tour.' And then he put in my hand a stone. It was smooth and flat, about the size of a new stick of surf wax. I could tell that it had something written on it, but it was too dark to see.

'Oh wait a sec,' he said as he pulled out his phone from his back pocket and shone the flashlight onto the stone in my palm. I looked down at it to see three words 'Follow The Feelgood' painted in green, with a blue wave curled around the words.

'Seth, this is beautiful! You made this?' I wasn't bullshitting, it was gorgeous.

'Yeah, I just wanted you to remember all the stuff we've talked about, and I thought this would be a good thing to put by your bed at night, to remind you. I guess it's a bit of added weight to drag all over the world, but hey...'

'No way! I love it so much. It's perfect!' I put my arms around him and let my lips touch his neck lightly. As I did, he quickly shoved his phone back in his pocket so that his hands were free to pull me in. His shirt was mostly unbuttoned and the soft skin on his chest was warm and delicious-smelling. I allowed myself to let go a little bit, and embrace the moment, kissing his neck softly, working my way up to his chin, his cheek, and finally, he tilted his head slightly so that his lips met mine.

In this warm, sweet embrace we had finally found our moment. He was so caring as he kissed me, brushing his lips softly on mine, teasing me a little bit before opening his mouth slightly to gently touch my tongue with his own. And then he went deeper in my mouth as he kissed me with a hungry, confident kind of intensity. I loved how he had taken control of the situation. It was hot!

I was slowly moving my hands from his muscular back, towards his chest, lost in the moment. He pulled his head back with what seemed like a sense of relief before saying, 'Oh my God, Zoe, I've wanted to kiss you like this for so long, you have no idea.' I could feel his heart pounding underneath my hand. I giggled a little bit, and finally admitted, 'Yeah, I think, me too.'

'Really? You, umm, don't show it most of the time. To be honest, I really wasn't sure.'

'Well, it just took me a while to admit it to myself, you know? I mean, you're my best friend's little brother, so I've been a little hesitant to be cool with it.'

'But you're cool with it now?'

'Yeah, I'm cool with it now,' I replied. 'I mean, I'm still not sure whether or not it's a *smart* idea, *he he he!* But I, um, don't think I'd be able to stop myself at this point anyway,' I said as I looked away, feeling vulnerable.

We held each other closely for a few more moments, until Seth pulled away from me to take my hand in his and guide me back to the house.

The porch lights were on, but the rest of the house was dark. I fumbled around, looking for the light switch just inside the sliding door, but Seth had his hands up my shirt and I was distracted by his touch. I blindly banged into the back of the dining table as he crashed into me from behind, nearly knocking the wind out of me. 'Ah!' We were laughing now.

I turned around and he lifted my shirt off. The sensation of his bare chest against mine. And those abs, mmm. His shirt was already mostly undone so I just ripped the last few buttons to peel it off completely. Letting go in this moment made him literally irresistible.

'Really? You had to tear my shirt?!' he whispered in my ear, with a playful tone of voice. He picked me up and carried me to the bedroom, placing me down gently before climbing on top of me and rolling us onto our sides. We intertwined our legs and kissed eagerly, excitedly.

'Wait, wait...' I said as I stopped him.

'What's wrong?' he said, surprised.

'I just... I want to see you, but it's too dark and I can't see anything!'

'Oh! Okay cool.'

It was tough to kill the moment, but I really needed to make this small little adjustment. I flicked on the lamp by my bed, found the lighter and lit the candles that had been on the windowsill all summer but that I'd never even thought to use until this moment.

Seth was sitting on the edge of the bed now, watching me fiddle with the candles, and I could feel his eyes on me. I came back to the bed and turned off the lamp. 'There. Much better, right?'

'Zoe, I'm so happy to be here with you, like this, right now.'

He grabbed my hands and pulled me in so that I was standing in between his legs. He looked up at me and smiled ever so sweetly that I swear my heart skipped a beat. He began kissing my stomach, using his tongue to gently move up to the space between my breasts, and I heard myself moan with approval. He was tender but confident in his movements. And I willingly received his touch.

We rolled around in the candlelight, enjoying one another throughout the night. Laughter, sweet kisses, conversation, connection. It was magical, mind-blowing. It felt beyond me, beyond us, if that makes sense. Once I let go and allowed myself to give in, it was like another force took over. We became so in sync it was as if we'd become one. It was effortless, beautiful, and I can honestly say that I've never experienced anything like it.

Chapter Forty-Three

I woke up with the sun shining through my window. I was curled up next to Seth, who was completely passed out. My head, awkwardly resting on his chest, was stiff. I lifted it slowly, glancing up at him as I moved, watching as he slept so soundly.

Is this for real? Did this really happen? I thought to myself unbelievingly.

I got up and made us some hot water with lemon, and a couple of pieces of toast with butter and Vegemite, and carried it on a tray back to the room. As I walked in, Seth's eyes opened.

'Morning!' he said sleepily as he sat up and rubbed his eyes.

'Morning!'

I put the tray down by the foot of the bed while Seth reached over to grab me and pull me in for a hug.

'OMG, you're so hot!' I said, feeling the heat of his skin on my chest.

'Why, thank you!'

'No, I mean... Well, that too, but... Argh!'

He was laughing while I continued to stumble on my words, 'It gets hot in here. Uh, um, you wanna go to the kitchen?'

'Well, I could probably hang out in here with you all day, but my stomach wants more food!' he said as he munched on some toast.

We ventured into the kitchen, giggly and pretty perky for two people who'd barely slept.

'Hey, I didn't know you could cook?' I said as I watched him throw together an omelet while I made a smoothie with the usual ingredients.

'There's probably quite a bit you don't know about me, Zoe,' he said smilingly, and I could tell he was throwing some honesty at me.

'True, I'm sure' I replied matter-of-factly.

'And I hope you'll still want to get to know me even when you're away.'

'God, you're so sweet!' I said, pleased that he was just so straightforward and not acting awkward at all, considering it was the morning after the night before. You never know how someone might close off after being so open and vulnerable, including me. Just when we were sitting down to eat, Sophie walked in the door. As I heard it open, I froze, looking at Seth, not sure how Soph was going to react.

'Mmm, that smells delish, what are you...?'

And then she stood there, motionless for a sec. I'm assuming she was putting together the pieces of the puzzle. I sat, waiting for her reaction.

'Hey sis! There's some omelet in the pan if you like,' Seth chirped as he shoved a forkful of egg in his mouth, not seeming to care at all about what his sister might think. I guess he knew her pretty well, because it only took a moment for her to respond.

'Alright, alright, nice, nice,' she said as she winked at me, while I still sat tense.

'Breathe, Zoe, breathe,' Seth whispered in my ear. I took a

deep breath in as he put his hand on my lap, helping me to chill out in a situation that didn't require any tension at all. It was just my fear trying to trip me up with thoughts; thoughts that apparently weren't real.

'Did you two have a nice evening then?' Sophie said as she helped herself to some eggs and joined us at the table. We just looked at one another and grinned.

'You know we did, c'mon! What about you?' He was smart to put the conversation back on her, if only for my sake.

'Yeah, it was all good! But I had to come back to take The Zozo to the airport, now, didn't I? Or did I?!' She looked over and winked at me. A bunch of times. She was being her usual self. And I was relieved.

'Wow, I can't believe I'm leaving.' I said, coming out of my insecure moment. 'Hey, are you coming with?' I asked Seth as I took a sip of smoothie.

'Love to, of course. I want every minute with you before you leave! And then he moved his arm from my lap and put it around my shoulder as he pulled me in to him.

And I almost fell off my stool.

Chapter Forty-Four

We arrived at the airport, and I was both excited as well as hesitant to catch my flight to Perth for the next comp, the Margaret River Pro.

'Are you sure you guys can't come?' I didn't want to leave them behind.

'I wish, babe,' Sophie said. 'But hey, you never know. I'll see how the schedule is looking at work and call you if I can make some changes.'

Seth was pulling my boards off the car at that point, so he didn't hear me ask about them joining me at Margies.

'Now Zozo, you take care of yourself, okay? Keep it real for us, and have fun on all your adventures. Oh, and here, everyone from the crew wanted me to give you this,' she said as she pulled out a card from her bag.

'They got me a card?'

'Yeah, you made quite an impression on them. You know how cool it was for a legend like you to hang out with all of us commoners? Ha!'

'Oh man, c'mon, S! But seriously, they're all awesome. You have a great crew, and an awesome life here. And S, OMG, Kiko is amazing. I know I said this already but I'm so stoked for you! Don't screw it up okay?!'

We hugged and said our final goodbyes, and then she turned to go wait in the car, while Seth helped me with the rest of my stuff.

'Well, Seth,' I began, 'I don't even know what to say, except that you're like magic!'

He started laughing. 'Magic?'

'Yeah, I mean, everything you say, and everything you do, is just, I dunno... You're like a light, and you carry around all this wisdom. It's so... well, inspiring.'

He grabbed my hands and spoke, 'Zoe, I don't want this to be a goodbye, okay? I want more of us, even though you're leaving for a while. What do you think?'

'Umm, yes please!' I said as I stood on the curb so that we were a more equal height.

I released my hands from his so that I could wrap my arms around his neck and look at him face to face without having to look up to meet his gaze. And his lips. I kissed him. And kissed him again. I wanted to remember the feeling of his lips, the softness, the love, the passion, and the feelgood. We hugged and held each other and just took a few moments to soak up the energy of our connection.

We said our goodbyes, and with his painted rock in my backpack, I turned and walked into the airport. I wasn't sure when I'd see him again, but I also wasn't going to discount the possibility of seeing him sooner rather than later. Well, that's what I was hoping for, anyway.

Waiting at the gate for my flight, I sat down and once again pulled out my 'everything book'. My emotions were running in circles and I needed to set myself straight. I wrote.

Wowzers, I'm all over the place! I need to come back to my Self. And I mean my true Self, the one that Teo talks about, where

I can shine as bright as he does. That's where it'll be possible to fulfill my true potential, and that's what I want.

Right, so I've learned that in order to do that, I need to let go and let the Universe lead the way.

What do I need to let go of?

Fear.

What kind of fear?

Worry, around not connecting with Seth again. He feels so good and I don't want to lose that.

Sadness and anger, which I feel when I think about Derek, who I still miss sometimes.

Doubt, because while I'm stoked with a second place finish at Snapper, can I do it again? What if that was a fluke? The ladies rip, and I know I have some catching up to do when it comes to adding newer, more challenging moves to my repertoire.

I paused. *Hmmm. I can work through this. I've got this*, I thought to myself as I looked up from the page and let my mind wander. *Listen to your heart, not your head, and feel what's being said.* I reminded myself, then glanced back down at the paper, ready to write again.

Everything is working out in my favor. My job is to relax and feel for the flow. 'Let the ocean move you' as Teo said. External gratification is a distraction from the awareness that I am complete and whole as I am. I embody the essence of Pure Love.

I don't know what the future holds, so there's nothing to control. Be present in the moment. Feeling good is the goal.

And suddenly the book flew out of my hands, as if by an unforeseen force. It landed face down with its pages spread. Picking it up I turned it over to see what page it had landed on. And wouldn't you know it? It was the page I wrote in, on the plane on my way here from Hawaii, right after I met Teo for the first time.

And there it was, right in front of me. My declaration:

* * *

*I WILLINGLY RECEIVE ABUNDANCE IN ALL ASPECTS
OF MY LIFE, THROUGH THE UNIVERSAL GATEWAY
OF MIRACLES AND MAGIC.*

* * *

I laughed quietly to myself, and in my mind, acknowledged Teo's presence.

Out of my confusion came clarity, and I now understood what Teo had meant when he said there's more to life than meets the eye. If these last few months had taught me anything, it was to trust that the Universe has my back, to have faith in the process, to believe in magic...

And more than anything, to follow the feelgood.

* * *

 Did you enjoy this book? Please consider leaving an honest review on amazon so that others may enjoy it too! It makes ALL the difference in the world for a small indie author to garner as many reviews as possible. We need that cred! **Scan the code to go straight to the review form for the book.**

Want to know Sophie and Seth's conversation after leaving Zoe at the airport? Great! You can grab it at: **www.tiffanyman-chester.com/surfacing-bonus-epilogue.**

Afterword

'OCEAN SPEAKS' - A SURFER'S MEMOIR

I was hesitant at first, because I knew that if I
    decided to be in this relationship I would
    have to commit to Her 100%.
And I wasn't sure I was ready for something that
    intense.
But the moment I entered Her I was instantly
    swept away, and knew there was no chance
    of ever turning back.

She is the Ocean and I am a surfer.

Of course, this doesn't mean our relationship is
    perfect.
In times of uncertainty, when it feels like our
    connection is lost, I'll consider breaking up
    with Her.
But then I take a moment to remember the many

*sweet, divine moments we've shared, and I
realize that leaving isn't the answer.*
I could never do it.

She is the Ocean and I am a surfer.

This Salty Goddess *known as the Ocean is a
great teacher who demands respect.*
*She may be soft and gentle one day, then fierce
and raging the next.*
But make no mistake about it - She is **always** *in
control.*
*And if I go out for a session and get my butt
kicked, I know it's because I let my ego take
over.*

That is, I'm distracted by my emotions *- with thoughts about the past
and concerns about the future - and therefore
I'm not focused on the present moment.*
*I can't 'see' what She is offering because my mind
isn't there, in the moment.*
*Ultimately it means I am working against Her
because I'm working against myself, and
that's how I end up in the wrong place at the
wrong time.*
*On the other hand, when I let go of my thoughts
and concerns with the world and the role I
play in it, finally the fear washes off of me,
allowing the peace to settle in.*
In these moments I can connect with Her vibe by

feeling her movements and listening to Her guidance.

'Being' becomes effortless - and that's always when the perfect wave lines up right in front of me.

She is my guru, and in this relationship I am learning how to live with more joy and trust in the process of life - to have patience while I accept and love myself at every moment.

I realize now the choice to be in this relationship never was mine to make, and I never could leave - because I love Her with all of my heart.

She brings me peace and I am committed to Her 100%.

She is the Ocean, and I am a surfer.

Tiffany Manchester, circa 2009

Resources

Yogananda, Paramahansa. *Autobiography of a yogi.* India: Yogoda Satsanga Society of India, 2001.

Al Huang, Chungliang (livingtao.org), Jerry Lynch (wayofchampions.com). *Thinking Body Dancing Mind. Taosports For Extraordinary Performance In Athletics, Business, And Life.* USA and Canada: Bantam, 1992.

About The Author

Tiffany Manchester is a new adult fiction author and surfer. She is also a former professional athlete, four times National Champ and a Bronze World Medalist in the extreme sport of freestyle whitewater kayaking. Before the glory of the professional scene wore off, she spent a decade traveling to remote places around the world on a shoestring budget, seeking the thrill of epic adventures on mountains, rivers, and jungles. Eventually she found herself embarking on a spiritual journey in Hawaii, one that introduced her to meditation, dance, magic mushrooms, angel tarot, and of course, surfing - and began the creation of Follow The Feelgood®, a simple system for connecting to one's intuition to make guided decisions with ease.

One night years later, she met a beautiful man on the dance floor of an electronic music festival. Still based in Hawaii, they have no kids or pets, enjoying instead the freedom to sleep and travel as they please.

Find her at www.tiffanymanchester.com

Printed in Great Britain
by Amazon

11780133R00164